D0835716

THE BLACKWELL PAGES

THE BLACKWELL PAGES

K. L. ARMSTRONG
M. A. MARR

LITTLE, BROWN BOOKS FOR YOUNG READERS
lbkids.co.uk

First published in the United States in 2013 by Little, Brown and Company
First published in Great Britain in 2013 by Little, Brown Books for Young Readers

Text copyright © 2013 by Kelley Armstrong and Melissa Marr
Interior illustrations copyright © 2013 by Vivienne To
Shield and logo by Eamon O'Donoghue based on the work of Lisseth Key

The moral right of the authors and illustrator have been asserted.

A CIP catalogue record for this book
is available from the British Library.

ISBN 978-0-349-00152-4

Printed and bound in Great Britain by
Clays Ltd, St Ives plc

Papers used by LBYR are from well-managed forests
and other responsible sources.

MIX
Paper from
responsible sources
FSC
www.fsc.org   FSC® C104740

Little, Brown Books for Young Readers
An imprint of
Little, Brown Book Group
100 Victoria Embankment
London EC4Y 0DY

An Hachette UK Company
www.hachette.co.uk

www.lbkids.co.uk

M. A.: To Dylan—
This one is for you and because of you
(also, yes, there will be goats).

K. L.: To Alex and Marcus—
Whatever parental horrors I may inflict on
you guys as you move into teenhood, I will never
make you fight a giant serpent. I promise.

MATT

"CONFRONTATION"

M

ONE

MATT

"CONFRONTATION"

Matt walked through the center of Blackwell, gym bag in hand, jacket thrown over his shoulder. It was dark now, with an icy wind from the north, but the cold felt good blowing back his sweat-soaked hair. After two hours of boxing practice, he'd been tempted to take a detour and jump in the Norrström River, even if he had noticed ice on it that morning. Ice in September. Weird. Even in South Dakota, winter never came *this* early.

A muscle spasmed in his leg, and he winced as he stopped to rub it. The upcoming tournament might be for charity—raising money to help tsunami victims in Hawaii—but Coach

Forde still made Matt work as hard as he would before a title match.

Matt started walking again, limping slightly. As much as he wished he could call for a ride, he knew better. He'd made that mistake last winter, when Coach had said a blizzard was coming. He'd gotten his ride—and a lecture on how his brothers had never needed one, even when it *was* storming. He couldn't catch a lift with his friends, either—that was worse because it set a bad example. If Sheriff Thorsen's boys weren't safe walking through Blackwell at night, who was?

Matt was reaching down to rub his leg again when something moved in the town square. His head shot up, eyes narrowing. Outside the rec center, two kids climbed onto the weathered Viking longship. Shields lined both sides as if invisible warriors rowed the old wooden boat, protection always within reach. A carved dragon arched from the hull.

The kids were probably setting up a prank, trying to beat the one Matt had done with his friend Cody at Sigrblot, the spring festival. The parade had arrived at the longship to find it covered in a tarp...and making honking noises. Underneath the tarp, they'd discovered a flock of geese wearing little Viking helmets.

Best prank ever, that's what everyone said. Unfortunately, Matt had to pretend he didn't have anything to do with it. If his parents had found out...well, they wouldn't ground him or anything. He'd just get "the talk." How disappointed

2

they were. How embarrassed they were. How much more responsible his brothers were. Personally, he'd rather be grounded.

In a few more steps, he saw that one of the kids was a guy with shaggy brown hair that needed cutting and clothes that needed washing. With him was a girl. Her clothes weren't in such rough shape, but her blond hair needed a trim just as badly.

Fen and Laurie Brekke. Great. The cousins were always getting into trouble. Still, Matt told himself they really might just be pulling a prank...until he saw Fen wrench at one of the shields.

There were a lot of things Fen could do and Matt would just look away, tell himself it was none of his business. That wasn't always easy. Being the sheriff's kid meant he'd had lectures about vandalism since he was old enough to carve his name into a park bench. But this wasn't a park bench. It was an actual longship—something the people in Blackwell were really proud of. And there was Fen, yanking on it and kicking at it.

As Matt's temper flared, his amulet flared with it. He reached for the silver pendant. It was in the shape of an upside-down hammer and almost as old as the longship. Thor's Hammer. Everyone in Matt's family had one. Thorsen wasn't just their name. They really *were* descendants of the Norse god.

As Matt looked at Fen and Laurie again, his amulet

burned hotter. He was about to yell at them, then he stopped and took deep breaths, sucking in cold air.

He could hear his mother's voice. *You need to learn to control it, Matty. I don't know why you have so much trouble with that. No other Thorsen has this problem. Your brothers could handle theirs even when they were younger than you.*

Controlling his temper—and Thor's Hammer—seemed especially hard around the Brekkes. It was like the Hammer knew they were related to the trickster god Loki. The cousins didn't know that, but Matt did, and he could feel it when he looked at them.

Matt took another deep breath. Yes, he needed to stop Fen and Laurie, but he had to be cool about it. Maybe he could just walk past, pretend he didn't notice them, and they'd see *him* and take off before they were caught.

Fen spotted him. Matt continued walking, giving them a chance to sneak off. Being fair. His dad would be proud—

Fen turned back to the longship and yanked on the shield again.

"Hey!" Matt called.

He didn't say it too loud, and he tried not to sound too angry. Just letting them know he saw them, giving them time to run...

"Yeah?" Fen turned and stared straight at him, chin up, shoulders back. He was shorter than Matt. Skinnier, too. The only "big" thing about Fen was his attitude, which was

5

always getting him into fights with larger guys...not that he seemed to mind.

Laurie stepped beside her cousin. Matt couldn't see her expression, but he was sure it matched Fen's. They weren't going to walk away. He'd been stupid to think they would.

"You shouldn't be doing that." Even as Matt said the words, he wanted to smack himself. It was exactly the kind of thing everyone expected the sheriff's kid to say. By tomorrow, everyone at school would have heard Fen and Laurie repeat it with a twist of their lips and a roll of their eyes.

Matt cleared his throat. "It's an artifact, and it's really important to the town." Yeah, like *that* sounded better.

"Really important to *your* town," Fen said. "Thorsen-town."

"Just...don't do it, okay?"

"But I want to. And if you want to stop me..." Fen stepped forward, giving a grin that was all teeth, and for a second, Matt thought he saw—

Matt shook it off. "Look, I'm just asking—"

"The answer's no." Fen jumped out of the ship with a leap that would make an Olympic athlete proud. "So what are you gonna do about that, Thorsen?"

Matt's amulet heated again. He took a deep breath. *Cool it. Just cool it.*

He remembered something Coach Forde had said during practice. He'd been trying to teach Matt how to intimidate an opponent. *You're a big guy*, he'd said. *Use that.*

It was hard for Matt to remember how big he was. At home, he only came up to his brothers' shoulders. But he *was* the tallest kid in eighth grade.

"What am I going to do?" Matt squared his shoulders, flexed, and stepped forward. "Stop you."

Something flashed in Fen's eyes, something cold and hard that made Matt hesitate, but only for a second. He finished his step, stopped in front of Fen, and pulled himself up to his full height.

Laurie climbed out of the ship and moved up beside her cousin. She leaned in and whispered something. Egging him on, Matt was sure.

Fen waved her off. When she hesitated, he said something so low it was almost a growl. Laurie looked at Matt, then backed into the shadows of the longship.

Fen moved forward. "You think you can fight, just because you've won a few in the ring? That's not *real* fighting. I bet you've never thrown a punch without gloves on."

"Then your memory sucks, because I'm pretty sure I beat the snot out of you and Hunter when you two ganged up on Cody."

Fen gave a short bark of a laugh. "That was what? First grade? I've learned a few things since then, Thorsen."

Matt took another step. He was sure Fen would back down. He had to. Taking on Matt was crazy. He hadn't just "won a few in the ring." He'd made it all the way to the state championship.

But Fen just planted his feet far enough apart to keep steady if he got hit. He wanted to fight. Really fight. Matt should have known that. Mom always said this is what got him into trouble—he never thought things through.

If he got into it with Fen, his dad would...Matt inhaled sharply. He didn't even want to think what his dad would do.

The power of respect. The power of authority. That's what let Thorsens walk through Blackwell at night. *Not* the power of violence. If he fought Fen Brekke, his dad would haul him in front of the council and let them handle it. The humiliation would be worse than any punishment they'd order.

"You really want to do this?" Matt asked.

Fen cracked his neck, tilting it side to side, and said, "Yeah, I do."

"Well, too bad. I've got a big match coming, and I need to save my strength for a real opponent."

Matt started to turn. As he did, he heard a growl like a dog's, and he saw Fen lunge, eyes glinting yellow, teeth bared. Matt wheeled. The heat of the amulet flared in a wave of fury that turned his world red.

8

He felt the power surge down his arm. Heard the crackle. Saw his hand light up and tried to pull the power back.

Too late.

The white-hot ball shot from his hand and exploded with a boom and a blast of wind that sent Matt tripping backward. Fen flew right off his feet. He hit the longship hard, his head whipping back, striking the side with a thud. Then he crumpled to the ground.

Laurie yelled something, but Matt couldn't hear the words. She raced to her cousin. Matt did the same. Laurie dropped beside Fen, took him by the shoulder, and shook him. Fen groaned, his eyelids fluttering.

"Is he okay?" Matt said, crouching beside her.

She stood up, lifted her bag like she was about to slug him with it. "You knocked him *out*."

"I didn't mean to. I'm sorry. I—"

"I don't know what kind of trick that was. Throwing that light thing to blind him before you hit him? You call that fair?" She scowled. "Exactly what I'd expect from a Thorsen."

"I didn't—"

"Whatever. Just go. Fen's not swiping anything tonight." She looked at him. "Or do you want to call your dad to lock us up?"

"Of course not. I just—" Matt swallowed. "We should get him to the doctor."

"You think he can afford a doctor?"

"I can. I'll—"

"We don't need anything from *you*. Just go away," Laurie snapped.

"But if he's—"

"Go. Get out of here."

He pushed to his feet and hesitated, but she was still glaring at him, and Fen was coming to. Matt probably didn't want to be around when Fen woke up. So he mumbled another apology, backed away, and left them alone.

TWO

LAURIE

"CHANGES"

Laurie helped Fen up from the ground. Her cousin wasn't ever good at accepting help, and being knocked on his butt by Matt Thorsen of all people wasn't helping matters. The two of them had a natural dislike of one another that she didn't always understand, but *this* time, she got it. Matt was a jerk.

"I'm going to kill him," Fen snapped for the third time in as many minutes. "He thinks he's so special, but he's just a spoiled rich kid."

"I know."

"I could take him." Fen climbed back over the side of the ship.

She didn't tell Fen he was wrong. She wasn't going to be disloyal, but they both knew Matt was a better fighter. Matt was like a Rottweiler to Fen's back-alley mutt: the mutt might try its best, but the bigger, stronger dog was the one likely to win.

All she said was, "We need to get out of here before he tells his dad and we get arrested."

He ignored her and continued ranting, "We'll see who's smart when I find him alone after school."

"Getting arrested *or* getting detention isn't going to make you seem very smart," she said, as calmly as she could.

"Maybe I won't get caught." Fen stared down at her. He had the bag in one hand, and the other hand rested on the shield he'd been prying loose when they'd gotten to the park.

Laurie dropped her gaze to the weathered ship that stood outside the Thorsen Community and Recreation Center. "What were you thinking? We could've ducked. I know you saw him."

"I'm not afraid of him." Fen stood aboard the ship and stared out at the town.

Laurie shivered. It wasn't hard to think of Fen as a Viking Raider. She wasn't shaking as badly as she'd been when she'd told Matt to shove off, but she still felt all twitchy, like the time she'd grabbed a frayed electrical cord in Uncle Eddy's garage. She stared up at Fen. "His dad is the *sheriff*. He could

13

send you away . . . or tell the mayor. You know Mayor Thorsen hates our family."

"I'm not afraid of any Thorsens." Fen straightened his shoulders and gave her a look that reminded her of Fen's dad, her uncle Eddy, which wasn't a good thing. Uncle Eddy never backed down from a challenge. She might not know exactly what he'd done to end up in prison, but she'd bet it had started with a challenge.

He tugged on the shield. "I can't get it loose."

"Just leave the shield alone!" She rubbed her hands again.

"Fine." He hopped over the side of the ship and came to stand beside her.

Laurie didn't always understand her cousin, but she knew that he had a stubborn streak that led him—and often her—into trouble. That wasn't what they needed. "Matt's not worth the hassle."

With a soft snort, Fen said, "You got that right."

"So you'll stay away from him *and* the shield? I don't want you to get into anything." She looked at him, hoping for a promise that didn't come, and when he stayed stone-silent, she gently bumped her head into his shoulder and immediately felt silly.

But then Fen butted her head with his and said, "I'm okay."

She paused. That's what she'd meant, some combination of *I'm worried, you fool. Are you okay?* and *Talk to me.* Fen got it. Her dad's side of the family always seemed better at communicating without words. Her dad did, too—when he was around, at least, which these days wasn't very often.

"Come on," he said. "You need to get home anyhow."

They started toward her apartment building. She wouldn't have time to walk Fen home, but even if she did, he wouldn't let her. He was the older brother she didn't have, determined to protect her even as he drove her crazy. Most of the Brekke side of the family treated her like she was something to be shielded. Even though she didn't see them, she knew they watched out for her. No one at school ever gave her grief, and she was pretty sure that Fen had let it be known that he'd pummel anyone who started anything with her.

"I miss seeing everyone," Laurie said quietly. Aside from Fen, she only really got to see her dad's family when she passed them in town. Fen was in her class, so they saw each other at school, but there were no family barbecues, no parties, no even stopping by for a chat. Her mother stayed clear of the Brekkes, and since her dad was off on one of his neverending trips, Laurie wasn't able to be around the family, either.

"Everyone misses you, too . . . and Uncle Stig." Fen didn't mention her half brother, Jordie, or her mom, of course. The Brekkes hadn't quite rejected Jordie, but he wasn't *family* to them. He was proof that her mother and father had separated, that her mother had tried to move on, but that hadn't worked out. Now, her mom let her dad move back in every time he came to town. *He* treated Jordie like a son, not as much as he did with Fen, but still he accepted Laurie's brother. The rest of the Brekkes weren't that cool.

"Has Uncle Stig called lately?" Fen asked. There was so much hope in his voice that Laurie wished, not for the first time, that her dad would try to remember to call Fen, too. Of course, he didn't remember to call her most of the time, so expecting him to do much else was silly.

"A few weeks ago. He's coming to see me soon. That was what he said, at least." Laurie ducked her head.

Fen nudged her with his shoulder. "He'll come."

"Unless he doesn't," Laurie added. Both were equally likely. Her father came and went as the mood struck him; he called or sent presents if he thought of it.

"Maybe he'll stay for a while," Fen suggested.

And Laurie knew the part he didn't say, *and then I can stay with you.* Fen had no real home. Uncle Eddy had been locked up the past few years for some crime no one would talk about in front of either of them, and Aunt Lillian had packed her bags years ago. Fen moved between the relatives like a bag of hand-me-down clothes. When Laurie's father was around for a while, he was likely to invite Fen to live with them. Once he left, Fen moved out. Laurie's mother never *said* he had to go, but Fen always did—and her mother never stopped him.

16

"Can you just try not to fight with Matt? Or anyone?" she blurted.

Fen stopped, gave her a look, and then resumed walking.

"It'll be easier if you don't fight with him." She grabbed Fen's forearm. "Mom worries about your influence on Jordie, and if Dad does stay, it'd be nice if you came home, too."

They rounded the corner and were almost at her apartment building. The drab beige building sat like a squat stone giant from one of the stories that they all had to learn in sixth-grade English class. Fire escapes that the landlord insisted were scenic balconies clung to the side of the building. The red and blue swaths of spray-painted graffiti were the only colors to be seen.

Fen gave her a quick hug, a sure sign that he was feeling guilty, before he said, "I'll try to keep out of trouble, but I'm not going to sissy out."

That was the best she could hope for. Fen didn't really look for trouble, but it found him—and her—more often than not. Or maybe they simply didn't resist trouble very well. That was what her mom thought. *I can stay out of trouble, though.* She'd had a few visits to Principal Phelps and that one little misunderstanding at the lockers, but mostly, she'd stayed out of trouble lately, which would totally change if she started spending more time with Fen.

He didn't have many friends, so she always felt bad when she didn't hang out with him, but she felt just as bad when

17

she was grounded all the time. He didn't get into half as much trouble when she was around him, but she got into twice as much. Like tonight, all she knew for sure was that he'd said he needed her with him, and she'd come along. She wasn't sure if he was trying to break the shield or take it. With Vetrarblot—the big festival for the start of winter—coming, either one would be a problem.

Laurie ran up the stairs to her apartment. Her mother was working nights at the hospital, so one of the neighbors, Mrs. Weaver, stayed with them after school, but she didn't really enforce the whole get-home-right-away thing. She did, however, insist that Laurie be in the apartment before Jordie went to bed. Laurie took a couple more deep breaths as she ran up the rest of the steps to their fourth-floor apartment. It wasn't quite high enough to have an elevator, but it was enough steps to complain about, as far as she was concerned. If they ever got hit by a tornado—which was a risk in South Dakota—she was pretty sure they'd all die. The apartments all had storage units in the basement, and her mother swore they could get downstairs fast enough if the time came, but that was five floors' worth of stairs. They'd waited a couple storms out in the storage unit, but mostly they stayed upstairs in the apartment, waiting and listening, and planned to run down all those steps if necessary. It was a bad plan.

She thought about that as she reached her floor, unlocked the door, and went inside. The lights were off, and the flicker of the television cast strange flashes of light into the room. Even though Mrs. Weaver would be leaving soon, Laurie still locked the door.

"You're late," Mrs. Weaver said as Laurie walked into the living room.

"Is Jordie asleep?"

Mrs. Weaver shook her head. "Unless he's started snoring in the sounds of explosions and spaceships, no, he's not asleep."

"Then I'm not late," Laurie pointed out. "Curfew is before Jordie's asleep, so—"

"Nice try, missy." Mrs. Weaver's mouth was trying not to curl into a smile, though.

Laurie opened the door to her little brother's room. Piles of books and toys were everywhere, but Mom wouldn't yell at him. Jordie was her "little angel," the baby who didn't worry her. If his school called, it was to say what a great job he did or what award he was getting. *He should've been a Thorsen.*

"Good night," she said. "Stop blowing things up."

"A volcano blew up for real!" Jordie squirmed in his bed, flopping over so he could see her.

"A what?"

"Volcano." Jordie made another explosion noise. "The whole top blew off like a rocket. Isn't that cool? Lava and smoke and—"

"Mom doesn't like you watching the news." Laurie sighed.

"And she doesn't like you being out this late. I won't tell if you don't," Jordie said, with the sort of bargaining powers that had kept him in gummy bears for months.

She rolled her eyes, but she still said, "Deal."

After she'd pulled the door shut, she went back out to the living room. Mrs. Weaver had gathered up her knitting needles and was slipping on her shoes. They said their good-nights, and Laurie curled up on the sofa with her math homework.

The sound of the lock turning woke her. Sort of. Sleepily, she let her mom direct her to bed. It wasn't like Laurie usually worried, but the whole episode with Fen tonight had freaked her out a lot. If Matt would've stayed out of it, she could've talked Fen into leaving the shield alone. *Maybe.* Either way, though, Matt didn't need to throw that light thing or whatever it was he did.

"Saw Fen," she told her mother.

"Laurie..." The tone that her mom always had when she talked about Fen was already there; even half-asleep, Laurie heard it. It meant *Fen's bad news, stay away from him.*

"He's family," Laurie murmured as she crawled into her bed.

Her mother pulled a cover over her. "One of these times he's going to get you into the sort of trouble you aren't ready for. Then what will you do?"

"Handle it." Laurie snuggled into her bed. "I can handle it."

A few hours later, Laurie woke with the vague sense of suffocation, which wasn't entirely unexpected because she had woken up as a ... *fish*—a salmon, to be precise.

I am a fish.

She'd gone to sleep as a perfectly average thirteen-year-old girl and woken up as a fish, and as much as she'd like to try to figure out how that had happened, she had a more pressing concern: air. Salmon needed water to get that, and since she was a girl when she'd crawled into her bed, she was now a fish nowhere near water.

Her fishy eyes spied a sports bottle, and she felt a flicker of hope, but the lack of thumbs and the inability to put a salmon in a bottle made that useless as far as solutions go.

She flopped around on her bed, torn between trying to figure out how not to be a fish and trying to decide if she could flop her way to water—and trying to wake up for real because the odds of this being a bad dream seemed pretty high ... except she felt awake.

I can't be a fish. It's a dream. No. I'm really a salmon.

21

The only water nearby was the toilet, and flopping her way into that germy thing sounded gross...but the need for air outweighed the sheer nastiness of trying to swim in a toilet.

With a burst of energetic wiggling, she managed to launch herself from her bed. She hit the floor, her fall cushioned by the piles of clothes strewn all through the room. She wriggled her way across the clothes, books, and accumulated junk on her floor—and hit the closed door.

I need help. I need Fen.

If fish could cry, Laurie would be weeping. The thought of dying as a fish, of her mother finding a stinky dead fish on the floor, was far from good.

Where is Fen?

Her cousin should be here; he should help her. That's how it worked: they helped each other, but he wasn't here, and she was going to die. Her gills opened and closed rapidly as she panicked, too exhausted to even try to figure out how a salmon could open a door.

The door opened, and Laurie stared up at her rescuer. *Not Mom. Not Dad. Not Fen.* Her little brother stood in her doorway. "Why are you on the floor?"

"Because I'm a fish," she said.

Jordie stared at her. He opened his mouth, apparently thought better of whatever he was going to say, and closed it. He shrugged.

"Can you open the bathroom door and put me in the tub? My fins—"

"You're kind of weird." He turned away.

"Is she awake?" Her mother called.

"Yeah, but she says she's a fish," Jordie yelled back to their mother.

Laurie took a deep breath . . . and realized that she had no gills. "I can breathe!" She looked around her room. The bedcovers were tangled, and she was on the floor. It had been a dream—a vivid dream, but not real. Girls don't turn into fish. She went over and sat on the bed—and was still sitting there half-dazed when her mother walked into her room.

"Honey? Are you okay?" Her mother leaned down and kissed her forehead, checking for fever. "Jordie said you had a bad dream."

"I was a fish," Laurie said, looking up at her mother. "Fen wasn't here, and I was going to die because Fen wasn't helping me."

Her mother sighed and sat next to her. Silently, she pulled Laurie into a hug and rested her cheek against Laurie's head. After a minute, she said, "You can't count on boys, especially your cousin Fen. I know you care for him, but Fen's trouble. He has no one teaching him right and wrong, and the way he's been raised . . ."

"We could let him live here," Laurie suggested.

Her mother's pause held the things her mother wouldn't

23

say—that she disliked Fen, that that side of the family made her uncomfortable, that the only reason she let any of them into the house was because she still loved Dad. Finally, what she did say was, "I need to think of what's best for my kids, and having Fen around Jordie isn't what's best. I'm sorry."

Laurie pulled away, got dressed, and walked out of the room. She didn't argue with her mother. That was something she tried not to do. She felt like she started enough trouble without meaning to, so causing problems on purpose was a bad idea. She stayed quiet. She wanted to tell her mother about the dream, but she felt silly. She'd wait and talk to Fen. He was her best friend, her almost-brother, and the only person who wouldn't think she was crazy for worrying over fish dreams.

Maybe.

THREE

❖

FEN

"DUES"

Fen spent the next day expecting the sheriff to come grab him and the evening hiding in the damp of the park looking for a chance to get the shield. Even though Thorsen apparently hadn't specifically ratted him out, he obviously had said something because there were patrols around the longship all night. Fen had tried to get the job done, but he'd failed.

And he wasn't much looking forward to telling Kris, but when he trudged home from the park and saw the rusty pickup truck, he knew he had no choice. His cousin was home from wherever he had been the past few days.

Fen didn't ask too many questions about where Kris

went. Lesson number one in the Brekke family: what you don't know, you can't spill. It wasn't a matter of trust, really, just common sense. Brekkes looked out for themselves first. They might do a good turn for someone—or not—but they weren't foolish enough to go sharing things that could land them in hot water.

He crossed the pitted gravel drive and stood in the doorway to the garage.

"Fen? That you?" The voice called out from under the shell of an old car. Kris had been working on it for the better part of the year. Music blared from an old stereo. Like everything in Kris' place, it hadn't been in good condition for years.

"Yeah."

"Grab me a beer." From under the car, one greasy hand pointed in the general direction of the rust-covered refrigerator in the back corner of the garage.

Fen dropped his bag on the floor. He shoved it to the side with the toe of his boot and went over to the fridge. The door creaked, and the old metal handle clacked as he opened it. He pulled out a can of beer and popped the top. He didn't understand why anyone drank it. Kris gave him some one day, but it was gross. Beer tasted like how he suspected dog urine would taste, but everyone in his family drank the stuff.

"I heard that top pop, boy. It better be full when you hand it to me," Kris said.

Fen walked over and held the can out. "It is."

"Good pup." Kris slid out from under the car. He lay stretched on the creeper, grime, oil, and grease covering him from boots to bandanna. He was in his twenties, but now that Fen was in middle school, one of the aunts had decided Kris was old enough to keep Fen this year. It was a lot better than the year he'd spent with Cousin Mandy. She was older than dirt and had some crazy ideas about how many chores he should have. Kris, on the other hand, was young enough to remember hating chores. He gave Fen things to do, but they weren't exactly chores most of the time.

Kris sat up, grabbed the can, and took a long drink. He wiped his mouth with a grubby hand. "So did you get it?"

"No."

Kris frowned. "It was a simple task, boy. Go steal a shield. Easy stuff."

"Thorsen...Sheriff Thorsen's son Matt was there yesterday, and today there were patrols all day." Fen squatted down so he was eye to eye with Kris.

"The last thing I need is Mayor Thorsen or the sheriff to come around here asking questions. You need to stay clear of that kid."

"I know, and I did. Last night was the only time Laurie could be there, though, and I need her to be a part of the job," Fen added. "What was I supposed to do?"

"You were supposed to get the job done. You better figure

that out fast, boy." Kris finished his beer and crumpled the can. "If you don't pay your dues to the *wulfenkind*, there won't be anything anyone can do to help you."

"I heard you the first three times you told me," Fen snapped.

"Don't be smart." Kris stood and walked back to get another beer. "Bet there aren't as many patrols during the day."

"I have school," Fen started.

Kris opened the second beer. "You think the *wulfenkind* are going to care that you had school?"

"I could try again tonight," Fen suggested. "But what about Laurie?"

Kris nodded. "She *did* help, so that term is met. Go get it on your own, and if you can't get it tonight, you miss school tomorrow."

"Right," Fen said.

"If you don't get the job done, Laurie will have to meet them," Kris threatened.

Years of protecting his cousin made his answer obvious. He said, "I'll get it. Promise."

Fen heard the alarm go off in the middle of the night, far too few hours after he'd set it. It was one of those horrible clocks that ticked, and the alarm was a little hammer that smashed back and forth between two bells. *Like Thorsen's little Hammer*

trick. Fen threw the alarm at the wall. *Like I could throw him.* Even as he thought it, though, Fen scowled. The sad truth was that Fen couldn't toss Matt at a wall. Thorsens were unnaturally strong, and even though every Brekke had a few extra skills of their own, they also knew not to tangle with Thorsens. Well, not *every* Brekke knew it. Laurie was still clueless. Fen had only known what was up for a few years, and he'd done his best to play dumb.

Like the Thorsens think we all are.

After Kris snarled about the alarm—and the *thunk* of the alarm hitting the wall—Fen figured he'd better make as little noise as possible. He carried his boots to the front door. When he stepped outside, he held the screen door rather than let it slap closed. A rush of relief hit him when he turned to face the darkness. He could pretend it was just because he'd avoided Kris' temper, but the truth was that Fen always felt a bit of stress vanish when he stepped outside. Wolves, even those in human skin, weren't meant to be inside. This time of night was the best. Most people were in their beds in their homes, and the world was his.

He sat on the stoop, shoved his feet into his boots, grabbed the sack and crowbar Kris had left out for him, and started off toward Sarek Park. If Fen didn't take care of what he owed the Raiders, there would be consequences. The Raiders—*wulfenkind* packs—lived a life of thievery and scavenging, roaming from camp to camp, barely a minute ahead of the law. They could join packs once they shifted, but from birth they owed dues. Usually their parents paid. If not, the pack held a running tally of dues. Fen, like every Brekke, had to either pay dues to the local pack of his age group, join it, or—once he was old enough—go lone-wolf. For now, he'd opted to pay dues—his *and* Laurie's. He wasn't going to offer obedience to anyone simply because they were the best fighter.

Laurie didn't even know a lot about the ways things worked. She didn't know what he was or what she might be—because she didn't know about their ancestor Loki. So she had no idea that Fen was sometimes a wolf. Unless Laurie changed, they didn't need to tell her.

Her dad, Fen's uncle Stig, didn't think she'd change. Her mother wasn't *wulfenkind*, so she might turn out to be just a regular person. If she didn't change, she didn't need to know. Fen wished he could tell her, wished she would be a wolf, too... almost as much as he hoped, for her sake, that she wouldn't be one. For now, he agreed to pay her dues to the *wulfenkind* during the transition window. Usually *wulfenkind* parents did that, but Uncle Stig was a lone wolf, so Fen had taken on the responsibility. It's what he'd have done if Laurie were *really* his sister, not just his cousin. It meant double payments, but he could handle it. Once they knew if she'd change, she'd take over her own payments, join a pack, or go lone-wolf like Uncle Stig. Laurie was even less likely than Fen to join, so if she changed, Fen figured he'd either help her with payments or they'd go lone-wolf together. The problem with being a lone wolf was that you couldn't stay in any one territory too long. He couldn't imagine going lone-wolf without her, and he certainly wasn't joining the Raiders.

For now, that left him with dues, and for reasons he didn't want to know, the Raiders said the old shield was payment enough for both of them. The only weird thing was that the wolf in charge of their age pack, Skull, had said Laurie had to be involved at least a little—and she had been. Now Fen just had to finish the job.

His feet hurt from too many trips between Kris' trailer and the park, but there were rules about running around Blackwell as a wolf, so he went as he was. Of course, even if he was allowed to shift to wolf, it would cause other problems. *What would I do? Bite it free?* He smiled a little at that image, and he ran the rest of the way to Sarek Park.

This late—*or early, really*—the patrol cars weren't passing by as often. He took the crowbar Kris had given him and applied it to the side of the ship with as much force as he could. The shield was already loose. It had to be that specific one, the third shield from the front with the weird designs on it. Viking symbols, Fen guessed. He didn't know why it had to be that shield; he didn't really care. He just put his strength into prying it free.

Fifteen minutes and several splinters later, Fen was starting to really worry. "Come on; come on." He gave another good tug, and the final bolt popped free. The shield dropped to the ground with a loud crash.

Fen jumped over the side of the longship, landing in a crouch with one hand flat on the ground, and grabbed the shield.

As he did so, a big gray wolf padded into the park. He was as large as a full-grown wolf, but even before he shook off his fur and stood on two feet, Fen knew who it was.

Skull grinned at him and said, "Not bad."

Skull was only a few years older than Fen, but he was a lot scarier than any of the guys at school. He had scars on his arms, and right now, he also had a red scrape on his cheek that kept company with a number of purple and yellow bruises. He wasn't skinny, but he didn't have any fat on him. Skull was nothing but muscle, scars, and attitude.

"Where's Laurie?"

"Not here." Fen shoved the shield into the bag he'd brought with him and held it out to Skull. "She helped the first time I tried to get it, but she doesn't need to meet *you*."

Skull didn't take the bag Fen held out. "You can carry it."

He turned his back and walked away without seeing if Fen had obeyed. Of course, they both knew that he could follow or fight Skull—and that fighting would either result in being hurt pretty bad or being in charge of this pack of *wulfenkind*. Winning a fight with the lead wolf meant replacing him. As much as Fen disliked Skull, he didn't know that he could beat the older wolf, and even if he could, he didn't want it badly enough to risk getting saddled with the responsibility of a pack.

They walked at least five miles, so on top of the lack of sleep, Fen was dead on his feet by the time they reached the camp. Small groups of *wulfenkind* looked up with interest.

Skull's twin sister, Hattie, walked over and held out a chunk of some sort of meat on a stick, probably elk from the smell. "Want a bite?" She took a bite out of it, chewed, and swallowed. "It's safe."

He accepted it with a nod. He wasn't as constantly ravenous as the older *wulfenkind* got, because he didn't change forms as much yet, but he was starting to notice a change.

Skull nodded at Hattie, and she put her fingers to her lips and whistled. Once everyone looked at her, she signaled different people and then different directions. "Check the perimeter."

Of the almost two dozen boys and girls there, half—in two groups of six—left. Fen watched with appreciation. They were a well-organized, obedient pack. The camp was impressive, too. Gear was in small piles, firewood was stacked tidily, and sleeping bags were rolled and stowed. Camp could break and depart in moments.

"You could stay with us," Hattie offered. Her attention had both flattered and frightened him for years. She was one

33

of the strongest *wulfenkind* he'd met, but she was also weird and kind of mean. When they were ten, he'd watched her kill several squirrels by biting their throats. If she'd been in wolf form at the time, he might not have found it so gross. She hadn't been, though.

"Here." He pulled the shield out of the sack and tossed it to her. He didn't expect it to hit her, but he might have hoped a little. Unlike fighting Skull, there were no downsides to fighting Hattie.

She caught the shield in midair. "You brought me a present?"

Skull laughed.

Fen shifted his feet and said, "No. It's the dues for me *and* Laurie."

Skull clamped a hand on his shoulder and squeezed, but he told his sister, "Leave Fen alone. You're scaring him."

Although he was trying not to get into too much trouble with Skull, Fen couldn't ignore the insult. "I'm not sc—"

"You belong with us, Fen," Skull interrupted. "You know something big is coming. We need it to come. We'll make it come."

Hattie laid the shield down on a piece of animal hide that one of the younger wolves had dragged over to her. She squatted beside it and looked over her shoulder at Fen. "This wood was from the bog. This will be used in the final fight."

"The *what*?"

"Ragnarök," Skull said reverently.

"Ragnarök?" Fen repeated. He shook his head. It was one thing to remember the old stories, to know where they came from, but it was another to think that the end of the world was coming.

"The prophecy is true," Skull said. "The final battle will change everything. It will be the sons—"

"And *daughters*," Hattie interjected with a growl.

Skull continued, without even glancing at his sister, "The children of Loki will rise up; the monsters will wake. We'll rule the world, and everyone will tithe to us. We'll reign over the world like kings."

And as much as Fen thought they were a little crazy before, right then he knew that they were far beyond simply crazy. The whole there-used-to-be-gods bit was true, but the gods were stupid. They were all dead. If the gods were dead, how could there be a final battle? It didn't make any sense. Of course, that didn't mean Fen felt like getting into it with Skull and Hattie. He tried to sound a little less disdainful than he felt as he said, "Right. Gods and monsters will fight, and a new world will be born. You'll be in charge. Sure thing."

Hattie stood and instantly arranged her body for a fight. "You doubt it?"

Ignoring her, Fen tossed the stick with the rest of the meat toward the fire and pointed at the shield. "I stole the shield. I carried it to your camp. We're square. My dues and Laurie's are paid. Whatever you do with it now is your business."

"We just need one more thing," Hattie started.

Fen looked from Skull to Hattie and back again. It was one thing not to start trouble with them; it was another thing to be their errand boy. "I *paid*," Fen said. "Those are the rules. I paid, and now I'm done."

Skull punched him.

Fen staggered. The whole side of his face hurt, and he knew he'd have a black eye for school. *Great. Just great.* He stepped backward.

Hattie walked over to stand beside Skull. Behind her, Fen could see other members of the pack watching. There would be no help here. They followed orders. They protected their pack and worked toward the goals of the pack.

"The final fight is coming. That changes things," Hattie added.

The temper Fen was trying to keep in check flared. "Rules are rules, so—"

"*You* can help, or we can go to Laurie, and *she* can help," Skull said. "The monsters will come, and they will fight alongside our champion. We need to be ready."

There was no way Fen was letting them near Laurie, especially after the things they'd just said. He lowered his gaze as meekly as he could. "What do you want?"

37

"A Thorsen. The youngest one," Skull said.

Every Brekke knew there were things the Raiders did, things that were better not asked about. That didn't mean that Fen liked the idea of helping them get at anyone he knew—even someone he disliked. Turning a person over to them was wrong.

"Why?" Fen asked, hoping that they would say something that didn't involve hurting Thorsen.

Hattie sighed. "Because he's *their* champion in the final fight."

"Right," Fen drawled. "You need to stop a kid from fighting in Ragnarök. What are you going to do, really?"

Skull and Hattie exchanged a look, and then Skull stepped forward and slung an arm around Fen. "The boss said to deliver the kid. We aren't dumb enough to ask what for, but"—he paused and grinned—"if you want to ask, we can deliver you and Laurie, too."

"No," Fen said carefully. "I'll get him."

Skull squeezed Fen's shoulder tighter, painfully so, and said, "Good pup."

FOUR

❖

MATT

"PREMONITION"

Matt lay in bed. It'd been a day since he'd unleashed Thor's Hammer. Fen hadn't said anything to anyone. Laurie hadn't, either. Matt wanted to believe that meant they were going to forget it, but he couldn't help thinking they were only waiting for the right moment. Then they'd tell everyone how he'd used something like a flash-bang and knocked Fen right off his feet, and Matt's parents—and every other Thorsen in town—would know exactly what had happened. Matt had broken the rules: he'd used Thor's Hammer.

Thor's Hammer was the only magical power the Thorsens still had. Sure, they were usually bigger than other people, and stronger, too, but that wasn't magic. The old books said there used to be other powers, like control over weather, but that was long gone. They were left with the Hammer, which for everyone else was like an invisible punch that they could throw whenever they wanted. Only Matt got the special-effects package—the flash and the bang. And only Matt wasn't able to control when it went off.

His grandfather had tried giving him different amulets, but it didn't fix anything. His parents were right: it wasn't the amulet messing up—it was him. The power was in the descendants of Thor themselves—the amulet was just a . . . Matt struggled for the word his family used. Conduit. That was it. The necklace was a conduit that allowed the power to work. Which should mean the solution was easy: take off the necklace. Except a Thorsen couldn't do that for long before he got sick. Matt could remove his in the boxing ring, luckily, but that was it.

He should just tell his parents what happened. He'd started to last night, then chickened out and told Dad he'd seen some kids messing around at the longship, and Dad said he'd have his men patrol for a while. He'd lectured Matt, too, about taking more responsibility for their town, how he should have done something about it, not come home and tattled to his parents. That stung, especially when Matt *had* done something. He already felt bad about it. He should have been able to handle Fen without setting off the Hammer.

Don't think about that. Focus on something else. Think of your science fair project.

Oh, yeah. That helped. Let's focus on *another* example of how badly you can mess up, Matty.

He'd totally blown his science project, and he needed to do a new one before tomorrow night's fair. He'd overcomplicated things, as usual. He'd been trying extra hard because his family always won the eighth-grade science fair. First his dad. Then his brothers, Jake and Josh. If it were any other subject, Matt would be fine. But, as usual, if his family was good at it, he wasn't.

Maybe if he slept on it. He got some of his best ideas at night, when he could relax and stop worrying.

When he finally fell asleep, he did dream about his science project... all the ways he could mess it up again and embarrass his family. He kept dreaming about building the best project ever, only to accidentally unleash Thor's Hammer and blow it to smithereens in front of the entire school. Then his brain seemed to get tired of that and plunked him down in the middle of a field.

It was daytime. He was standing there, staring up at the sky. He wasn't alone; he could sense someone behind him. But he didn't turn to see who it was. He was busy staring at the sun—and at the wolf chasing it.

The wolf was a huge, black shadow, all gleaming red eyes

41

and glistening fangs. The sun was a glowing chariot pulled by three white horses.

"It's Sköll and Sól," Matt murmured.

"Huh?" said a girl's voice behind him. He felt like he should know the voice, and in the dream, he seemed to, but his sleeping self couldn't place it.

"A Norse myth. The sun circles the earth because she's trying to escape the wolf Sköll. And the moon—" He squinted against the bright sun. Behind Sól's chariot, he could make out a paler version, chased by another shadow wolf. "There he is. Behind her. Máni, chased by Hati."

"Looks like the wolves are catching up."

Matt shook his head. "That won't happen until Ragnarök."

"Ragnarök?"

"The end of the world. It's supposed to begin when Loki kills Balder. Then Sköll catches Sól, and Hati catches Máni, and the world is plunged into endless night and winter. But that's not going to—"

The wolves leaped and closed the gap. The chariot riders whipped their horses, and they pulled ahead.

Matt exhaled. "Okay, it's just—"

The wolves lunged again. They caught the chariots in their powerful teeth and wrenched. The chariots toppled backward, horses flying. The sun and moon tumbled out. The wolves dove after them, opened their jaws, and...

Darkness.

Matt bolted up in bed, his heart thudding so hard he swore he could hear it.

Ragnarök.

The end of the world.

He blinked hard. Then he shook his head. Yes, his family did believe in Ragnarök, and the Seer was always looking for signs, but they'd been looking since before the old gods had died. Because the gods had been…well, *stupid*, they'd all managed to get themselves killed long ago. According to the Seer, that meant that when Ragnarök did come, some of the descendants would have to stand in for the original gods in the final battle. They'd be filled with the gods' powers and would fight the monsters as it had been foretold. Luckily, Ragnarök wasn't coming in his lifetime. What *was* coming was the science fair. Not exactly apocalyptic, but it sure felt like it.

He rubbed his face and yawned. Every time he closed his eyes, though, he saw the wolves chasing the sun and the moon.

He shook his head. That wasn't going to help his science… Or could it?

Matt smiled, stretched out again, and fell asleep.

"Rakfisk!" Josh yelled, thumping open Matt's door. "Hey, Mini-Matt. Don't you smell that? Mom's making rakfisk."

43

Matt lifted his head, inhaling in spite of himself. He groaned and clenched his teeth to keep from barfing into the pillow. Nothing smells as bad as raw fish. Unless it's raw fish that's been left to rot for months, then served on toast. For breakfast.

Jake grabbed Josh's shoulder. "Don't wake the baby. More for us."

Josh was seventeen and Jake a year younger, but they were both so big that Josh practically filled the doorway by himself, and all Matt could see of Jake was a shock of red hair over his brother's shoulder.

They took off, thudding down the hall. Matt lifted his head, nose plugged. He tried breathing through his mouth, but that didn't help, because then he could *taste* the rakfisk. If there was one thing that totally ruined Norse holidays, it was the food. Ancient Viking traditions, his mom would say. Traditions the Vikings should have kept to themselves, he thought.

He found his mom in the kitchen, working at the counter while his brothers sat at the table and devoured plates of rakfisk on toast. He opened the fridge and found two milk containers. The first was filled with a thin, bluish-white liquid. Whey—the stuff that's left over after you curdle milk for cheese. He groaned and shoved it back in.

"Whey's full of protein, Matty," his mother said. "You won't get any bigger drinking pop."

44

"Oh, he won't get any bigger no matter what he drinks," Jake said. "Or no matter how many weights he lifts. Josh and I were both bigger than Matt at his age."

Josh shrugged. "Not by much. There's still time. Maybe if he'd join the football team…"

"I like boxing."

His mother tried not to make a face. She didn't like boxing. Or wrestling, which Matt also did, although he wasn't as good at it. She said she worried he'd get himself hurt, but he knew she just didn't get it. Football was the only real sport in the Thorsen house. Or in all of Blackwell.

"Oh," she said. "Your granddad asked about you last night. You haven't had any more…" She gestured to his amulet. "Outbursts?"

Matt struggled to keep his expression blank. "No, not since the last time." Which, technically, was true. Just not the "last time" she knew about.

His mom exhaled in relief. "Good," she said. "Now, let me get you some rakfisk for breakfast."

Science fair night. There were about a hundred people milling about the gym, pretending to be interested in the projects.

Hunter stood beside Matt's table. "I don't get it."

"That's 'cause you're too lazy to read." Cody waved at the explanation Matt had posted. "Which isn't a surprise, since you're too lazy to even do your own project. Did you think no one would notice you borrowed your brother's?"

Hunter's project was supposed to be a volcano, but after three years in storage, the "lava" kept running out through the holes mice had chewed.

Matt heard a snort. He glanced over to see Fen, who sported a fresh black eye. He was there with Laurie, keeping his head ducked down like he was trying to hide his shiner.

As Laurie approached Matt's table, Fen scowled. Laurie just gave him a look, and then asked Matt, "What's it supposed to be?"

Matt started to explain, but then noticed his granddad and two of the Thorsen Elders heading over, so he switched to his grown-up lecture.

"It's from a Norse myth," he said. "The wolves, Sköll and Hati, chase the sun, Sól, and the moon, Máni."

He waved to the board, where shadow wolves were supposed to be chasing two glowing balls on a modified railroad track. It hadn't quite worked, though, and they weren't actually moving. Biting off more than he could chew, his dad had said. Still, it looked okay. Granddad and the others had stopped now for a better look.

"In the story, they finally do catch them." Matt leaned over to push the wolves around the track, and they picked up speed until they moved over the balls, and the toy globe in the middle went dark. "That marks the beginning of

Ragnarök. The battle of the gods. From a scientific point of view, we can see this as an explanation for eclipses. Many cultures had a myth to explain why the sun would disappear and how to get it back."

He motioned to a second board, covered in eclipse pictures and graphs and descriptions. It was a rush job, and it looked like it, but it wasn't as bad as some...or so he kept telling himself.

"That's very interesting, Matty," his grandfather said, putting a hand on his shoulder. "Where did you come up with an idea like that?"

Matt shrugged. "It just came to me."

"Did it?"

Granddad's blue eyes caught Matt's, and under his stare, Matt felt his knees wobble. His grandfather studied him for another minute, his lips pursed behind his graying red beard. Then he clapped Matt on the back, murmured something to the Elders, and they moved on.

Matt got a B, which was great for a rushed project that didn't actually work right. His teachers seemed happy. His parents weren't. They'd headed out as he packed up his project, and he'd taken it apart carefully, slowly, hoping they'd get tired of waiting and leave.

"So it just came to you," said a voice behind him.

It was Granddad. The gym was empty now, the last kids and parents streaming out.

Matt nodded. "I'm sorry I didn't win."

His grandfather put his arm around Matt's shoulders. "Science isn't your strongest subject. You got a B. I think that's great." His grandfather pointed to the honorable mention ribbon on Matt's table. "And that's better than great."

Of the thirty projects at the fair, five got an honorable mention. Plus there were the first-, second-, and third-place winners. So it wasn't really much of an accomplishment, but Matt mumbled a thanks and started stacking his pages.

"So, Matty, now that it's just us, tell me, how *did* it come to you?"

Matt shrugged. "I had a dream."

"About what?"

"The wolves devouring the sun and moon. The start of the Great Winter."

"Fimbulwinter."

Matt nodded, and it took a moment for him to realize his grandfather had gone still. When he saw the old man's expression, his heart did a double-thump. He should be more careful. With the Elders, you couldn't casually talk about dreams like that. Especially not dreams of Ragnarök.

"I was worried about my project," Matt said. "It was just a dumb dream. You know, the kind where if you fail your project, the world ends." He rolled his eyes. "Dumb."

"What exactly did you see?"

Sweat beaded along Matt's forehead. As he swiped at it, his hands trembled.

Granddad whispered, "It's okay, Matty. I'm just curious. Tell me about it."

Matt did. He didn't have a choice. This wasn't just his granddad talking—it was the mayor of Blackwell and the lawspeaker of the town.

When he finished, his grandfather nodded, as if...*pleased*. He looked pleased.

"It—it was only a dream," Matt blurted. "I know you guys believe in that stuff, but it wasn't like that. I didn't mean to—"

Granddad cut him off by bending down, hands on Matt's shoulders. "You didn't do anything wrong. I was just curious. It's always interesting to hear where inspiration comes from. I'm very proud of you. Always have been."

Matt shifted, uncomfortable. "Mom and Dad are waiting...."

"Of course they are." After another quick hug, Granddad said, "I've always known you were special, Matty. Soon everyone else will know it, too."

He pulled back, thumped Matt on the back, and handed him the box. "You carry this, and I'll take your papers. It's windy out there. We don't want them blowing away."

Matt started across the gym, Granddad beside him. "I saw ice on the Norrström a few days ago. Is that why we're having Vetrarblot so soon? Winter's coming early?"

"Yes," Granddad said. "I believe it is."

FIVE

MATT

"CHOSEN"

After the science fair, Granddad came to the house and took Matt's parents for a walk. By the time they came back, Matt was heading off to bed—early wrestling practice—but they called him out to the living room and gave him a long speech about how proud they were of him for getting a B and an honorable mention. As a reward, they'd chip in the forty bucks he still needed to add to his lawn-cutting money so he could buy an iPod touch.

He knew they weren't really proud of him. He'd still messed up. But his parents always did what Granddad said. Most people in Blackwell did. Anyway, he wouldn't argue about the money. Now he could start saving for a dirt bike, and maybe if he managed to win the state boxing finals, Granddad would guilt his parents into chipping in for that, too. Not likely—his mom hated dirt bikes almost as much as she hated boxing—but a guy could dream.

Vetrarblot. It wasn't as cool as Sigrblot—because Sigrblot meant summer was coming, which meant school was ending—but it was a big deal. A really big deal this year, for Matt. He'd just turned thirteen, which meant he'd now be initiated into the *Thing*.

The *Thing*. What a dumb name. Sure, that's what it had been called back in Viking days—the word *thing* meant assembly—but you'd think one of Blackwell's founding fathers would have come up with a new name so the town meetings wouldn't sound so stupid. They hadn't.

In Viking times, the *Thing* was an assembly made up of all the adult men who weren't thralls—what the Vikings called slaves. In Blackwell, women were members, too. And by all "adults," they meant all Thorsens past their thirteenth birthday.

As for what exactly the assembly did, well, that was the not-so-exciting part. It was politics. They'd decide stuff. Then the town council—which was mostly Thorsens—would make it happen.

They discussed community issues, too—ones you couldn't bring up in a town council, like "That Brekke kid is getting into trouble again" or, he imagined, "Matt Thorsen still can't control his powers." Which was why he'd rather not be sitting there listening.

And during Vetrarblot, he'd really rather not be there. They held the meeting just as the fair was starting. Cody and the rest of Matt's friends had a nine-o'clock curfew, which meant he wasn't even sure he'd get out of the *Thing* in time to join them. Which was totally unfair, but his parents wouldn't be too happy if he began his journey into adulthood by whining about not getting to play milk-bottle games.

He'd already gotten a long talk from them that morning about how he was supposed to behave. Matt was pretty sure they were worried it would be a repeat of the disaster at Jolablot. That was the winter festival where they retold all the old stories, and Granddad had asked Matt to tell the one about Thor and Loki in the land of the giants, just like Josh and Jake had when they were twelve. His parents hadn't wanted him to do it, but Matt insisted. He knew the myths better than his brothers did. A lot better. He'd make them proud of him. He'd really tried to—memorizing his piece and practicing in front of his friends. Then he got up on the stage and looked out at everyone and froze. Just froze. Granddad had to come to his rescue, and his parents weren't

53

ever going to let him forget it. This festival, he'd just keep quiet, keep his head down and out of the spotlight, and do as he was told.

Between the parade and the *Thing*, there was food. Real food, not corn dogs and cotton candy. At that time, everyone who wasn't a Thorsen went home or filled the local restaurants or carried picnic baskets to Sarek Park. The Thorsens took over the rec center. That's when the feasting began. There was rakfisk, of course, and roast boar and elk and pancakes with lingonberries. Mead, too, but Matt didn't get any of that.

Inside the rec center, there were a bunch of smaller rooms plus the main hall, which was where the feast took place. The hall would have looked like a gym, except for the mosaics on every wall. Matt's granddad said they were nearly five hundred years old, brought over from some castle in Norway.

The mosaics showed scenes of Thor. Fight scenes mostly—when it came to myths about Thor, that's what you got. Thor fought this giant, and then this giant, and then this giant. Oh, yeah, and a few dwarves, but they were really mean dwarves.

Back when Matt had signed up for boxing and wrestling, he'd pointed this out to his parents. Sure, people loved and respected Thor because he was a great guy, but more than a little of that came because he sent monsters packing. And he didn't send them packing by asking nicely.

His parents hadn't bought it. Physical strength was all very good—they certainly wouldn't want a bookworm for a son—but the Thorsens weren't like Thor. They had each other, so it was a team effort, and those skills were better developed through football.

Still, those mosaics were what Matt grew up with. Thor fighting Hrungnir. Thor fighting Geirrod. Thor fighting Thyrm. Thor fighting Hymir. And, finally, in a mosaic that took up the entire back wall, Thor's greatest battle with his greatest enemy: the Midgard Serpent.

According to legend, Thor had defeated the serpent once but hadn't killed it. He'd fished it out of the sea and thrown his hammer, Mjölnir, at it, leaving it slinking off, dazed but alive. According to the myth, when Ragnarök came, the serpent would return for vengeance. The mosaic on the wall showed how the epic battle would play out, ending with Thor delivering the killing blow. As Thor turned his back, though, the dying serpent managed one last strike: it poisoned Thor. And the god staggered away to die.

Matt kept looking at the Midgard Serpent scene as he sat with his family at the head table. The hall was filled with wooden folding chairs and long tables set up for family-style feasting. A small stage stretched across the front of the room.

The Seer was already up there with her assistant. At first look, he always thought the Seer could be a grandmother, but when he'd look again, he'd think she barely looked old enough to be a mother. She had that kind of face. For the festivals, the Seer and her assistant both dressed like women from Viking times, in long, plain white dresses with apronlike blue dresses overtop. White cloth covered their blond hair. Otherwise, they looked like a lot of women in Blackwell, and he was sure he passed them all the time on the streets and never even recognized them without their Viking dresses.

As the feasting went on, the Seer stood on her platform, throwing her runes and mumbling under her breath, making pronouncements that her assistant furiously jotted down. Matt noticed some of the younger members of the *Thing* had taken seats near her. They were hoping to hear something important. They weren't allowed to talk to her. No one could. And they really, really weren't allowed to ask her anything.

Divining the future through runes was a very serious matter, not to be confused with fortune-telling, a lesson Matt had learned when he'd bought a set of fake ones and charged kids two bucks to get their futures told. That scheme got him hauled in front of the *Thing*, and he'd had to miss the next festival. He should have known better. Okay, he *did* know better. But it was like pulling pranks—he knew he should just behave and make his parents proud, but he couldn't seem to help himself. It was hard, doing the right thing all the time, trying to live up to his brothers when he knew he never could—not really—and sometimes, he just got tired of trying.

As dinner wound down, more people moved to sit cross-legged around the Seer. Others shifted to the Tafl tables set up along the sides of the room. When Granddad asked Matt to play a match against him, it was no big deal—Matt played Tafl with his grandfather all the time. Maybe not at the festivals, but only because Granddad was usually too busy. As they walked to a table, though, Matt could hear a buzz snake around the room, people whispering and turning to look, some making their way over to watch.

Tafl—also known as Hnefatafl, but no one could pronounce *that*—was a Norse game of strategy, even older than chess. It was called the Viking game because that's where it came from, and it was based on the idea of a raid, with each player getting two sets of pieces as his "ship" and the king and his defenders in the middle.

Matt wasn't worried about people watching his match with Granddad. Tafl was like boxing: he knew he was good at it. Not good enough to win every time, but good enough that he wouldn't embarrass his family.

He didn't win that match. Didn't lose, either. The game had to be called on account of time—kids were itching to get out to the fair before dark, and it was Granddad's job to officially end the feast. As Granddad did that and the kids took off to the fair, Mom led Matt over to the chairs that had been set up as the tables were cleared.

When Granddad stepped onto the stage, everyone went silent. Someone carried a podium up and set it in front of him. He nodded his thanks, cleared his throat, and looked out at the group.

"As some of you know," he began, "this will be very different from our usual assemblies. No new business will be brought forward tonight. Instead, we will be discussing a matter that is of unparalleled importance to all of us."

Some people shifted in their chairs. Were they worried about what Granddad was going to say? Or did they know something Matt didn't, namely that *important* meant "you're going to be stuck in those chairs for a very long time"?

Granddad continued, "As you know, our world has been plagued by natural disasters for years now, but recently the rate of these disasters has increased to the point where we barely have time to deal with one before we are hit with another."

That was the truth. It seemed like every day there was a new school fund-raiser for a newly disaster-torn country. So far, Matt had helped out with two dances, a dunk tank, a bake sale, and now the charity boxing match … and it wasn't even the end of September yet.

Was that what this was about? Raising money for disaster

relief? Or maybe looking at the town's emergency plan? His parents had totally redone theirs after all those tornadoes went through in the spring.

Granddad was still talking. "Last week, a volcano erupted that scientists had sworn was dormant. Today, they closed down Yellowstone Park because the hot springs and cauldrons are boiling over, releasing deadly amounts of poisonous gas into the atmosphere." His grandfather paced across the tiny stage. "Dragon's Mouth is one of those. The Black Dragon's Cauldron is another. Aptly named, as our history tells us, because what keeps those cauldrons bubbling—and what makes fire spew from the mouths of mountains—is the great dragon, Nidhogg, the corpse eater. For centuries, his destruction has been kept to a minimum because he is otherwise occupied with his task of gnawing at the roots of the world tree. But now he no longer seems distracted. We know what that means."

Matt felt icy fingers creep up his back.

This was his fault. He had the dream, and it was just a dream, but now his grandfather believed it, was using it to explain the bad things that were happening in the world.

"Nidhogg has almost bitten through the roots of the world tree. One of the first signs of Ragnarök."

Matt gripped the sides of his chair to keep from flying up there and saying Granddad was wrong. He'd misunderstood.

He'd trusted some stupid dream that was only a dream; Matt was only a kid, not a prophet, not a Seer.

"And we understand, too, the meaning of the tsunamis and tidal waves that have devastated coastal cities around the world. Not only has Nidhogg almost gnawed through the world tree, but the Midgard Serpent has broken free from its bonds. The seas roil as the serpent rises to the surface. To the final battle. To Ragnarök."

Matt sucked in air, but it didn't seem to do any good. He started to gasp. Mom reached over and squeezed his hand. On his other side, Dad eased his chair closer, his arm going around Matt's shoulders as he whispered, "It's okay, bud." Josh leaned around Dad and gave a wry smile.

On Mom's other side, Jake snorted and rolled his eyes. Scorn for the baby who was freaking out because bad things were coming and he couldn't handle it, which was how it would look to everyone else.

Matt disentangled his hand from his mother's and shrugged off his father's arm. Then he pulled himself up straight, gaze fixed on his grandfather, who was saying something about nations in Europe breaking their promises on an environmental treaty and rumblings of conflict. All signs of Ragnarök. Oaths broken. Brother turning against brother. War coming.

"In that final battle, we have a role." Granddad looked over at the mosaic, and everyone's gaze followed to the epic confrontation against the Midgard Serpent. "For centuries, the Thorsens have worked together, stayed together, fought together. But this battle is different. This job is for one and only one. The Champion of Thor, who must win the battle, defeat the serpent, and save the world from destruction."

Dad's hand went to Matt's leg and squeezed. When Matt looked over, his father's face was tight and unreadable as he stared straight ahead.

"We have waited for the signs that point us to our champion," Granddad said. "We had seen some, but we were still unsure. Now, though, the prophecy has been fulfilled and the runes..."

He moved back, and the Seer shuffled forward. She didn't step up to the microphone, so her reedy voice barely carried past the front rows. Matt had to strain to listen.

"The runes have spoken," she said. "I have cast them again and again, and the answer remains the same. We have chosen correctly. We have our champion."

Matt glanced at his father. Tentatively, his father slid his hand around Matt's and held it so tightly that Matt had to fight not to pull away.

On the stage, the Seer's voice rose, so all could hear. "Our champion is Matthew Thorsen, son of Paul and Patricia Thorsen."

Matt froze.

There was a moment of stunned silence. Then whispers slid past. *Did he really say the Thorsen boy? He's just a kid. No, that can't be right. We heard wrong. We must have.*

Granddad's voice came back on the speakers. "I know this may come as a surprise to some of you. Matt is, after all, only thirteen. But in Viking times, he would have been on the brink of manhood. The runes have chosen Matt as our champion, as the closest embodiment of Thor. His living representative. And they have chosen others, too, all the living embodiments of their god ancestors, all children born at the turn of the millennium. Young men and women like Matt. The descendants of Frey and Freya, Balder, and the great god Odin. They will come, and they will fight alongside our champion. And…" He pointed at the mosaic of Thor's death. "That will not happen, because they will win and they will live."

Another moment of silence, like they were processing it. Then someone clapped. Someone else joined in. Finally, a cheer went up. It didn't matter if they thought Matt was too young—the runes called him the champion, so that's what he was. However ridiculous it seemed.

Matt looked around. People were turning and smiling, and his mother was pulling him into a hug, whispering how proud she was. Josh shot him a grin and a thumbs-up. Jake's glower said Matt didn't deserve the honor and he'd better not mess this up.

So Ragnarök was coming? And he was the Champion of Thor? The chosen one? The superspecial kid?

I'm dreaming. I must be.

Once he figured that out, he recovered from the shock and hugged his mother and let his dad embrace him and returned Josh's thumbs-up; then he smiled and nodded at all the congratulations. He might as well enjoy the fantasy. Too bad it wasn't real, because if he did defeat the Midgard Serpent, he was pretty sure he could get a dirt bike out of the deal. He laughed to himself as he settled back into his seat. Yeah, if he fought and killed a monstrous snake, Mom really couldn't argue that a dirt bike was too dangerous.

He looked around as everyone continued congratulating him.

It had to be a dream. Anything else was just...crazy. Sure, Matt believed in Ragnarök, sort of. He'd never thought much about it. That's just how he was raised, like some kids were raised to believe an old guy named Noah put two of every animal on one boat. You didn't think much about it—it just *was*. So Ragnarök must be real, even if it sounded...

He looked around. No, everyone else believed it, so it must be true.

Maybe it wasn't an actual serpent. Maybe it was a... what did they call it? A metaphor. That's it. Not an actual snake, but some snake-like guy who had to be killed or he'd unleash nuclear war or something.

Except that wasn't what Granddad was talking about. He meant the Midgard Serpent. Like in the picture. An actual serpent.

That's the story, Matt. Don't you believe it? You've always believed it.

His head began to throb, and he squeezed his eyes shut.

Let Granddad handle it. Just do what you need to do.

Do what? Be their champion? No. He'd make a mess of it. He always did.

The *Thing* ended, and every Thorsen lined up to shake Matt's hand. He *was* awake, and he was the chosen one—and he was going to fight the Midgard Serpent and save the world. First, though, he was going to throw up.

Every time someone shook his hand, he felt his stomach quiver, too, and he thought, *I'm going to do it. I'm going to barf. Right on their shoes.* The only way he could stop it was to clamp his jaw shut and keep nodding and smiling his fake smile and hope that the next person who pounded him on the back didn't knock dinner right out of him.

After the others left, his grandfather talked to him. It wasn't a long discussion, which was good, because Matt barely heard any of it. All he could think was *They've made a mistake. They've made a really, really big mistake.* He even tried to say that, but his grandfather just kept talking about how Matt shouldn't worry, everything would be fine—the runes wouldn't choose him if he wasn't the champion.

Check again. That's what he wanted to say. *If a kid has to fight this . . . whatever, it should be Jake, or even Josh. Not me.*

Granddad said they'd talk more later, then he slipped off with the Elders into a private meeting, and Matt was left alone with his parents. They told him a few more times that everything would be fine. Then Dad thumped him on the back and said Matt should go enjoy the fair, not worry about curfew, they'd pick him up whenever he was ready.

"Here's a little extra," Dad said, pulling out his wallet. "It's a big night for you, bud, and you deserve to celebrate."

When he held out a bill, Matt stared. It was a hundred.

"Uh, that's—" Matt began.

"Oh. Sorry." His dad put the hundred back, counted out five twenties instead, and put them in Matt's hand. "Carnies won't appreciate having to cash a hundred, will they?" Another slap on Matt's back. "Now go and have fun."

Matt wandered through the fair, sneakers kicking up sawdust. He didn't see the flashing lights. Didn't hear the carnies hustling him over. Didn't smell the hot dogs and caramel corn. He told himself he was looking for his friends, but he wasn't really. His mind was still back in the rec hall, his gaze still fixed on that mosaic, his ears still ringing with the Seer's words.

Our champion is Matthew Thorsen.

Champion. Really? No, really? I'm not even in high school yet, and they expect me to fight some giant serpent and save the world?

This isn't just some boxing tournament. It's the world.

Matt didn't quite get how that worked. Kill the serpent; save the world. That's how it was supposed to go. In the myth of Ragnarök, the gods faced off against the monsters. If they defeated the monsters, the world would continue as it was. If the monsters won, they'd take over. If both sides died—as they did in the myths predicting Ragnarök—the world would be plunged into an ice age.

What if the stories weren't real?

But if the stories aren't real, then Thor isn't real. That amulet around your neck isn't real. Your power isn't real.

Except it obviously *was*. Which meant . . .

Even thinking about that made Matt's stomach churn and his head hurt and his feet ache to run home. Just race home and jump in bed and pull up the covers and hide. Puke and hide: the strategy of champions.

Matt thought of his parents catching him, and his heart pounded as he struggled to breathe. They expected him to do this, just like they expected him to walk home after practice and make his own science fair project. They expected him to be a Thorsen.

Something tickled his chest, and he reached to swat off a bug. Only it wasn't a bug. It was his amulet. Vibrating.

Um, no, that would be your heart, racing like a runaway train.

The tickling continued, and he swiped the amulet aside as he scratched the spot. Only it wasn't his heart—it really was the pendant. When he held it between his fingers, he could feel the vibrations.

Weird. It had never done that before.

"You are looking for Odin," said a voice behind him.

Matt wheeled. There was no one there.

"You are looking for Odin," the voice said again, and he followed it down to a girl, no more than seven. She had pale blond braids and bright blue eyes. She wore a blue sundress and no shoes. In this weather? She must be freezing. Where were her parents?

"Hey," he said, smiling as he crouched. "Do you need help? I can help, but we should probably find your parents first."

The girl shook her head, braids swinging. "I do not need your help, Matthew Thorsen. You need mine."

Strange way for a kid to talk. Formal, like someone out of an old movie. And the way she was looking at him, so calmly. He didn't recognize her, but in Blackwell, there were so many little blond kids that it was impossible to keep them all straight.

"Okay, then," he said. "You can help me find your parents."

"No, you must find Odin. He will help."

"Help what?"

She frowned, confused. "I do not know. That is to come. That is not now. I know only what is now, and *now* you must hear."

"Hear what?"

She took off into the crowd.

Matt bolted upright. "Wait!"

The girl turned. She looked at him, her blue eyes steady. Then she mouthed something, and he understood her, like she was standing right there, whispering in his ear: *You must hear.*

She turned and ran again. Matt hesitated, but only for a second. As safe as Blackwell was, no kid her age should be wandering around alone.

He raced after her.

SIX

LAURIE

"OWEN"

At the parade, Laurie had seen that the shield was missing, and she'd known that Fen must have gone back for it. She wasn't sure if that's where he got the black eye, and he wouldn't tell her what had happened. All she got out of him was that he was "handling it," but he looked like whatever it was had handled him.

Her temper wasn't often horrible, but as she waded through the carnival games and crowds of people standing in lines to buy food or tickets to the rides, she was shaking mad. Even the smells of popcorn, funnel cake, and cotton candy didn't distract her. Admittedly, she still kept looking at all the games of chance that were set up to convince people to spend all their money on games with pretty lame prizes. She won at those. She had a weird luck with carnival games and had toted home enough stuffed bunnies and creepy dolls over the past few years that her mother had taken a trunkful to the kids at the hospital. Maybe if Laurie wasn't so mad she could stop and play just one, but she *was* mad. If Fen got caught with the shield, he would put them both at risk. If her mom weren't so adamant that Fen wasn't welcome, or if her dad was around, or if Matt weren't the sheriff's kid, or if…well, if Fen weren't being so stupid, things would be better, but none of the *if*s were truths. The worst possibility was that Matt told the sheriff and she and Fen were both arrested. The best case was that Fen would get in trouble—and she'd lose him. So, even the best case was horrible.

Unless Matt doesn't tell.

Even before this, Laurie had needed to talk to Fen about the weird fish dream, but she hadn't been able to get him alone since the other night at the longship. Even at the science fair, he wasn't available. He'd actually invited his friend Hunter to join them. She wasn't going to be ignored any longer. She'd talk to him whether he wanted to hear it or not. Maybe if they turned the shield in, Matt would keep their secret.

As she walked around the festival, she kept a lookout for Fen. She stopped at the Ferris wheel, the Tilt-A-Whirl, and the teacup ride. No Fen. She wandered through the petting-zoo area. No Fen.

"Where are you?" she muttered. She'd call him, but he didn't have a cell phone.

"Hello." A boy a few years older than her stepped up beside her. "I wondered where you were."

"What?" She paused.

He looked like he belonged...well, anywhere but Black-well. He wore a pair of black-and-blue tennis shoes, black trousers that hung low, a blue shirt that looked silky, and slightly longish hair that was dyed blue. Odder still, the boy had on jewelry that was almost girly: a pair of tiny black bird earrings in one ear and a twisted metal ring on his finger.

"Are you looking for me yet?" he asked.

"No." She scowled. "I don't know you. Why would I look for you?"

"I'm Odin."

"Uh-huh. Odin." She did laugh then. Anyone who grew up in Blackwell knew the basics of their mythology. Between school, parents, plays, a well-stocked myth section in the library, and some pretty terrible videos in every grade, it was impossible to completely avoid myth in Blackwell. That didn't mean it was real.

"So, *Odin*, I guess there's another play this year?" She hadn't picked up any activities listing for the fair, but even if she had, she wasn't so much up for watching another play on some battle or other. Some people in Blackwell took their Scandinavian heritage far too seriously.

"Would you like to play a game?" Odin looked around for a moment and then pointed to a booth where some sort of gambling game was set up. "You'd be good at that one."

It was supposed to be a game of luck, but she'd been banned from it the year before when she won every time. The man running it insisted she was cheating somehow; she hadn't been. This year, she was staying out of trouble—no games of luck for her. This boy obviously had heard about the ugly scene last year when she'd had to give up every dollar she'd won *and* the money she'd paid to play.

"Very funny," she said.

Odin gave her a weird little smile, but didn't reply. He just stood there waiting. It seemed odd, but she didn't have the time or interest to waste on some blue-haired boy. She shook her head and turned away.

"You're leaving already?" he asked.

"I need to find someone."

"Not me?" He sounded sad.

She looked back at him. "No."

"Oh. I must be early then." The boy calling himself Odin frowned. "They won't like me, unfortunately."

Laurie stepped a little farther away from him. He was starting to make her nervous, and she wasn't used to talking to boys without Fen showing up to snarl at them anyhow.

Her whole family was overprotective in one way or another, and talking to Odin made her think maybe they were right. "I think I'm going to go now. Good luck with your play or whatever."

"It's real, you know," Odin said. "That's why you're good at those games. I know. You don't cheat, but you win."

At that, Laurie didn't know what to say, so she gave up. "I'm not allowed to play gambling games. My cousin will probably be a jerk to you if he sees you talking to me, and even if he doesn't, I'm not looking for you, so please just go away."

He studied her for a moment. "I expected you to be less of a rule follower, but I guess we're still becoming."

"Becoming *what*? What does that even mean?" She looked around for Fen—or even Hunter at this point. All she could see was the crush of people milling around the sawdust-covered paths of the festival. Blackwell itself wasn't that big, but the festival always drew in people from outside the area. It made sense, she supposed. The fair might celebrate Scandinavian heritage, but it still had the trappings of a lot of festivals. There were wooden booths where volunteers manned games of chance and skill; there were all kinds of good foods, and usually there were bands and fireworks and whatever else the committee felt would add to the overall excitement and appeal.

As Laurie looked, she saw a few of the odd acrobats who

74

were running through the festival, doing tricks that made her think of the extreme sports games Fen liked to watch. They didn't have bikes or skateboards, but they did handstands, weird half jumps, and crazy flips as they ran.

"Becoming more than we are," Odin said.

"Okaaaay, *Odin*, I'm not in your play or whatever, so I'm going to go now," she said.

"You can call me Owen, if you'd feel better," he offered. "I'd rather you call me my true name, but you're not ready. Maybe next time I see you."

She stared at him and said, "I don't need to call you Owen or Odin or whatever other name you want to use. I won't be talking to you. Now *or* later. Go away before my friends show up."

"They *would* misunderstand." The boy nodded to himself. "I just wanted to see you. You're the one who will understand me. I hoped...I hoped you'd be ready. Soon, though, we can talk as we are meant to."

He turned and disappeared into the crowd.

She watched him go; his blue hair made him stand out enough that it was easy. The acrobat kids seemed to be following him, but not with him. It was weird. They trailed him, and he walked as if he were alone. For a moment, she had a flash of worry for him. *What if they aren't with him? What if he's in trouble?* But they didn't seem to be trying to hurt him, and he didn't act like he was worried. *And it's not*

my problem. Still, she watched them as they headed toward the exit.

Owen was barely out of view when another, more important person caught her eye. "Fen!"

She pushed through the crowd, not caring that she was drawing attention or being rude. She shoved between him and the ever-present Hunter and grabbed Fen's wrist. "I need to talk to you alone...." Her words died. Fen had flinched from her touch. She let go of his arm and said softly, "Please, Fen?"

He looked directly at her.

And she said the magic words, the words that they'd both used over the years: "I need your help with something."

Her cousin opened his mouth, but before he could ask, she spoke. "I need to talk to Fen alone. If you could—"

"Go away, Hunter," Fen finished for her. Then, he started through the crowd away from Hunter. He was pulling her with him as he had on who-knew-how-many adventures over the years, and she felt such relief that she almost hugged him. Everything would be okay now. She had Fen at her side again.

By the time they'd reached the edge of the festival, behind a row of booths where the tangled wires for the strands of temporary lights were stretched, Laurie was bursting with the words she'd been waiting to say. The music over the loudspeakers made it impossible for anyone in the booths to hear them, but that didn't mean they wanted witnesses.

They both knew that if the other one said "I need your help" that meant they also needed privacy.

After he confirmed that no one was watching, Fen let go of her and tucked his hands in the pockets of the torn jacket he was wearing. He looked around to make sure no one was nearby. "What happened?"

She didn't want to start by accusing him—that never went well—so she started with her other worry. "I thought I was a fish," she blurted.

"Okay." Fen nodded, and then he paused, blinked, and said, "*What?*"

"A fish," she whispered.

He stepped closer to her and said, "Say that again."

"I woke up in the middle of the night, and I was a fish and I couldn't breathe and you weren't there." She sounded crazy even to herself. "I know it was just a dream, but it was so real, and all I could think about was telling you."

Fen stared at her.

"Say something," she half begged.

"Maybe you should keep a bucket of water by your bed, because Aunt Janey isn't going to let me stay with you unless Uncle Stig is around." Fen folded his arms over his chest.

Laurie stared at him.

The music on the loudspeaker was interrupted by some sort of squeal that caused them both to jump. After a minute, Fen said, "What I mean is maybe you really were a fish."

"It was a dream; it had to be," Laurie said.

"Maybe. Maybe not." Fen shrugged. "There's weirder stuff out there."

"Like what?"

"The Raider Scouts," he said.

"Who?" Laurie couldn't always follow the way his mind jumped around, but she knew he usually got to his point. "I don't get it."

"Those weird people who just camp and stuff all the time," Fen said.

Laurie shook her head. "You think turning into a fish is *less* weird than camping?"

Fen shrugged. "They say they're wolves, you know."

Laurie laughed. "Right. Well, maybe they are, and I'm a fish. Do you think I ought to join them? Can you imagine Mom's face? I dreamed I'd turned into a fish, and Fen says maybe I'll be a real fish, so I'm going to drop out of school and camp with these kids who say they're wolves."

"No, you shouldn't join them, but..." The way Fen looked at her seemed off, but maybe that was just because his face was so bruised. He smiled, but it didn't look quite right. "What if the Raiders really *are* wolves, Laurie? What if you really are a fish, or your dream means you will be?"

For a moment, she stared at him, and then she burst out laughing. "You don't know a guy named Owen, do you?"

Now it was Fen who looked confused. "No. Why?"

"Everyone seems crazy tonight. He was a stranger who acted like he knew me, got into his role for the play too seriously. It was weird. Now, you're telling me that there are kids who might be wolves, and . . . well, I'm telling you I am freaked out by a dream about being a fish. Crazy. Everything just seems crazy."

"Some of the cousins joined them."

"The Raiders?" she asked.

"Yeah." Fen folded his arms over his chest. "Dad was one, you know."

"So Uncle Eddy is a wolf? That makes you one, too."

"Maybe," Fen hedged.

"Okay, so I'm a fish; you and Uncle Eddy are wolves." She shook her head. "I know it's silly, but I feel better for having told you. I've never had such a realistic dream."

For a moment, Fen said nothing. He stared at her as if he would, but then he grinned. "Come on. I stole some tickets earlier for the rides."

She paused. Fen was relaxed enough for her to ask him about the other thing, but that didn't mean he'd like it. She put a hand on his forearm. "You still need to tell me what happened." She pointed at his swollen and blackened eye. "And about the shield. If Thorsen tells the sheriff, we're going to get in so much trouble."

Fen ignored her, as he always did when he didn't feel like answering.

"Seriously, Fen! If they go to your house and find it, we're going to—"

"It's not at the house," Fen interrupted. "I don't have it, and *if* I knew anything, that's not enough to get me—or you—in trouble."

She rolled her eyes.

"Trust me. I won't ever let anything happen to you. You know that, don't you? You're my sister even though we don't have the same parents." Then he head-butted her. It almost hid his blush. He was embarrassed every time he admitted to having feelings.

For a moment, Laurie didn't react. She knew he'd stolen it, but she also knew he looked out for her.

The look on his face was nervous, and he pulled his arm away from her—but he still tried to sound like he wasn't hurt when he said, "Come on, fish. Or are you afraid you'll slip off the Ferris wheel?"

"Jerk." She shoved him carefully. Hugs weirded him out, but a gentle shove, punch, or head-butt he was okay with. "I'm not afraid of anything...as long as you're not."

SEVEN

✦

MATT

"PAST, PRESENT, AND FUTURE"

When Matt saw the little girl racing into the rec center, he yelled at her to stop, but she kept running, bare feet slapping on the pavement, blond braids streaming behind. He flew through the entrance—only to see her running for the closed door into the private meeting his grandfather was having with the Elders.

Great. They choose me to stop Ragnarök, and what's the first thing I do? Prove I can't even stop a little girl from bursting into their meeting.

He could just turn around and walk away. Pretend he hadn't seen where she was going. Or pretend he never met her in the first place. The easy way out, which meant he'd never take it, even if he wished he could.

He raced across the main room as fast as he could. But the girl had stopped at the meeting-room door and was just standing there, waiting patiently as she watched him with those weirdly grown-up blue eyes.

"Now you hear," she whispered. She pointed at the door. "Listen."

He started to tell her they had to leave when he caught the word *Ragnarök*. Then his name.

He leaned toward the door. Yes, he shouldn't eavesdrop. Totally disrespectful. But the conversation was about him, which kind of made it his business. If he was caught, well, he'd just chased this little girl inside so he could return her to her parents. *That's champion-worthy behavior, isn't it?*

"... no need to tell the others yet. What I told them at the *Thing* is enough for now," his grandfather was saying. "Those who need to know the truth already do. For the rest, it will come as a shock, and we must ease them into it."

Was he talking about Matt being chosen as champion? That they had to tell the Thorsens who didn't live in Blackwell? In Matt's opinion, it was the ones who did live there—and *knew* him—who'd be the most shocked, and they'd already heard.

"We must begin a quiet campaign to convince them that Ragnarök is not the end of the world. It is a change. A cleansing. Ultimately, it is an event that will benefit our people, present and future."

He leaned closer.

"Ragnarök, as it is foretold in the myths, will not end the world. We must remind them of that. It will be a time of great turmoil and upheaval and a tragic loss of life, but the world will emerge the better for it. America is corrupt, from Wall Street to Washington, and it is the same in every country around the world. No politician or advocacy group can change that. Our world needs cleansing. Our world needs Ragnarök."

The other Elders chimed in their agreement.

What? No. I'm hearing wrong. The champion is supposed to stop Ragnarök.

"We know how this must work. Matt must fight the serpent. Matt must defeat the serpent . . . but he must be defeated in turn. The champions of the gods must die, and the monsters must die, as the prophecy says, so the world can be reborn."

Matt had stopped breathing.

They don't want me to win.

His grandfather continued. "I do not take this lightly. I will be honest in saying that when I first realized Matt was the champion, I prayed that the runes would tell me I was mistaken. But I have come to realize that this is right. The boy is strong and he is good, and he is deserving of this honor. That is how I must see this. My grandson is being honored in the highest fashion, and he will do us proud, and he will take his place in the halls of Valhalla as a champion with the long-dead gods. As a hero. Our hero."

Matt stumbled away from the door.

They expect me to die. They want the ice age to come, the world to end. I'm not their champion. I'm their sacrifice.

Of course I am. That's why they chose me. Because I'm guaranteed to screw this up.

He'd been planning to tell Granddad exactly that: *You made a mistake.* But there'd been a little bit of him that hoped he really was the champion, that he'd finally show his family and everyone else—

The little girl took his hand and tugged him across the room, and he was so dazed, he just followed. When they were at the door, she whispered, "You seek Odin."

Odin? Why would I . . . ?

Because Odin was the leader of the gods. The most powerful of them all. The father of Thor.

He stared at the little girl. Who was she? *What* was she? Not just a little girl—he was sure of that now.

"Odin will tell me how to fix this, right?" Matt said. "He'll tell me how to defeat the Midgard Serpent and survive."

Again, she looked confused. "I do not know. That is to come. That is not now. I know only—"

"You only know what is now. Yeah, I got that the first . . ." His gaze shifted to the mosaic on his left. A scene of Thor asking the Norns for advice.

The Norns. Three women who knew the destiny of gods and humans. In a lot of the old stories, Future was the youngest. But their tradition—and the mosaic—followed one from the old sagas. The oldest was Past. Then came Future. And finally, the youngest Norn—Present.

He turned to the little girl, and his heart started thumping again. By this point, he was pretty sure it was never going to beat at a normal rate again.

"Who are you?" he asked as the hairs on his neck prickled.

"You know."

"One of the Norns. Present."

She nodded. "I said you know."

"And *you* don't know anything except what's happening now. Or what should be happening now. So where do I get the rest?"

"From Future. She waits."

"Where will I find her?"

"I do not know. That is to come—"

"All right, all right. Where is she *now*?"

The little girl pointed. "Out there. She waits."

Matt followed her finger to the door. "Where exactly out there?"

No answer. He turned. The girl was gone.

86

This time when Matt walked into the fair, he still didn't notice the smells, the sights, the sounds, but only because he was focused on his task. Find the Norn.

Find the Norn? Are you crazy? A Norn? Like in the stories? That's all they are, you know. Stories.

Earlier, when he'd thought of fighting the serpent, he'd tried not to focus on what he believed. It was easy when they were old stories, like Noah's Ark. You could say, "Sure, that could happen." But then you thought about it, really thought about it, and said, "Seriously? One boat with two of every animal on Earth? How does that work?" It was easier to just not think about it. Accept it. That's what he'd done his whole life.

That's what he had to do now. Accept it. Believe it. He was looking for a Norn.

Which would be a lot easier if he had any clue what she looked like. The mosaic wasn't much help. In it, the youngest Norn had been about his age, and the only thing she had in common with the little girl who had actually appeared was her blond hair. Blond hair in Blackwell was as rare as fleas on a homeless mutt.

He weaved through the crowds. Normally, that would be easy. While people knew who he was, they wouldn't do more than nod or smile. Now Thorsens would stop mid-carnival-game to say something, and of course he had to be polite and respond.

With so many Thorsens talking to him, others noticed, and they said hi, too. Any other time, that would have been great. The center of attention. Can't argue with that, especially when you're usually only there if you've done something wrong. But right now, when he was on a mission, it was kind of inconvenient.

Finally, he spotted her. The Norn on the mosaic had been about his mom's age, but this girl didn't look older than Jake. She was dressed differently from the other girls at the fair, too. She wore a skirt of rough cloth, and her hair was piled up on top of her head in a heap of tiny braids. She sat on a bench, legs swinging as she watched kids on the merry-go-round.

So how did he know it was her? Because his amulet started vibrating. The same way it had right before he'd met the first Norn.

Still, he had to be sure. So he walked up as casually as he could and said, "Hey," but she only smiled and said, "Hello."

"Are you waiting for me?" he said.

She got that look of confusion, a mirror image of the little girl's. "I do not know. That is—"

"The present. You only know the future. Got it." And got the right girl, apparently. "Kind of feels like it should be Christmas, don't you think?"

She tilted her head, frowning.

"Scrooge? The ghosts of Christmas past, present, and future?" He shook his head when she continued to frown. "Never mind. Okay, so I should be looking for Odin, because he's going to tell me...what exactly?"

"How to defeat the Midgard Serpent."

Matt exhaled as relief fluttered through him. "And stop Ragnarök? So things don't need to happen the way they do in the myth, with all of us dying and the world ending?"

"Some parts cannot be changed. Some can. You must discover which is which."

"But you can foresee the future, right?"

"There are many futures. I cannot tell which will come to pass. You will try to change what the myth foretells. You will succeed in some parts and fail in others."

"Right. Except the whole die-defeating-the-serpent thing. I can definitely survive, despite what the myth says?"

"Yes," she said.

"And if I do, the world doesn't end?"

"It does not *end*, even if you fail," she said carefully. "However, almost all life on it will perish."

"Same thing. But if I defeat the serpent and survive, that doesn't happen, right?"

"Correct."

"Good. Now, where do I find him?" He paused again. "Is

it really Odin? I mean, the gods died, didn't they? Did Odin survive?"

She smiled. "No, the gods are dead. The one you seek is like yourself: a descendant. He is Odin as you are Thor. Yet he is not Odin, as you are not Thor."

Which made perfect sense.

"So he's a kid then. Where is he?" Matt asked.

"I do not know. Where Odin is, that is present. I know only what is to come."

Matt exhaled. They really weren't making this easy. "I *will* find Odin, though. That's a guarantee, which means I don't need to look for him."

"You may find him, or you may not." She had a faraway look in her eyes as she spoke. "There is more than one future."

Great.

Before he could try another tactic, the Norn said, "This is the best future. This is the one we wish for you: that you will find Odin, and you will find the others; that you will fight, and you will win."

"The others? But they'll come here, right? The *Thing* is going to gather them up."

"They will gather possible champions, but they will not gather the right champions. That is your task."

"And, let me guess, you have no idea where I'll find anyone."

"That is how. I do not know how. Only—"

"That I will or won't," he interrupted. "Do you know how completely useless that is? I'm thirteen. I can't just hop in my car and let my magical god-descendant-finding GPS guide me."

She looked at Matt blankly.

"Can I get one clue?" he said. "A bread crumb to start me on the trail? An e-mail address, maybe?"

"E-mail...?"

"Anything. I'll do what you tell me, because while saving the world and all would be great, I'm not keen on the dying part, either. I'd like to live long enough to get out of middle school."

She nodded. "That would be wise."

"So, the other descendants. It'd be nice if I could find them all in Blackwell, but it's only Thor and Loki here, isn't it?"

"You will not find the others here. *Around* here, yes, but not here."

Matt tried to be patient as he asked, "Around here...? In the county? The state? The country? The continent?"

"In the place known as South Dakota."

At least she hadn't said "continent."

The air beside her shimmered, and the little girl took form again.

"I know where Loki is," the little girl said.

"Okay, that's great, but I don't need Loki. Sure, he's to be at Ragnarök, but he leads the other side."

"That is not the present," said the girl Norn.

"Okay so…" He turned to the older Norn. "Am I right that Loki—or his descendant—will lead the monsters?"

"Loki may, or he may not. That is up to you," she said.

"Meaning he could help us, which would sway the battle our way, so I need to get him on our side. Got it." He turned to the youngest. "Where is he?"

"Loki is there." She gestured.

Matt followed her hand to see Laurie and Fen standing in line for the Tilt-A-Whirl. *Fen? No way.*

"Right *there*. Now?" He pivoted to watch Fen and Laurie as they climbed into one of the red cars. "But you said there were other champions. Maybe you can find another one for Loki, because Fen is not ever, in a million years…"

He turned back and found he was talking to himself. The Norns had vanished.

"…going to help me with anything," he muttered.

EIGHT

✦

MATT

"ALLIANCE"

Right after the Norns vanished, Cody and the others found him. While the last thing on Matt's mind was hanging out at the fair, right now, being part of a group might be the best thing. No one would bug him if he stayed with his friends, who also wouldn't really notice if he was quiet. He wasn't exactly loud at the best of times. He could just retreat into his thoughts. And he had a lot of thoughts to retreat into.

He had no idea what to do next. Apparently, he was supposed to buddy up with Fen. Which was not happening. Fen wanted nothing to do with any Thorsens, and Matt's family was worst of all—his dad had been responsible for putting Fen's father behind bars.

Speaking of his parents, what did they think of all this? He remembered his grandfather's words. *Those who need to know the truth already do.* His dad and mom would need to know, obviously. So they must. That's why they'd been so nice to him. That's why Dad had given him a hundred bucks for the fair.

Enjoy yourself, son . . . while you still can.

The Norns had said that he didn't have to die fighting the Midgard Serpent, but Granddad believed the prophecy was fated to come true. That meant he couldn't go to his grandfather or his family for help. He needed to do this on his own. Gather up the other kids and find Odin. Train. Fight. Win. There was no other way. If they failed, the world as they knew it would end. Which was kind of a big deal.

He was supposed to start with Fen. And then what? He had no idea. He only hoped something would come to him.

He was waiting for Cody and their friends to get off the Avalanche—his stomach sure couldn't handle that tonight—when saw Fen trudge past without Laurie, his gaze on the ground, boots scuffing the sawdust as he headed for the exit, looking like he'd had a really bad day.

Matt figured Fen had a lot of bad days, with his parents gone, being passed from relative to relative. Even if Dad said that's because Fen was too wild for anyone to handle, maybe all the moving around *made* him a little wild. And those cuts and bruises on his face . . . Matt had heard Fen was staying with his cousin Kris, and everyone knew Kris was quick with his fists.

Thinking about that put Matt in the right state of mind to talk to Fen. Not to tell him about Ragnarök and the Midgard Serpent, of course. That'd be crazy. If Matt had any chance of winning Fen over, he had to take it slow. He'd just happen to be leaving the fair at the same time and bump into Fen and offer him some . . .

Matt looked around. Corn dogs. Sure, that might work.

He told Cody he wasn't feeling great and was catching a ride home. Then he grabbed a couple of corn dogs. By that time, Fen was leaving. Matt jogged to catch up, but one aunt and two cousins stopped him on the way.

When he reached the exit, Fen had veered right, passing the parking lot and heading into the field. The sun was almost down, but the sky was oddly bright with a faint tinge of yellow. The wind seemed to be picking up, promising another cold night.

Fimbulwinter was coming.

Matt shivered and walked as fast as he could toward Fen, who'd disappeared around some trees. Matt broke into a run then, slowing only when he'd passed the trees, and saw Fen just ahead, trudging along.

"Hey," Matt called. "Fen? Hold up!"

Fen glanced over his shoulder. Then he turned back and kept walking.

"Fen!"

"Shove off, Thorsen."

Matt jogged in front of Fen and held out the tray of corn dogs. "I was just leaving, too, and I thought you might want these. I bought them, but I'm stuffed."

"And I look like I'd want your leftovers?"

"They're not leftovers," Matt exclaimed. "I never touched them. Even the ketchup's still in the packets. See?"

"You don't want them?" Fen asked.

"No, I thought I did, but I ate so much at the feast. . . ."

"Fine." Fen took each by the stick and whipped them into the field. "The crows can have them. They're scavengers. Not me."

Fen walked around Matt and kept going. Matt looked out at the corn dogs, yellow blobs on the dark field, and felt his amulet warm. Maybe offering Fen food hadn't been a good idea, but he didn't need to do that. He—

Loki may, or he may not. That is up to you.

Whether Fen led the monsters into the final battle depended on Matt. He took a deep breath, broke into a jog, and called to Fen, but a sudden gust of wind whipped his words away and nearly knocked him off his feet. He recovered and caught up to Fen again, this time walking beside him.

"I noticed your face looks kind of messed—" Matt began. "I mean, you have some bruises."

"Do I? Huh. Hadn't noticed."

"About that..." Matt cleared his throat. "If you're having problems—with Kris or anyone else—you should talk to the counselor at school. No one should do that to you. You've got rights."

Fen stopped and turned. A gust of wind whipped past, and Fen's hair fell over his eyes. "Excuse me?"

"If someone's hitting you, you should talk to Ms. Early at school. She can help. It's against the law for a grown-up to hit a kid. You don't need to take that."

"No one knocks me around, Thorsen, unless I'm knocking them back. I got into it with someone, okay? Someone who fought back. Someone with more guts than you." Fen didn't shove Matt, but he looked like he was considering it.

"More guts than me? Um, you know what I said last week, about your memory? It really does suck, because I'm pretty sure I *did* fight back. You jumped me, and you didn't land a single hit before I knocked you flat on your butt. Which is where you stayed."

Fen lunged. Matt ducked, swung around, and nailed Fen with a right hook that sent him stumbling. As Matt watched Fen recover, he reflected that this might not be the best way to make friends.

Matt clenched his fists at his sides and held himself still. "I don't want to do this, Fen."

"Really? Because it sure looks like you do."

Fen charged. Matt told himself he wouldn't hit him back. Defensive moves only. Except, as Coach Forde always said, he really wasn't good at the defensive stuff. So when Fen charged into Matt, they both went down.

Fen went to grab Matt by the hair, but Matt caught his arm and tried to hold it—just hold it—but Fen started thrashing and kicking, teeth bared, growling, and the only way Matt could stop him was another right hook that sent him skidding across the grass.

Then a blast of wind hit, so strong that it knocked Matt to his knees. He struggled up, blind, his eyes watering. When they cleared, he could make out figures. At least four. Surrounding them. The one in the middle towered over him.

Grown-ups. Someone at the fair had seen the fight and come over, and now Matt had been caught fighting Fen, and his dad was going to kill him before the Midgard Serpent even had a chance—

He blinked as the figures came clear. Not grown-ups. Kids. Six of them. Wild-looking kids, some in well-worn military surplus, others in ripped jeans and T-shirts. *Raider Scouts*. A weird Boy-Scouts-gone-bad kind of group. His dad and his deputies ran them off every time they found their campsite. Raiders didn't get their name because they thought it was cool: they really were like old-fashioned Viking Raiders, swooping into town, stealing everything that wasn't nailed down before disappearing into the woods again.

The biggest one looked about sixteen. He wore shredded jeans, hiking boots, and a skintight sleeveless shirt that showed scars on both arms. The group leader. Had to be. As Matt tensed, he kept his gaze on him. First sign of trouble, that was his target.

The leader reached down and picked up Fen by the scruff of his neck. He leaned over to whisper something before tossing him aside. Fen hit the ground, and Matt took a step toward him. It didn't matter that Fen had been trying to beat the snot out of him; Matt wasn't going to stand there and let outsiders treat a Blackwell kid like that.

But as soon as Matt stepped forward, the boy to his right lunged. Matt wheeled and nailed him with a left. There was a satisfying *thwack* and a grunt of surprise as the kid staggered back. Matt started toward him, but another kid leaped onto his back.

Matt yanked the kid over his shoulder, thinking as he did that the kid seemed awfully light. When Matt threw him down, he found himself standing over a boy no more than ten. Matt froze then, his gut clenching, an apology on his lips. The boy grabbed Matt's leg. Matt tried to kick him off, but halfheartedly. When you grow up bigger than other guys, you learn really fast that if you so much as shove a little kid you'll get hauled down to the office for a lecture on bullying and a call home.

The kid sunk his teeth into Matt's shin. Matt yelped and tried to yank back, but another kid jumped him. He wheeled to swing, but this one was a girl, and seeing her face, even twisted into a snarl, made his hand stop midpunch. Hit a little kid? Or a girl? He knew better than that.

The wind howled past, stinging his eyes again, and he dimly saw the girl go flying. For a second, Matt thought he'd accidentally hit her, but when he blinked, he saw Fen slamming his fist into her gut. Then he turned on Matt.

"I need to rescue you from a little kid and a girl? Really?" Fen grabbed for the boy, still snarling on Matt's leg, but another kid jumped him from behind. As Fen hit him, he yelled back at Matt. "Fight, Thorsen!"

Matt shook his leg, trying to disengage the boy. Behind him, another one snickered, taking in the spectacle as he waited his turn.

"Thorsen!" Fen snarled.

"But he's just a—"

"He's a *Raider*!" Fen yelled.

The boy lunged to bite again, and Matt grabbed him by the arm and threw him to the side. Then he looked up to see the leader smirking. The boy was twisting, scrambling to his feet, and to Matt's left, another was getting ready to take a run at him—a kid closer to his age, but scrawny, half a foot shorter. Matt glanced back at the leader, just standing there, arms crossed.

Matt charged. He heard Fen shout "No!" but Matt didn't stop. At tournaments, Coach Forde always tried to arrange it so Matt took on his toughest opponent first. Take care of the biggest threat while you're fresh. If you win the round, you're left with weaker guys who've just seen you knock out their best fighter.

As Matt rushed the Raider leader, he saw surprise flash across the Raider's face. Matt barreled into the guy and sent him staggering. It was only a stagger, though, and the guy came back swinging. Matt managed to duck the first blow, but he took the second to the side of his face, his neck wrenching.

Matt swung. He landed three blows in quick succession, the last one hitting so hard the guy went flying.

As the Raider leader fell, the wind whipped up again. This time it sent Matt stumbling. His ankle twisted, and he went down on one knee. He started to rise again and—

A low growl sounded behind him.

Matt lifted his head to see a wolf standing there. A giant wolf with gray fur and inch-long fangs. The guy he'd thrown to the ground was gone.

Matt could tell himself that the wolf had somehow run in without him noticing, and the Raider leader had taken off, but one look in the beast's eyes and he knew better. This *was* the Raider leader. The guy had turned into a wolf. Now it was hunkering down, teeth bared, ready to leap and—

Someone screamed. A long, drawn-out wail of a scream that made the wolf stop, muzzle shooting up, ears swiveling to track the sound.

Not a scream. A siren. The tornado siren.

Matt looked up and saw that the sky had turned yellow. Distant shouts and cries came from the fair as people scrambled for cover. Then, far to the left, a dark shape appeared against the yellow sky. A twister. It hadn't touched down, but the gathering clouds seemed to drop with every passing second.

A howl snapped Matt's attention back to the wolf. It wasn't the beast howling; it was the wind, shrieking past, as loud and piercing as the siren. The wolf's eyes slitted against the wind as it sliced through his fur, and he turned away from the blast.

Matt charged. He caught the wolf with a right hook to the head. The beast staggered, but only a step, better balanced on four legs than two. Then it lunged, teeth flashing. Matt caught it with an uppercut. A yelp, but the wolf barely stumbled this time, and its next lunge knocked Matt down, with the wolf on his chest. He grabbed its muzzle, struggling to keep those jaws away from his throat as the beast growled and snarled. Matt tried to kick it in the stomach, but his foot wouldn't connect.

Someone hit the wolf's side and sent it flying off Matt. Matt scrambled up and tackled the wolf. His rescuer did the same, both of them grabbing the beast and trying to wrestle it down. It was only then that Matt saw that it was Fen who'd come to his aid.

"Attacking a *wolf*?" Fen grunted as they struggled. "You're one crazy—" The wind whipped the last word away.

Matt looked across the field. The tornado had touched down. They needed to end this and get to safety. Now.

With a sudden burst of energy, the wolf bucked. Matt lost his grip and slid off. Fen stayed draped over the beast's back.

"Use your thing!" Fen shouted.

"What?"

"Your—" Fen's face screwed up in frustration as he struggled to stay on the wolf's back. "Your power thing. What you hit me with."

How did Fen—? Not important.

Matt clenched his amulet. It had barely even warmed since the fight had begun, and now it just lay in his hand, cold metal. When he closed his eyes to concentrate, something struck his back. A chunk of wood hit the ground. A sheet of newspaper sailed past, wrapping around his arm. The next thing that flew at him wasn't debris—it was one of the Raiders. Matt slammed his fist into the kid, then turned back just in time to see the wolf throw Fen off.

The wolf looked at Matt. Their eyes met. The wolf's lip curled, and it growled. Even as the sirens drowned out the sound, Matt swore he could feel it vibrating through the air. Matt locked his gaze with the wolf's. It didn't like that, snarling and snapping now, but Matt held its gaze, and as the beast hunkered down, Matt pulled back his fist, ready to—

A black shadow leaped on the wolf's back. Matt barely caught a flash of it before the two went down, rolling across the grass. Then all he could see was fur—gray fur and brown fur.

Two wolves. The big gray one and a smaller brown one. Matt looked over to where the wolf had thrown Fen, but he wasn't there.

Loki. The trickster god. The shape-shifter god.

Fen was a wolf. These kids all were—which wasn't possible. The Thorsens all said that the Brekkes didn't know about their powers. You can't use powers if you don't know about them.

He looked at the wolves again.

Apparently, everyone was wrong.

Matt ran at the leader wolf. Another Raider jumped into his path. It was the little kid from earlier, but Matt was beyond worrying about fighting fair. He hit the boy with a blow to the stomach, followed by an uppercut to the jaw, and then shoved him aside.

Now the big wolf had Fen pinned, jaws slashing toward

his throat. Matt jumped on the beast's back. It reared up. Matt grabbed two handfuls of fur, but that was really all he could do. He didn't have claws or fangs, and he wasn't in any decent position to land a punch. Just get the thing off Fen. That was his goal. Just—

He saw something sailing toward them as fast as a rocket. A branch or—

"Duck!" he shouted to Fen as he leaped off the wolf's back.

He hit the ground hard. He heard a yelp and rolled just in time to see the wolf staggering, a piece of pipe hitting the grass beside him. The beast snarled and tried to charge, but it stumbled and toppled, blood trickling from its ear. It hit the ground, unconscious.

Fen leaped up and they turned to face the other Raiders, who'd been standing back, letting their leader fight. Half of them were wolves now, and they were closing in, growling and snarling, eyes glittering.

A figure jumped one of the human Raiders. It was Laurie. The Raider grabbed her and threw her aside. Two of the wolves jumped Fen. The biggest ran at Matt, but he veered aside and raced toward Laurie. He caught her attacker in the side and knocked him away.

He put out a hand to help Laurie up.

She waved off the help and glowered at him. "I could have handled it."

"I was just—"

"I'm here to help you two. Not to be rescued," she said.

Before he could answer, the bigger Raider was on him, and Laurie's attacker was back on his feet. Matt managed to take down his, and Laurie seemed to be doing okay with hers, but when he went to help her, a hand grabbed his shoulder.

Matt turned, fist raised. It was Fen, now back in human form. He pointed to the east, and Matt saw the twister coming. The dark shape was stirring up a debris cloud, making it seem even bigger than it was.

"We gotta run," Fen said.

"What? No. We're—" He slammed his fist into a charging attacker. "We're fine. That twister—"

"Not the twister," Fen said as he ducked a blow. He jabbed his finger east again, and Matt made out a group of figures racing across the field. Coming their way. More Raiders. He faintly caught a groan to his left and glanced over to see the big wolf rising.

"We need to *run*." Fen gave Matt a shove in the right direction and went after Laurie.

Matt turned to help, but Laurie had thrown off her attacker. Fen grabbed her by the arm, and they started to race toward the fair. Matt took one last look around—at the twister, the Raiders, the giant wolf.

At this rate, I'll be lucky if I make it to Ragnarök, he thought, and tore off after Fen and Laurie.

NINE

LAURIE

"TORNADO TOSSED"

L aurie shook off Fen's arm. Hailstones pelted them as they ran. Everyone knew not to run from tornadoes, but tornadoes *and* wolves? That changed things, but maybe not everything.

"I don't want to get separated," Fen yelled over the wind. He grabbed her hand and twined his fingers with hers.

She yanked away from him again. She was hurt and angry that Fen had kept such a huge secret from her.

"Then hold Matt's hand," she yelled back and got a mouthful of the sawdust that was lifting and swirling in the air.

He was family, her best friend—and he'd lied to her. *He's*

a wolf. How could he not tell me! She felt tears sting her eyes as the wind slapped her face.

She wasn't sure which of the shrieks and howls in the air were wolves and which were from the tornado sirens and the storm itself. She wasn't going to look back for either threat. If she'd been at home, she'd have gone into the basement of the building. Here, she wasn't sure what to do, but Matt seemed to have a plan. She'd never expected to be following a Thorsen, especially after the fight Matt and Fen had had the other day, but right now they were all on the same side: the three of them versus the wolves.

"Over here." Matt gestured toward the longship.

Climbing up seemed crazy, but the ship would protect them from the hail, flying things, and maybe even the wolves. It wouldn't protect them from the tornado. The roar of it was awful, and being higher up seemed like a great way to fall farther.

"We can get inside it." He scrambled up the side of the ship. Matt tapped in a code on a lockbox mounted on the wall. It popped open, and he grabbed a key. "Come on."

Would Fen go with him? She wasn't sure, and her loyalties were divided. She might be mad at Fen, but he was still Fen—and Matt was the kid who had thrown Fen at the longship. *Was that magic, too?* She felt like an idiot. They both knew things. Matt wasn't freaked out about the wolf thing, either. She wasn't sure what was going on, but right now, the two people who had answers were both staring at her. A new burst of hurt and anger filled her.

She ignored the hand Matt held out to help her over the side of the ship, and she didn't say a word as Fen climbed over after her. They crawled across the deck of the ship on their stomachs, keeping themselves as low as possible; the sides of the longship protected them from the worst of the wind and kept them hidden from the wolves.

Matt fumbled at the lock, taking far too long for her liking.

The wind ripped at their clothes and hair; rain and hail pelted them. She opened her mouth to say "Hurry," and the air took her breath away. She snapped her lips closed.

Behind her, she felt Fen move closer. He had put his body behind her to shelter her from flying branches and hailstones. Because he was blocking her from the storm, his mouth was directly beside her ear. "I wanted to tell you," he said. "Wasn't allowed."

She didn't answer. Later, they would have to talk—or yell, more likely—but right now, she couldn't say anything. If she did, she might start crying, and she wasn't going to look all wussy in front of the two of them.

Matt looked back and said something, but all she caught was "Fen, pull."

Fen yelled, "What?"

"Pull," she shouted, turning to him as she did so.

Fen glanced behind him, and then he nodded, apparently satisfied with what he saw—or with what he didn't see.

As her cousin reached past her, she looked back, too, and realized that no one had followed them onto the ship. She wasn't sure where the wolves had gone, but they weren't here now. Maybe they'd had the sense to seek shelter, too. Being caught in a tornado could be deadly for a wolf, just as it could for a person.

Together, Matt and Fen tugged the door open. Matt's arms were tight as he held on to the door, and Fen had to brace a foot on the wall, but they had the door open. Fen gestured with his head, and even though she couldn't hear what he was saying, she knew it was some version of *You go first*.

She scrambled inside, fumbling in the dark, and felt someone bump into her almost immediately.

"Sorry," Matt muttered as he steadied her. "Steps. Be careful."

The door crashed shut, taking away any light. She'd already seen that there were steps. They were all standing on a small landing, and another foot in front of her steps descended into the still deeper darkness of the ship. "How many steps?" she asked Matt.

"Maybe twelve. Just follow me."

"You can't see any better than I can." She rolled her eyes, even though neither of them could see. Boys had some pretty ridiculous ideas about what girls could do. She might not be able to wrestle—or turn into a wolf—but she was just as capable of climbing down the steps as they were. Unless . . . "Can either of you see?"

Fen snorted. "My vision is better than regular people's, but when it's this dark, I'd need to be a wolf to see."

"Right," she murmured. She started to laugh at the strangeness of . . . well, *everything* today, but stopped herself. Fen was prickly on the best of days, and he was as likely to think she was laughing at him as not. The sound that started as a laugh ended like a cry.

"Are you hurt?" Fen sounded less worried than he would have if Matt weren't there, but she knew him well enough to know that he was alarmed.

"I'm fine." She sighed. It was hard to stay mad at him sometimes; he'd made it his personal goal in life to look out for her, to be there whenever she needed anything. He was a combination of her best friend and brother. She tried to push the hurt further away and said, "Bruises, but that's all. I think. You two?"

Matt shrugged. "Like going a few rounds in the ring. No big deal."

Fen snorted. "Yeah, right."

Matt ignored him and said, "Just feel with your foot. We're right behind you."

"Let me pass," Fen demanded. "I can go first in case—"

"I got it," she cut him off, and eased her foot forward. The only way he was going to stop trying to shelter her from everything was for her to push him more.

Between the darkness of the storm and the lack of lights inside the ship, she had only her sense of touch to guide her. She made her way down the steps, counting as she went.

"Twelve," she said when she reached the bottom.

She heard and felt them reach the bottom, too. They stood there in the dark, not speaking. Behind them and above them, she could hear the *ping*ing and *thump*ing of things hitting the wood, and the roar of the storm outside. She wasn't sure if the boys were scared, but now that they were out of the storm and away from the wolves, the fear of what could have happened hit her, and she shuddered. *We're fine*, she reminded herself. *Right now, we're just fine.*

She felt around with her hands, but she wasn't sure what would be down here. Was it storage? Things she'd knock over? And even if it wasn't, did she want to fumble around in the dark and then have to fumble back to the steps when the storm ended? She ended up standing still.

She hated waiting in the dark while a storm tore around outside. Twisters were scary in a way that blizzards weren't. They had those in South Dakota, too, but those mostly just meant school was canceled or delayed. Sometimes, there were whiteouts, where the wind blew the snow, and everything was a white blur outside. That was the thing, though:

it was outside, and she was safe inside. Tornados were different. Inside wasn't the same sort of protection from a storm that destroyed buildings. She shivered.

Immediately, Fen's arm went around her. "It'll be okay. We'll get out of here."

She nodded even though he couldn't see it and then whispered, "I'm mad at you."

He growled, and now that she knew he was a wolf sometimes, it sounded somehow more like a real growl. "There are rules. I couldn't tell you unless you changed, too."

Quietly, she asked, "Does the whole family change?"

Fen was quiet for a minute. "No, only some of us." He butted his head into hers, and for the first time, she realized that the gesture was one an animal would make. She'd known it was an odd thing that the Brekkes all did, but she hadn't made the connection before now. Their version of affection was because they were part animal.

When she didn't respond, Fen added, "Don't be mad. Please?"

Matt's voice saved her from answering. "We can sit over here."

There was no way to tell how long they would have to wait. They were all wet and cold, and once the storm left, they still had to deal with werewolves—*Were they werewolves? Or were they just wolves?* She wasn't sure the term even mattered. "So are you a Raider, too, then? That's what they all are, right? The Raiders are all wolves."

"I'm not one of them," Fen spat. "I follow my *own* rules, not theirs. They're *wulfenkind*, too, but I'm not joining them. I pay my dues...and yours, so I don't have to join them."

"*My* dues?"

She felt him shrug next to her, but all he said was, "No big thing. Once we figure out if you're going to change, you'll either pay, join, or go lone-wolf—like Uncle Stig."

"*Dad* is...that's why he's always gone?" Laurie felt like everything she'd known was suddenly different. Maybe it wouldn't have made things easier, but so much made sense now that she knew the family secret. "He could pay them and stay here? Why doesn't—" She stopped herself. They had other things than her father to deal with right now, but she couldn't help adding, "I'm not joining them. I can tell you that...and neither are you, Fen Brekke. You think I'm mad now? If you join them, I'll show you mad."

He didn't answer, but he gave her a brief one-armed hug. She'd told him she cared about him. That was all Fen ever really needed when he was worried: to know she cared.

A click in the dark was followed by a flash of fire. In Fen's hand was a lighter. It wasn't exactly him saying *Let's change the subject*, but it did the trick all the same.

"How long have you had *that*?" Matt asked.

Fen shrugged.

The light it cast was scant, but she could see stacks of boxes and more than a few cobwebs. Nothing particularly interesting, and then the light went out.

"Did you see any candles?" Matt asked. "Or a lantern?"

"We could burn one of the boxes," Fen suggested.

"Don't even think about it," Matt said. "Give me the lighter, and I'll look for—"

"Yeah, right. I don't think so, Thorsen."

"If we're going to work together—"

"I don't remember agreeing to that," Fen interrupted. "I saved your butt with the Raiders, but that doesn't mean—"

"You saved me? Were we at the same fight?"

"Stop. Just *stop*," Laurie interrupted. "You're both better than the other one. Now, we can stay here and wait for the monsters to—"

"Wolves," Fen muttered. "Not monsters."

"Well, since you didn't even tell me, how would I know that? And they weren't being friendly, were they? How would I know what you act like as a wolf, since you hid it from me?" She poked him repeatedly as she spoke.

Fen flicked the lighter again and looked at her.

"You lied to me." Laurie folded her arms over her chest.

"Um, planning?" Matt reminded them quietly before her glare-fest with Fen could turn into an ugly argument. "Laurie's right. We need a plan." He took a breath. "I know this is going to sound crazy, but we need to work together. Quick version: Ragnarök is coming. We have to find the rest of the gods' descendants. We have two already—I'm the stand-in for Thor, and Fen is for Loki. That's what the Norns told me tonight."

"The Norns?" Laurie interjected.

"They're the ladies in charge of everyone's fate," Matt said. "I talked to them, and that's how I knew I needed to talk to Fen." He stopped, took a breath, and added, "Look, I know Loki and Thor weren't always friends in the myths, but they could work together." He paused and turned to Fen. "I'm guessing you know the Brekkes are descended from Loki."

The lighter clicked off, so they couldn't see each other again. Laurie was glad they couldn't see the shock on her face. *Loki? The god Loki? From the myths?* She pinched her arm to make sure this wasn't like her weird fish dream. It hurt, but she was definitely awake—and apparently the only one surprised that their ancestors were real gods.

"Yeah, and that Thorsens don't think we know." Fen sounded smug. "Guess you didn't know some of us kept Loki's skill in shape-shifting, either. We might have only kept the wolf, but it's a lot more useful than most of Loki's shapes."

Matt let it drop. "So we need to find the other descendants and stop Ragnarök. If we don't do something, the world will end. They're not here in Blackwell, so we need to go find them. Are you in?"

Laurie tried to not freak out over the things they were talking about. It was bad enough that Fen had hidden that he was a wolf, but then Matt said the god thing and the whole world-is-ending thing. She'd thought the worst trouble they had to face was theft of a shield. These were much bigger problems. When she could finally speak, she asked, "Why were the wolves after us?"

Neither boy said anything for a moment. Then Matt said, "Maybe they know we're the god stand-ins."

"Or they're just out starting trouble," Fen added. "You're a *Thorsen*, and that means you're the enemy to *wulfenkind*."

"I'm not your enemy, Fen."

At that, Fen flicked the lighter on again. "Why should I believe you about any of it?"

"I don't lie," Matt said simply.

"Fen, I think we can trust him," Laurie started.

The lighter went out.

Laurie knew that Matt was telling the truth. Somehow, it just made sense to her. Believing it was as easy as believing that she and Fen were descendants of the long-dead god Loki. She wasn't sure why she was so sure, but she was. The question was how she could convince her stubborn cousin.

Before Laurie could say anything else, though, Fen said,

"Fine. If it's a choice between working with you or the world ending, I can put up with you for a while."

Although Laurie knew Fen was trying to sound like he didn't really care, she knew him. That was the voice he always had before he was about to go and do something colossally stupid. It meant that he expected something crazy or dangerous to happen. Proof positive that he expected true trouble if he joined up with Matt came in Fen's very next sentence: "We need to get Laurie home first and—"

"Are you *joking*?" All of her anger and frustration came roaring back. She shoved him so hard he fell sideways.

Fen flicked the lighter on and glared at her.

"No," she snapped. "Don't even start! You can't expect me to stay here."

He sat up, lighter still flickering with its small flame, and began his list of objections. "Come on, Laurie. You're not the one who has to do this. It's dangerous, and you don't have a way to protect yourself." He jabbed Matt in the arm. "Thorsen has his knockout thing. I have teeth and claws. You're just a girl, and Uncle Stig will kill me if you get hurt."

"You're not going anywhere without me," Laurie insisted. Fen might think he was keeping her safe by leaving her behind, but she *knew* that he wasn't safe without her. Between his temper and his recklessness, there was no way he could avoid trouble when he was here in Blackwell. Once he was on the road running from other wolves and who knows what—or who—else, he'd be in trouble she couldn't even begin to imagine.

The lighter died again.

"Why would I risk you getting hurt?" Fen asked. She heard the fear in his voice that he always thought he hid, and she understood, but it didn't matter. She wasn't letting fear—his or hers—stop her. He needed her.

Laurie tried to think of an argument. She felt like she was missing something obvious, and then it hit her. "I met Odin," she blurted. "Oh. Wow. I thought he was just a weirdo, but I met *Odin*. Remember? I told you I met a stranger who acted like he knew me." She filled them in on her whole conversation with Odin and was surprised by how quiet Fen still was when she was done. "Fen?"

Fen flicked the lighter on one more time.

"I'm coming with you, Fen," she said. "I know what Odin looks like, and he said I'd see him again, so I'm *supposed* to come."

Fen opened his mouth to say something, no doubt an objection, but she folded her arms over her chest and used the one thing she knew he couldn't ignore: "What if the Raiders come back, and I'm here alone? They know who I am, and I'm not a wolf. How am I supposed to fight them on my own?"

"I don't have a problem with it," Matt said. "We can take care of her."

"Take care of me?" Laurie sputtered.

"Yeah," Fen snarled. "If you're coming, next time there's a fight you stay out of it. If they're up there right now, you let Thorsen and me handle it. Or you can stay here, where it's safer."

"Safer?" Laurie echoed. "Did you listen to *anything* I said?"

"About as well as you did to what I said," Fen muttered.

They sat in tense silence for a few moments until Matt pointed out, "Sounds like the storm's ended. Let's get out of here."

Cautiously, they started up the stairs. Matt was in front, and Fen was behind her.

When they stepped outside, they stopped and looked at the destruction all around. A lot of the shields on the side of the ship were thrashed. Trees were uprooted. A car was overturned. The stop sign at the intersection had been flung halfway down the block.

Laurie didn't see any wolves, but people were already appearing, and she wasn't sure which ones were the ones who became wolves. Fen hadn't technically agreed to her coming, but she wasn't going to wait for him to stop being difficult. She looked at him and said, "We need to get out of here before the wolves find us. We'll stop at home, grab some clothes and whatever money we have, and then figure out where to go." She glanced at Matt, who was now squirming. "Look, if you'd rather tell your dad, we can—"

"No," he interrupted. "It's just...I can't go home."

Laurie and Fen exchanged a look.

"You're a Thorsen. Just walk in, get your stuff, and pretend like you're going to the gym or something." Fen shook his head. "I know you've probably never told a lie in your perfect life, but I can talk you through it. Easy as falling off a pedestal."

Laurie hid her sigh of relief. If Fen was focused on Matt, he'd stop being a pain about her going with them. She felt a little bad for Matt, but better Matt having to put up with Fen's teasing than her needing to fight about being left behind in Blackwell.

"I'm okay with lying, Fen," Matt was saying. "It's just... My family..." He took a deep breath. "They don't expect me to kill the Midgard Serpent. They expect me to die. And, apparently, they're okay with that."

For a moment, no one spoke. Fen's characteristic rudeness vanished, and Laurie wasn't at all sure what to say. The Thorsens were perfect; Matt had a family, a big family, who treated him like he could do no wrong. Carefully, she repeated, "They're okay with you dying."

"They told me I was going to be the one to stop Ragnarök, but I overheard my grandfather"—he paused, and then he spoke really quickly, all his words running together, as he looked at them both—"when I was with one of the Norns. My grandfather and the town council *want* Ragnarök to happen. Granddad wants me to fight the Midgard Serpent. He wants me to defeat it—so the monsters don't take over the world—but he expects me to die trying, just like in the myth. Then an ice age will come, and the world will be reborn, fresh and new."

"After almost everyone dies. That's messed up." Fen shook his head. Then he looked at Laurie and said, "We'll go to your place first. It's closest. He and I will stay outside. Aunt Janey won't let you go anywhere with me. Then we'll stop by the garage for my stuff."

They didn't have to worry: her mom wasn't home, so Laurie left a note and they headed to Kris' place. Leaving Blackwell seemed scary, but the other descendants weren't here—and the Raiders were. Plus, there was the whole Matt's-family-wanting-the-end-of-the-world problem. Leaving home was necessary.

But she was still nervous, and she was sure the boys were, too.

Once they had backpacks and a couple of sleeping bags they'd borrowed from Kris' garage, she turned to the boys and asked, "Okay, where to?"

The boys exchanged a look. Neither spoke. Day one and

they were already lacking any sort of plan. They had no idea what to do. They were kids and supposed to figure this all out...because Matt said his family and some women claimed he and Fen were to defeat monsters. It was crazy. No one was saying it out loud, but she suspected they were all thinking it.

Fen turns into a wolf.

There was that one detail, proof that the crazy was real, that kept her from thinking it was all a great big joke. The rest of her "proof" was just her instincts and a conversation with a blue-haired boy. It wasn't much. The wolf thing was real, though. She'd seen it.

After a few moments, Matt said, "I can do this."

"Riiiight." Fen drew out the word. "Didn't we already decide that?"

"Not *that*," Matt said. "Maybe I can..." He stood straighter. "I'll talk to my brothers. They'll know about this. They're smart. They can help."

"Are you sure?" Laurie asked.

Matt nodded, but she didn't believe him, and from the look on Fen's face, neither did he.

"I'll go with you," Fen suggested. "You"—he looked pointedly at Laurie—"need to stay out of sight in case the Raiders come back."

She wanted to argue, but she was pretty sure that Fen

wouldn't need much of an excuse to decide to leave her behind. She nodded as meekly as she was able. "Fine."

This time, she added in her head. *I'll hide and wait* this time.

Fen and Matt both looked tense, but she knew they were trying to hide it. They had a start of a plan of sorts. For now, that would have to be enough.

This is going to be a disaster. The world is going to end because we don't know what to do.

TEN

MATT

"NIGHT FRIGHT"

att stood on the corner, looking at his house. For the first time in his life, he realized how much it looked like every other house on the block. Each was painted a different color, but otherwise, they were identical—split-level houses with single-car garages and exactly the same size lawns, sometimes even the same flowers now dying in the same size gardens.

"Come on," Fen whispered. "We don't have all night."

Matt tried to hurry, but his feet felt like they were made of lead. Shame burned through him. Some champion he was, too frightened to even face his family. That was nothing new, but—like looking down this street—it felt different now. Maybe it was because Fen was here, and he was seeing things like Fen would, just a bunch of nice houses, all in a row. Just an ordinary family living in the third one down. Nothing special. Nothing to be afraid of. Not for a kid who was destined to fight a giant serpent.

Matt took a deep breath and imagined Jake standing there. *Man up*, he'd say, like he always did, with that look on his face, like he couldn't believe they were actually related.

Man up. Matt wasn't sure what that meant exactly, but he was pretty sure Fen would say the same thing. *Stop dragging your feet like a baby and start acting like a man.*

Matt straightened and started forward before Fen noticed him hesitating.

"Wait," Fen said. He was even more prickly now that Laurie wasn't with them.

Matt ignored him. He wasn't trying to be rude; he needed to keep moving or it'd be morning and he'd still be on this street corner.

"I said *wait*," Fen snapped, and moved in front of Matt. He looked left and right, head swinging. *Like a wolf*, Matt thought. *Watching for trouble.*

"Back," Fen said.

"What?"

Fen shot him a glare and motioned him back around the corner, behind the Carlsens' garage.

"Raiders," he said.

"What?" Matt repeated, and then caught himself before he sounded like a total idiot. He took his voice down a notch like Jake did sometimes. "The Raiders are there?"

"Watching the house. We gotta go back."

Which was, Matt admitted to himself, exactly what he wanted. Forget grabbing stuff from his house. He'd happily stay in the same shirt and jeans for a week if it meant he didn't need to face his family.

Coward.

He peered out.

"I said—" Fen began.

"Just taking a look."

"Because you don't believe me?"

"No, I just—"

"Who's the guy who can see better at night?" Fen asked in a voice that sounded a lot like a warning growl.

"I know, I just—"

"Look at the house on the other side of yours. By the garage."

Matt peeked out and saw a young Raider hiding in the shadows.

"Three of them," Fen said. "Maybe more. Skull's not with them this time."

"Skull?"

"The leader. He was at the field."

"Right." Matt remembered the big Raider and was glad

at least he wasn't here, but still, three Raiders were three too many. "We need to draw them off."

"Um, no, we need to get out of here before they see—"

"You go," Matt said. "They're looking for me. If they don't see me come home, they'll think I snuck in later. They might go after my family."

"So?"

Matt looked at him.

"Isn't this the family that was going to sacrifice you to a dragon?" Fen asked.

"Serpent. Well, it's kind of like—never mind. My brothers don't know. They can't."

"Are you sure?"

He was certain Josh didn't know. But could he help? He was only sixteen. No. He had to do what Jake would. Man up. Protect his family. Prove to them that he could do this.

"I'm drawing the Raiders off," he said. "They need to know I never went home. That'll keep my family safe."

Fen snorted.

He thinks I'm an idiot. I shouldn't care. But I do. Matt shook his head. *Doesn't matter. I'm still a Thorsen. Family comes first.*

"You go on," Matt said. "I'll—"

"Walk," Fen said.

"What?"

Fen made a move, as if to shove him. "Go. Move. Pretend you're walking home."

Matt stepped out and started down the sidewalk. It took a moment to realize Fen was beside him. When he did, he started to protest, but a look from Fen shut him up.

"So, um, how's . . ." Matt struggled—and failed—to think of any sports or clubs Fen was in. "School. How's school?"

Fen looked at him like he'd asked how he liked ballet lessons.

"Mr. Fosse is being a real jerk this year, isn't he?" Matt continued.

"What the—?" Fen began.

"I'm making conversation."

"Seriously? We're on the lam together, Thorsen. Not buddying up."

"I'm doing it for them." Matt jerked his chin at the Raiders. "So it looks normal."

"Us talking does *not* look normal," Fen pointed out.

They continued in silence. It took a minute before the Raiders noticed them. Matt kept going, like he hadn't seen the figures sliding from behind the neighbor's garage.

"I'll just grab some clothes and a toothbrush," Matt said, as loudly as he dared. "Then we'll run away together. I mean—"

"Shut it, Thorsen," Fen hissed. "Just shut it."

There were five Raiders. They'd all come out now. Matt looked straight at them.

"Uh, Fen?" he said. "Aren't those the—?"

"Go." Fen wheeled and ran, Matt racing after him, the Raiders giving chase.

They managed to ditch the Raiders before they got back to Laurie. Then, as they were heading out of town, they saw them again. It didn't seem as if the Raiders noticed them, but they weren't taking a chance. They ran from Blackwell and didn't look back.

Late that night, Matt awoke smelling the sharp tang of wet grass. A distant coyote yipped. Beside him, someone groaned in sleep. *Camping*, he thought. *I'm camping.*

He started to drift off again, then he felt the wet grass, dampness seeping through his sleeves, and he bolted upright, remembering his father yelling at him for leaning his knapsack against the tent.

Anything touching the tent lets in the rain. You're not a child, Matthew. It's time you stopped acting like one.

Matt scrambled up, trying to see what he'd left against the tent this time. But there was no tent. He was looking up at shards of night sky through the treetops. He blinked hard as he struggled to focus. Then he looked over, saw Laurie and Fen, and it all came back.

He heard the Seer's voice: *Our champion is Matthew Thorsen.*

Then Granddad: *My grandson is being honored in the highest fashion, and he will do us proud, and he will take his place in the halls of Valhalla as a champion with the long-dead gods. As a hero. Our hero.*

Matt's stomach lurched. His foot slid on the wet grass, and he went down on his knees, his stomach tumbling with him. He fell onto all fours, retching.

Mistake. It's gotta be a mistake. They wouldn't do that. Not Mom. Not Dad. Especially not Granddad.

But even as he denied it, his stomach kept heaving, a thin trickle dripping as he coughed.

"Matt?"

He pushed up fast, his hand swiping the dribble from his mouth. Laurie sat blinking at him.

"You okay?" she asked quietly. After a moment's pause, she added, "Or is that a dumb question?"

"I'm fine." He wiped his mouth harder and straightened, letting his voice drop an octave. "Sorry about that. Just... fair food. Corn dogs taste great, then you wake up in the middle of the night, feeling like they were made from real dogs."

She didn't smile, just kept peering at his face in the darkness. He tried to straighten more. He couldn't let her see he was scared. She was a girl. She had to be protected. That's what Dad always said.

"Everything's fine," he said.

"Um, no. It's not," she said. "You and Fen nearly got killed by Raiders. We all nearly got killed by a tornado. And

134

now we're sleeping in the woods, resting up so we can fight to stop the end of the world. Things are *not* fine."

"But it will be. Everything is under control."

No, it's not, you idiot. You have no idea what you're doing. No idea where you're going. Morning's going to come soon, and they're going to find out you don't have a good plan. You don't have any plan at all.

"Everything is under control." *Say it often enough, and I might even start to believe it.* "Just go back to—"

"Shhh!"

Matt looked over at her. "Huh?"

Laurie opened her mouth to say something, but another *Shhh!* came from beside her as Fen sat up, scowling. His head cocked. He motioned around them.

When Matt frowned, Fen's scowl deepened. "Are you deaf, Thorsen? Stop yammering and listen."

Matt did and heard the faint rustle of grass. He was about to say it was just the wind, but Fen already thought he was a clueless rich kid. When he listened more closely, he heard a *thud*, like...

He wasn't sure what it sounded like. Not the wind. Not a scurrying rabbit, either. It *was* familiar, but only vaguely, some memory locked deep in his brain.

Then another noise: a *click-click*, like dice knocking together.

"I'm going to take a look," he whispered.

Fen shrugged. "Whatever."

When Laurie gave Fen a look, he said, "What? He offered."

Laurie began getting up. "I'll come—"

Fen caught her arm. "The more of us go, the more noise we make. Thorsen can handle it."

Matt squared his shoulders and gave what he hoped was a confident nod. Then he slipped to a patch of bushes, crouched, and made his way along. He'd gone only a few steps when he heard the clicking again. Then a snort. A bump. All three sounds came from different directions. He tried to take another step, but his body wouldn't listen, frozen in place.

His amulet had started to vibrate again, like it had with the Norns, only it felt different. It felt like trouble.

A whisper sounded behind him. Matt looked back to see Laurie leaning toward her cousin, her gaze on Matt as she whispered something. He couldn't hear the words, but he could imagine them. *Thorsen can't do it. He's scared.*

He wasn't usually so jumpy—he'd been camping plenty of times. But after last night, he couldn't be sure it was just a wild animal out there. It might be . . . well, there were lots of things it might be. Norse myths were full of monsters.

He gritted his teeth and resumed walking, straining to see in the dark, leaning forward until he almost tripped. Then he glimpsed a huge pale form just beyond the forest. It had to be at least seven feet high and almost as long.

That's not possible. Nothing's that big.

Nothing natural.

But there was nothing natural about giant serpents and kids who turned into wolves.

Something had tracked them down. Some monster. His mind whipped through his mythology books. Trolls. Frost giants. Berserkers.

Another snort to his left. When he turned, he could make out a second huge pale shape. And a third behind it. And a fourth...

He swallowed.

They were surrounded. These things had found them, and now—

"I come for Thor's son. Send him out!" It was a woman's voice. But not like any woman's voice he'd ever heard. There was no softness to it. It was as harsh as the caw of a crow.

He took a slow step back.

"You!" The pale beast moved to the forest edge. "I see you, boy. You cannot be the one I seek. The son of Thor does not cower in shadows."

Anger darted through him, and he almost barreled out to confront her. He stopped himself, but after that first jolt of *Are you nuts?* he thought maybe that wasn't so crazy after all.

Fen must be able to hear the woman. He'd know they were in danger and that Matt was the target. He'd take his cousin and run. And that, Matt reasoned, was probably their only chance.

Matt strode from the forest. "I am a son of…"

As he stepped into the moonlight, he found himself staring up at a white horse bigger than any he'd ever seen. On its back was a woman. But not like any woman he'd ever seen, either. She had bright red hair that rippled and snarled around her pale face. Her cheeks were stained with what looked like handprints. The horse was painted with them, too, handprints and lines and swirls that shone blue in the moonlight.

The horse snorted and shifted, and when it did, he heard that clicking noise and looked over. The horse's bridle. It was… it was made of bones. Finger bones strung together. More bones hung from the saddle, which almost looked as if it was made of… nope. He wasn't thinking of that. It was leather. Just regular leather.

"Are you Matthew, son of Thor?" the woman asked.

He looked up at her. He had to. Even if his heart was pounding so hard he could barely breathe.

He noticed then how young she was. Not much older than the elder Norn. Pretty, too. His stomach twisted as he thought it. He didn't want to think it. She shouldn't be pretty with that wild hair and blue-stained face. She should be terrible—and she was. But as she sat there, perfectly straight, blue eyes flashing, shield over one shoulder, sword gripped in her free hand, he didn't see a monster, he saw…

He swallowed as he realized what he saw. What she was. They had mosaics of her, too—her kind—in the rec center. Only they didn't look like this. The women in those pictures were tall and beautiful with long blond braids and horned hats and breastplates that didn't totally cover...well, he remembered how much his friends liked that picture. And maybe he'd kind of liked it, too.

The only thing this woman had in common with them was her sword and shield, but Matt remembered an older painting in a dusty book his granddad kept in his private library. In that painting, the women were wild-haired and painted, riding great winged steeds through the battlefields, stripping trophies from the enemy dead.

"Valkyries," Matt whispered.

"Huh?" said a voice behind him.

Matt spun to see two women on foot leading Fen and Laurie around the forest patch, as if they'd tried to escape out the other side. Laurie was struggling and snarling. Fen just walked, as if he'd realized he couldn't fight.

"They're Valkyries," Matt whispered as he stepped back beside Fen.

ELEVEN

❖

FEN

"READING MOUNT RUSHMORE"

Valkyries?" Fen echoed. That explained how the women had managed to sneak up on them. He looked back at the woman who held him. She was blond, but otherwise looked like the red-haired rider, right down to the blue war paint.

"The son of Thor is correct," the red-haired Valkyrie said in her rough voice. "The son of Loki knows too little of his heritage." She turned to Laurie. "And the daughter?"

Laurie pulled herself straight. "I'll learn."

"The descendants of Thor are taught their heritage." Fen pulled away from the Valkyrie holding his shoulder. "Not all of Loki's descendants are taught—because of the sons of Thor."

He sent a glare Matt's way.

"You must learn," the Valkyrie said. "I am Hildar of the Valkyrie. We are pleased to see you have accepted the challenge. We have come to offer assistance."

Fen looked around as a half-dozen horses and riders drifted in from the shadows. His gaze went not from face to face but sword to sword. He smiled. This was the kind of help they needed. The *wulfenkind* would be in for a surprise next time they came sniffing around. "So, how does this work?"

The Valkyrie gave Fen an amused look.

Laurie cleared her throat; Fen pretended not to hear. "Do we lead—"

Matt interrupted. "I know we need to find Odin. That's what the Norns said."

"One cannot rely on the Norns to set the order of battle plans—they jump forward and back and do not see the proper path," Hildar said. "Odin is not your concern yet; your priority is finding the other descendants of the North. We will help you."

Matt exhaled. "Thank you. I was wondering how we'd—" He stopped and glanced at Fen and Laurie. "I mean, I had a few ideas of how to do that, but I appreciate any help you, um, ladies can offer."

"Yeah. Me, too." Fen felt a guilty rush of relief. So far the entire plan had been to run and hide and stumble around in the dark without a clue. They'd avoided the Raiders for now, and they would have to keep doing so because he was pretty sure that Skull was going to deliver them all to his boss if they were caught. Fen had told Skull he'd deliver Thorsen, but instead he'd fought Raiders to *help* him. He wasn't entirely sure why he'd done that—other than the obvious fact that he didn't want to work for the Raiders—but it had been a sort of last-minute decision. Still, last-minute or not, it would have consequences if Skull caught up with them.

So we need to be far enough ahead that they can't catch us.

Fen stepped forward. "Do you have extra horses, or do we share with you?"

"It is not our place to take you to the descendants. You must find them yourselves," Hildar said.

"So you'll tell us where they are?" Matt prompted.

The Valkyrie frowned. "No. We will tell you where you can go to learn where they are."

"Uh-huh." Fen's hopes of real help were quickly vanishing, but maybe it was a case of the Valkyries just not understanding. "Could you make it a little less complicated? We're talking about the end of the world here."

The look she shot him made him step backward, but all she did was say, "First, you must be tested."

"I haven't studied," Matt said.

Fen stifled a laugh, but either Hildar didn't get the joke or didn't think it was funny.

"It is not that kind of test," she said. "You must win a war."

"I get that," Matt said. "But I'm pretty good at fighting already. Can you just skip the scavenger hunt and do this the old-fashioned way? Mano a mano. I take on a challenger."

The other Valkyries murmured among themselves in a language Fen didn't know, and Hildar shook her head. "You are indeed a son of Thor: you think you can overcome any obstacle with a hammer in one hand and a stein of mead in the other."

"I don't think they'll let me have mead, but I wouldn't mind the *real* Hammer." Matt fingered his amulet.

All the Valkyries just stared, stone-faced. Fen felt just as frustrated as they looked. Sure, Thorsen didn't know what Fen had risked or what trouble awaited if the Raiders caught up with them, but here they were with an offer of help that was being dashed as quickly as it had arrived. He didn't feel like arguing the matter, either, but Matt was persistent. Fen had to give him credit for that. He was ready to walk away, but Thorsen was obviously still clinging to the hope that the Valkyries could be convinced to offer genuine aid.

Matt sighed. "Come on. It's a war. The Midgard Serpent isn't going to let us settle this over a game of Tafl." He paused. "Unless that's a possibility, 'cause I'm pretty good at that, too. Would save a lot of trouble. Lot less messy, too. So, what do you think?"

"I think you are not taking this seriously enough," Hildar said.

She seemed to think that Thorsen was being flip with her, but she'd already said it wasn't a fight. It only made sense to come up with other possible types of challenges. Fen didn't figure pointing that out would earn them any favors, though, so he kept his mouth shut and waited.

"The fate of the world is in your hands," one of the other Valkyries said.

Laurie stepped forward, drawing everyone's gaze to her. "Then *help* us."

Fen felt a flash of worry and eased closer to her. She was where his loyalty should be—and would be. Hildar saw his movement and smiled.

"You're the descendants of gods," Hildar said, almost kindly. "They died, and it's up to you now to fulfill the roles in the great fight. Ragnarök comes. This is your duty. We can't assume your duty for you."

"I didn't sign up for this. None of us did," Fen objected. It was like the world had spun backward a thousand years and they were now old enough to leave home and get married, old enough to fight, old enough to die. They were being asked to risk death because somewhere forever ago they had relatives who were gods. Worse still, those gods had died and left them a mess to handle.

"Did you not?" Hildar asked.

And Fen wondered briefly how much she knew. He *had* made a choice. When the Raiders came at Thorsen, Fen had chosen. When they were on the longship and Fen had heard Thorsen talk about Ragnarök just like Skull had talked about it, Fen had chosen. He'd decided to throw in on the side of the gods, the side that the prophecy said would lose. There was a part of him that wanted to be better than the god who was his long-gone ancestor, be a hero instead of a troublemaker, and maybe in doing so keep the monsters from winning. Being *wulfenkind* didn't make Skull or anyone else a monster, but wanting to destroy the world certainly did.

"What are we supposed to do?" Matt asked.

"We would prefer you to win," Hildar replied, not quite answering the more practical question Fen suspected Matt was asking. The Valkyrie continued, "If you are to win, you must be ready. You must not be children, waiting for things to be handed to you. You must find the others. In time, you must find Odin. You must collect Mjölnir, a feather from each of Odin's ravens, and the shield. These things will help you fight the serpent."

"Mjölnir? You mean…*the* Mjölnir? Thor's Hammer?" Matt looked like someone had offered him a great big prize, which, Fen supposed, she kind of had. A god's hammer would be pretty handy in a fight with monsters. It was a shame that no one was offering him a superweapon, too.

146

After another of those glances that made Fen think Hildar knew more than he'd like, she looked back at Matt and her lips twitched with the faintest sign of a smile. "That is what you wanted, is it not, son of Thor?"

"I was kidding," Matt said in a half-shocked voice. He took a deep breath. "So Mjölnir, feathers, and some shield. And the other kids. And Odin."

"You'll give us a clue, though, right?" Fen interjected. "That's what you said: you'd help."

Hildar nodded. "Indeed." She looked at them each in turn and then said, "Seek the twins first. To find them, go see the presidents. Their faces hold the answer."

Then she lifted her hand, and all the Valkyries turned away.

The riders swung onto their horses' backs. In an instant, hooves pounded; the horses and their riders were a blur, and then they were gone.

"Seriously?" Fen said, spinning around to face Laurie and Matt. "Seriously? Answers on the faces of the presidents? What kind of riddle is that?"

"It's not a riddle," Laurie said evenly. "It's Mount Rushmore."

"Yes!" Matt already looked calm again, and Fen wished briefly that he were that sure of himself—not always or anything, but sometimes.

Matt continued, "They mean we'll find the answer at

Mount Rushmore. That's got to be it. Something there will lead us to the twins."

"What twins?" Laurie had a nervous look on her face. "Sorry. My mom was anti–Blackwell history because my dad gets so into it. I had no idea it would ever matter."

Fen felt another flash of guilt. He hadn't had a choice about keeping secrets, but he also hadn't tried to convince her to pay attention to the myths, even though he knew she might turn into a wolf like him. Now she was caught up in a dangerous situation with a lot less information than she needed to have.

Uncle Stig is going to kill me ... unless the Raiders do it first.

While Fen was stressing out, Matt seemed perfectly calm now that Laurie had asked a question he could answer. He launched into explaining the myths: "The twins are Frey and Freya. In the old stories, Freya is the goddess of love and beauty. Frey is the god of weather and fertility. We need to find their descendants, who are apparently also twins." Matt paused. "Two for one. That'll make it easier."

Fen scowled at him. "I don't think any of this is going to be easy."

"And that's the point," Laurie murmured.

"Okay, then," Matt said. "I guess we visit the presidents."

Blackwell wasn't too far away from Mount Rushmore, but it was a long enough walk that Fen wished he could change into a wolf and run. He wasn't about to leave his cousin behind, though. He'd promised Uncle Stig that he'd keep an eye on her, especially around boys. The idea of telling any of the family that he had left her alone with a Thorsen made his stomach twist inside him. He glanced at Matt and Laurie talking animatedly while they walked toward Mount Rushmore. It seemed like just friendship, but even that would anger the family.

And they'd blame me.

Fen was all on board with the stop-the-end-of-the-world part, and he hoped his family would be, too. They were mostly lone wolves or tithed. That had to mean his dad and Uncle Stig wouldn't side with the crazy let-the-world-end plan, right? Fen wasn't entirely sure about some of his family. What he did know, however, was that the Raiders definitely wouldn't be forgiving of any *wulfenkind*'s decision to side with a Thorsen.

And Thorsen won't be forgiving if he finds out I was supposed to capture him and deliver him to them.

His whole family would be angry if they found out he was running across the state with a Thorsen. They might not all like the Raiders, but *wulfenkind* didn't help Thorsens. That part was just the way it was, the way it always had been. Matt didn't seem like most Thorsens, though. They'd fought side by side against the Raiders, and they'd stood side by side in the face of warrior women. Both times, Matt seemed to want to win more than be a show-off. It reminded Fen of what packs were supposed to be like, what families were supposed to be like. It wasn't what Fen would expect from a descendant of Thor. Surprisingly, Matt seemed like he was kind of an okay guy. Fen wasn't about to tell him that, but he really didn't want Matt or Laurie to know that he'd considered helping the Raiders capture Matt. Matt would hate him—and Laurie would probably be mad, too.

He hadn't wanted to deliver Matt to them, and he'd been trying to think of a solution. Throwing in against his own kind wasn't the one he'd meant to pick, but it had seemed like a good idea at the time. Still, if Laurie and Matt learned that Fen had given them the shield and that he was supposed to deliver Thorsen to the Raiders, they wouldn't understand. He knew it.

So they can't find out.

He knew how to keep a secret. He'd been dealing with knowing he was Loki's descendant for years, turning into a wolf the past year, paying tithe to the Raiders, keeping secrets from Laurie, and alternately hoping and not hoping that she'd be a wolf like him.

"Are you still with us?" Laurie looked over her shoulder at him.

"Sure." He thought about telling her the truth, or at least some of it, but Thorsen was watching, and Fen wasn't about to tell him. Fen would just continue to keep an eye out for

Raiders, and they'd deal with any trouble if it came. What he could tell them was, "I know where the shield is."

"The shield the Valkyries said we need?"

A car passed, with music blaring, and Fen almost growled at how close it came to Laurie. He moved to walk beside her, and she stepped onto the gravel along the road. He nodded. "The Raiders have it. It's the one I was trying to get."

"Why didn't you tell me that's why you were trying to steal it?" Matt asked.

Laurie hugged him. "You could've at least told *me* you were trying to keep it out of their hands."

Gratefulness shot through him: their misunderstanding of his role in the shield's theft was the perfect cover.

"I never wanted you to know anything about the Raiders," he told her. That part was true. The part where he was trying to *protect* it from the Raiders, not that he stole it and delivered it to them, wasn't exactly true, of course.

He looked from Matt to Laurie and then added, "I don't know how we're going to get it from them, but at least we know where it is."

"And we know that Odin says we'll talk again, and even I know that Odin is supposed to be all-seeing in the stories. I'm guessing he'll be able to get us the feathers from his ravens." Laurie laughed. "Is it weird how easy it is to believe that all of this is real?"

"Don't know," Fen hedged. "I've always known some of it. Thorsen probably has, too."

Matt nodded.

"Well, I haven't, and I still think we can do this," Laurie said. She stared at the giant carved presidents in the distance and smiled.

After a friendly smile at her that made Fen want to snarl protectively, Matt said, "Let's go find our clue."

Fen shook his head. They'd barely survived a fight with the Raiders, and he didn't expect a tornado to pop up and save them the next time. He knew the Raiders, knew how well patrolled their camps were, knew that the way Hattie and Skull were about the shield meant that it would be well guarded. He couldn't tell Laurie and Matt any of that without admitting how well he knew the Raiders, and he wasn't willing to do that. He'd figure out a way around the shield problem later, but for now, he kept his mouth shut and followed Laurie and Matt through the visitors' entrance to Mount Rushmore.

They walked past the tall gray columns. On one side was a wall with names carved on it, and on the other was a statue of the guy who was behind creating the monument.

There were more stone columns, with state flags on top of them, and at the end was a big open space where people stood staring at the presidents' faces. Fen wasn't really much into school stuff, but they'd come here on a field trip, and he'd been impressed by the idea of making such an enormous sculpture. These were the sort of giant carvings that meant explosions and giant power tools were needed. Far cooler than sitting there with a tiny blob of clay, trying to make a sculpture, which is what they'd had to do in art class. He smiled at the idea of getting to use explosives in art class. *That* would be cool.

The three of them stood there with the people, all staring up at Washington, Jefferson, Teddy Roosevelt, and Lincoln. He felt like one of them should have a camera so they'd blend in, but no one was staring at them like they were doing anything wrong. And they weren't...yet.

They had to wait for a while until they were able to get closer to the faces—where the Valkyrie had said the clue was—so they killed time until the park closed, watching the movie in the visitors' center two times, and then buying something to eat using money that they'd all brought. No one asked where he'd gotten his, and he didn't tell them he'd taken it from Kris' stash. Laurie had hers and some jewelry she said they could sell if they needed to. Matt had used a cash machine to add to the money he still had from his dad.

"We'll hide and wait," Matt said.

They crept into the woods and settled in for a few hours. This part of their quest was far from exciting. Fen was a lot more at ease fighting Raiders than sitting in silence. He wasn't great at staying still in general, but from the looks of it, neither was Matt. He fidgeted almost as much as Laurie and Fen did. They exchanged an almost-friendly nod.

Eventually, the statues were lit up, and then people started leaving. But the guard didn't leave. So they kept waiting.

Unfortunately, the waiting part was a lot harder than the hiding. They had a number of places to hide over in the wooded area, but that guard not only watched the visitors' area but also the monument itself. Plus, there were cameras aimed at the monument and around the area.

Earlier that day he had overheard someone talking about some sort of environmental protest a few years ago that had resulted in new security. Fen was all for taking care of the environment, especially since he was a wolf part of the time, but he wished they'd staged their protest elsewhere because the extra security meant getting close to the presidents' faces was seeming pretty impossible. There was no way they were going to be able to climb up there with a guard watching and who knows how many *more* scanning the security feed from wherever the cameras sent their signal.

A couple of hours passed, and they were no closer to progress than when they'd arrived. The guard stayed alert, and the cameras weren't going to vanish. It was ridiculous.

"I could get up there," Fen said in a low voice.

Matt shot Fen a warning glare.

"No one's going to stop a wolf." He turned to his cousin. "I wish you could change, too."

Then he turned his back on them and became a wolf.

It would be so much better if she was a wolf, too. He'd hoped in a weird sort of girly way that if she changed, too, Uncle Stig would take them with him. Then they could all three live together like a normal family. Laurie wasn't happy with her mom and brother, and Fen wasn't happy moving from house to house, and Uncle Stig surely wasn't happy alone. Laurie hadn't turned into a wolf, though, and he didn't know if she would. He felt sad, which made him want to howl.

She was already crouched down, so they were face-to-face. "Be careful," she whispered. "Don't do anything too stupid."

He butted his head against her shoulder, and then he was off. He walked right up to the guard, who looked at him with the sort of respect that he saw more often from the American Indians in South Dakota. Ranchers weren't usually keen on wolves, but the Sioux were more likely to respect nature—which included wolves.

The guard watched him warily, and then looked around as if he were seeking shelter. Fen didn't like that he had frightened him, so he smiled, which he always forgot never looked very friendly when he was a wolf, and the guard took a step backward. Fen felt a little guilty about scaring the

guard, but he had no intention of hurting the man. He kept the man's attention, hoping that Matt and Laurie were moving farther into cover.

Then he leaped over a low wall and started toward the monument. He knew the guard was watching him. The weight of the man's attention felt good, almost as good as stretching his muscles after hours of sitting and doing nothing. He grinned. Getting close enough to see whatever clue was on the presidents' faces was going to be easy.

He left the tourist section of the monument—and the guard—well behind him as he made his way up closer to the mountain, enjoying the feel of the ground under his paws, and was almost there when movement caught his eye. He stopped and looked. Rocks were raining down from the faces.

He waited, torn between natural caution and rushing forward to look for the clue before an earthquake or avalanche hid it even more. Several more rocks fell. Then, it looked like a giant part of the rock face was about to come crashing down. He was glad the guard was well out of range, but when he looked back, he couldn't see where Laurie was.

Whether it was an earthquake or avalanche, he didn't know. What he did know was that if there was a disaster of any sort starting, he needed to be with Laurie to keep her safe. He turned his back to the mountain and started to race back toward Laurie. He could hear a rumble behind him as he picked up speed.

TWELVE

❖

MATT

"TROLL CONDO"

When Thomas Jefferson's nose dropped off, Matt's first thought was: avalanche. He'd never actually experienced one, but he'd seen plenty in movies, and if pieces start falling off the faces at Mount Rushmore, that'd be the only natural and logical explanation. Then, when George Washington's nose dropped, he thought *It's an earthquake*, immediately followed by *It's Ragnarök*. More natural disasters. More signs—as if he needed them after being visited by Norns and Valkyries—that the world was indeed sliding into Fimbulwinter.

His first reaction, he was ashamed to admit, was to look around and see who was handling this. Who was in charge.

Who'd tell them to get to safety. Then he realized that was him.

He was turning to warn Fen and Laurie when Teddy Roosevelt's mustache got up and stretched. There was a second where Matt just stared, sure he was seeing wrong. The gray lump on the lip of the twenty-sixth president of the United States could not be stretching. It must be rolling or something, breaking loose.

Except it wasn't. It was *stretching*. And Abraham Lincoln's beard was dangling from what looked like thick gray arms. Then it started going up and down, like it was doing chin-ups. Using Lincoln's chin.

They'd gotten as close as they could, but the faces were still so far away you'd need binoculars to really see them. Those lumps *were* definitely moving, though, and the more they moved, the less they looked like hunks of stone. The one that had been Roosevelt's mustache now crouched on the president's lip, long, apelike gray arms dangling. Then the arms swung, and it leaped down to the rocks below.

"Trolls," Matt whispered.

"Right," Fen said. "Mount Rushmore is really a giant troll condo. Makes perfect sense."

Laurie looked at Matt. "The trolls must have the answer. That's what the Valkyrie meant, don't you think?"

"They didn't say the answers were written on the faces. Just that the answers were on the faces." Matt looked at the

squat stone figure lumbering over the piles of broken rock, and he realized what he had to do.

"We need to get ourselves a troll," he said.

As they picked their way across the forested mountainside, Matt kept waiting for Fen or Laurie to argue. He'd just told them he planned to capture and question a troll. Fen should say it was a dumb idea, or Laurie should say it was too dangerous. At the very least, Fen should say *Go for it, Thorsen,* and walk away. But there he was, right beside Matt, peering through the dark forest, head tilting to listen, nostrils flaring to...to sniff the air? Could Fen smell things, like a wolf? Matt thought of asking but figured it was safer to keep his mouth shut. Just because they weren't trying to hit each other anymore didn't make them friends.

Laurie was right there, too, on Fen's other side, looking and listening. The night forest was a scary thing at any time—hooting owls and creaking branches and patches of darkness so complete you had to walk with your hands out, feeling your way. Add trolls, and his own heart pounded in time with his footsteps. He was sure Laurie had to be terrified. She didn't look afraid, though. Just cautious, like them. Maybe she didn't really believe there were trolls. Maybe she was humoring him—maybe they both were. Playing along, waiting to laugh at him when his trolls turned out to be piles of rock.

Almost as embarrassing was the fact that he was kinda hoping he *was* wrong. Otherwise, he had to carry through and actually catch a troll, and he had no idea how to do that.

This time, he was the one who heard something first. His arm shot out to stop Fen, who plowed into it, then turned on him, snarling. Matt lifted his hand to motion for silence.

Off to their left, a twig cracked. Matt pointed.

Fen rolled his eyes. "We're looking for a walking pile of rock," he whispered. "It's gonna make more noise than that."

True, if a troll was in the forest, they should all hear it, crashing through the undergrowth like a boulder rolling downhill. Maybe it was the guard? But there weren't any paths here, and they'd seen no sign of guards since they'd come into the forest. Matt guessed that if the trolls came to life at night, they were careful to do it when the guards wouldn't be watching.

Matt felt his amulet heat. It didn't get red-hot, like before a hammer flare, but it was getting warmer. He touched his cold fingers to it.

"There's a troll coming," he said, before he could even think it.

"What?" Fen waved at the amulet. "Now it's a monster detector?"

"Giants," Laurie whispered. "You must pay even less attention in class than I do. Trolls are a kind of giant. Thor was known as the giant-killer."

"Right." Fen sized up Matt. "We'd better hope they're very *small* giants."

Matt plucked at the shirt he was wearing. It was Fen's—Laurie had made her cousin grab extras for him. The tee rode at the top of Matt's jeans and stretched across his chest and biceps. When he'd come out wearing it, Laurie had giggled, which had made Fen scowl and say it was an old one that he'd outgrown, and she couldn't expect him to let Matt wear his good stuff. Now Matt didn't respond to Fen's crack. He just tugged at the shirt. Fen's scowl returned, and he opened his mouth before his cousin cut him off.

"Do I need to separate you two?" she muttered.

Laurie was stepping between them when the ground vibrated under Matt's feet. He tensed and looked around.

"What now?" Fen said.

"Didn't you feel that?"

Matt didn't wait for an answer. He dropped to his knees and pressed his hands to the ground. It was vibrating. So was his amulet. He closed his eyes, one hand on the necklace, the other on the ground. Fen snickered and said something about troll-whispering, but Laurie shushed him. Fen was right, though, it looked stupid. It *was* stupid. Matt let go of the necklace, opened his eyes, and started to rise, but Laurie crouched in front of him.

"What do you feel?" she asked.

He shook his head. "Nothing. I just thought—"

"Try again," she said.

He paused. *Fen won't ever follow you if he thinks you're an idiot.*

"Try again," she said, more firmly this time. She met his gaze. "We're descended from gods, so we've all got some sort of god powers, right? We just need to figure out how they work."

"It might not be—"

"But it might be. If you're wrong, no one's going to laugh at you." She shot a warning look at Fen.

They've been following me so far, haven't they? They don't know me well enough to realize I don't know what I'm doing. I can worry that they'll find out I'm a fraud, or I can try to prove that I'm not. Try to be something different, someone different.

Matt shut his eyes and stretched his fingers against the ground. The vibrations were getting stronger now, and even if he couldn't hear so much as another twig cracking—which made no sense if a troll was nearby—he *knew* it was nearby. He could feel it walking across the earth.

"Which way?" Laurie whispered.

He started to hesitate, then stopped himself and pointed. Almost as soon as he did, another *crack* came, this one close enough that they all heard it.

"Okay," Matt whispered as he stood. "They're going to be big, so we need to make sure it's just one. If this guy has friends, we have to find another troll."

Fen pressed his lips together, and Matt knew he didn't like the idea of running from a fight to search for an easier one. Maybe he even thought Matt was being a coward.

Am I? No. That has to be part of leading. Knowing when something is too risky.

At least Laurie seemed to agree, as she nodded and waved for Matt to lead the way.

"You stay here," he said. "Fen and I—"

"Stop," Laurie interrupted.

"I'm just suggesting—"

"Suggestion noted. And rejected. I'm going with you, and the more times you do that, Thorsen, the more ticked off I'm going to get." She glanced at Fen. "Same goes for you."

"But you're—" Matt began.

"Don't you dare say 'a girl.'" She made a grumbling noise and then waved into the darkness. "Go."

Matt hesitated and glanced at Fen—who only shrugged.

When Matt didn't move, Laurie gave him a shove and muttered, "You know what you need, Thorsen? A sister." She gave him another shove, harder this time, and they headed into the deep forest.

Matt crouched behind an evergreen stump and peeked out at the troll. If he didn't know better, he'd think it was a big pile of rock. The troll was hunkered down next to a stream, staring at something in its hands. It turned it over, grumbling, the sound like stones clattering together. Then it reached out a long arm into the stream and scooped up a handful of rock and silt. It jiggled its hand over the water to let the silt rain down. Then it clenched its fist, dipped it into the water, and shook it.

Panning for gold. Or some kind of treasure. Maybe even just sparkly rocks. The old stories said trolls loved anything shiny. Matt didn't care much what it was doing; he was too busy staring at that hand. The troll itself wasn't a real giant—crouching, it wasn't taller than him. That hand, though, was huge. Bigger than his head. With claws as long as steak knives and probably just as sharp.

The troll opened its massive hand and poked at the rocks on its palm. Its grumbles grew louder when it found nothing of interest.

"What if we can't communicate with it?" Laurie whispered, coming up behind him.

Matt looked over at her.

"That doesn't sound like a real voice," she said. "It's just making noises. If we can't talk to it, how are we going to find out—"

The troll's head swung their way, and Laurie stopped. As the troll peered into the darkness, Matt got his first real look at the thing. It had a gray, misshapen, bald head with beady, sunken eyes and a nose that hooked down over a lipless mouth. The nose twitched, as if the troll was sniffing the air. Then the mouth opened, revealing rows of jagged teeth.

The troll rose to its full height. It would tower over Matt now. At least eight feet tall and half as wide, standing on squat legs, its long arms dangling, claws scraping the ground. It kept looking in their direction but just stood there, head bobbing and swaying, nostrils flaring. Then it charged.

There was no warning. One second it was standing there, and the next it was barreling toward them so quickly and so quietly that for a second, Matt thought he was seeing things. Then Laurie grabbed his arm, and Fen shouted, "Run!"

Matt lunged from behind the stump, breaking free from Laurie's grasp, and then he did run—straight at the troll. There wasn't a choice. It was coming too fast for them to escape. So Matt ran toward it, yelling.

The troll skidded to a stop. Its beady eyes went as wide as they could, its stone jaw dropping.

Matt kept running. As he did, his fears and worries seemed to fall behind. This was the part he understood, the part he'd always understood. This was when he really felt like a son of Thor.

That's why he loved boxing and wrestling. When he got into the ring, he didn't feel like a loser, like a screwup. His family was never there, watching and waiting for him to make a mistake. They didn't care. Win or lose, they didn't care, and if that kind of hurt, it also felt good in a weird way. It felt like freedom.

He ran at the troll, and he didn't think *I can't do this*. He didn't think *I can do this*, either. He just thought what he always did in the ring: *I'm going to give it my best shot*.

He concentrated on Thor's Hammer and imagined throwing it at the troll. Nothing happened. So he kept going. When he was a few feet away, he pitched forward, dropping and grabbing it by the leg. It was a good wrestling move, one Coach Forde had taught him for dealing with a bigger opponent.

The bigger they are, the harder they fall. In theory. A theory that, apparently, didn't apply to trolls, and when Matt grabbed it by the leg, it barely stumbled. Then it pulled back its thick, short leg, kicked, and sent Matt sailing into the undergrowth.

Matt hit the ground in a roll and bounced up. He wheeled to see the troll charging. Matt feinted to the side. He heard a *clunk* and saw a fist-sized rock bounce off the back of the troll's head. The troll staggered, its charge broken. As it turned, snorting, Matt saw Fen lifting another rock.

"What is it with you and attacking things that can kill you, Thorsen?" Fen yelled. "Next time, I'm not saving you."

Matt could point out that he hadn't needed saving. Not yet, anyway. But the troll was now charging Fen. So he ran at the monster. His first impulse was to jump on its back. One quick look at that solid stone slab told him he wouldn't get a handhold. So he dove again, this time landing in the troll's path. It ran into him, its feet hitting his side like twin sledgehammers.

The troll tripped. As it went down, Matt flew to his feet and jumped on the monster. It was like body-slamming a bed of rock. He was scrabbling for a hold when the troll leaped up.

Matt rolled off. He bounded to his feet and faced off against the thing.

"Now what?" Fen said from behind the troll. "It's a pile of rock, Thorsen. You can't fight that."

Matt ignored him and kept his gaze fixed on the troll's. They circled. The troll was grumbling and muttering.

The troll swung one long arm. Matt managed to back away enough that it should have only been a glancing blow. And it was—a glancing blow with a sledgehammer. It caught him in the stomach and sent him whipping into a tree and slumping at the base, doubled over, wheezing and gasping.

Out of the corner of his eye, he saw the troll coming at him. He leaped up and lunged. Except it was more of a stumble-up-and-stagger. It got him out of the way, but barely in time. His foot caught a vine. As he slid, he saw that massive stone hand heading straight for him—

"Hey!" a voice called as stones rained down on the troll. "Hey, ugly, over here!"

It was Laurie. The troll spun, and Matt launched himself at the thing's back, only to slide off. He saw Laurie holding up something that glinted in the moonlight. A coin. She threw it. The troll dove for the treasure. Matt clenched his amulet in one hand and concentrated on launching the Hammer. Nothing happened.

Why wasn't it working? Not now and not with the Raiders. But it had worked when he'd fought Fen at the longship. What was different?

At the longship, Fen had come at him, and he'd reacted without thinking. He'd reacted in anger. That was the difference. He hadn't been angry at the Raiders, and he wasn't angry with the troll. Sure, he was scared, but he also felt… good. In a weird way, even as he panted, stomach aching, what rushed through his veins wasn't anger. It was fear and excitement.

The troll scooped up the coin and turned on Laurie. Matt instinctively started to charge but stopped himself. Fen rushed forward, yelling and waving. Matt planted his feet, and he thought of what would happen if the troll got to Laurie. If the troll hurt her. If it hurt Fen. Matt would be angry *then*. Angry with the troll and angry with himself for dragging them into this, and if he couldn't even fight a single troll, how could he ever hope to—

The amulet's heat shot through him and now he ran forward, flinging out his hand, feeling the energy course down it, seeing it leap from his fingertips like a bolt of electricity.

It knocked the troll off its feet. Sending the thing flying across the clearing would have been even more satisfying, but it did go down. And it didn't get up. It lifted its head and looked at Matt, gaping and blinking as he stood there, fingers still sparking, amulet glowing through his shirt.

"Hammer," the troll said in a deep rumble. "You have god Hammer."

"Thor's Hammer," Matt said, and he pulled it out, the metal glowing bright blue. "I'm a descendant of Thor, and I demand—"

"Want Hammer." The troll used its long arms to push to its feet, like an ape rising. "Leaf want Hammer."

Again, it charged so fast that it caught Matt off guard. This time, he stumbled back, hand going to his amulet, other fingers shooting out to . . .

To do nothing.

Panic pounded through him, and he stepped back. Then he stopped himself.

Don't give in to the fear. Use it. This troll wants your Hammer. It'll take your amulet, and then what? You'll lose your only power in your first giant-fight? Against one troll? Oh, yeah, you were tested, Matty. And you failed on the first question.

The energy shot out and hit the troll. This time the thing

did sail off its feet, hitting the ground so hard the earth shook.

Laurie stumbled as if her knees had almost given way.

Matt advanced on the fallen troll. "You want the Hammer? *That's* the Hammer. You go after any of us again, and I'll give you a bigger taste of it. Now, I have questions, and you're going to answer, or you'll *get* the Hammer."

The troll said nothing, just stared at the amulet as if transfixed.

"We are looking for . . ." He remembered the term Hildar used. "The descendants of the North. Specifically, a pair of twins. From the gods Frey and Freya. They're about our age. Do you know where they are?"

Even before the troll answered, Matt could tell by its reaction that it did.

Finally the troll said, "Leaf knows." Then it narrowed its eyes. "Leaf could tell son of Thor. *Will* tell son of Thor. For Hammer." It pointed at the still-glowing amulet. "Give to Leaf, and Leaf will tell."

Matt tucked the amulet under his shirt again. "The only Hammer you're getting is the one I just gave you. Now answer the question."

"No."

Matt launched the Hammer again. It was easier now—he was honestly getting angry—and when the troll refused, he got madder, which made him launch it a second time, almost without meaning to. But the troll just sat there, absorbing the blows and refusing to talk.

Before he could try again, Laurie came up behind him and whispered, "I have an idea."

He was about to say no, he could handle it, but she stepped forward and announced, "There *is* a way you can have Thor's Hammer, Leaf."

THIRTEEN

LAURIE

"SLEIGHT OF HAND"

Laurie was unexpectedly calm as she smiled up at the troll. She took three steps toward him. "You're right: we *can* make a deal. We can trade with you."

Matt started to object, but she shot him a look over her shoulder, and he quelled. Fen was back in wolf shape, but the gaze he leveled on her made it pretty clear that he wasn't particularly in favor of her approaching the troll, either.

"You give god Hammer," Leaf demanded.

"Maybe," she said.

Both Matt and Fen had followed her. From the corner of her eye, she could see them standing on either side, but slightly behind her. She glanced quickly at them, hoping they wouldn't mess this up. Fen's expression was impossible to read, since he was a wolf, and Matt was definitely tense. "We need to find the two descendants of the North. The Valkyrie Hildar sent us to you. Do you know where they are?"

The troll glared down at her from its unsettling rocklike face. "Yes."

"And you will tell us where they are if we give you the god Hammer?"

The deep gravel voice said, "Yes! Want it."

Laurie nodded. A small flash of guilt filled her. She'd promised her mother that she wouldn't trick people like her dad's family did—*like the descendants of Loki did*—but this was a pretty extreme set of circumstances. Ragnarök was coming. That *had* to change the rules.

She turned to face Matt, who reached up to cover the Hammer with one hand.

"Trust me," she said.

Warily, he removed his hand.

Laurie stepped behind Matt and undid the knot of the cord. "Stay still," she said loudly. She moved closer to Matt, angling her body so the troll couldn't see her lips, and whispered, "It's just the Hammer, right? The cord doesn't matter?"

"Right," Matt said.

"What?" the troll grumbled at them.

"I was saying she's right. I need to stay still." Matt managed a smile. "See? I'm staying still now."

The mammoth creature frowned. It might not know what it had missed, but it was obviously not sure about trusting them, either.

Excitedly, Laurie removed the necklace from around Matt's neck and held it up so the troll could see the Hammer dangling from the black cord. The troll's attention left Matt and zeroed in on the Hammer.

"So, if I give you this, you'll tell us?"

"Leaf wants," the troll rumbled.

"I know." Laurie switched the necklace to her right hand and slid the cord free of the pendant itself. As she stepped from behind Matt, she slipped the Hammer into his hand; at the same time, she held up her left hand. The black cord dangled from her closed fist.

She stepped in front of Matt.

"I'll give you this. You have to bend down, and I can tie it on you." Laurie shook the hand holding the cord, making Leaf look at her hand again. With her right hand she reached into her pocket, where she had the necklaces she'd brought to sell. She nimbly slipped a pendant off one.

"Now," Leaf demanded. He bent forward.

"Just hold still, and I'll tie it on you." She slid the pendant, a tiny silver unicorn, onto the cord while Leaf's gaze was on the ground. As she approached him, she let the metal of the pendant flash briefly into his line of sight and then quickly palmed it again.

She peered at his neck, all the while trying not to inhale through her nose. Trolls, or at least this troll, did not smell good at all. She smothered a gag. "I don't think it will fit around your neck."

"Twins near," the troll cajoled. "Leaf made deal!"

Laurie tilted her head and stared at Leaf. "I suppose I could put it on your ear." She brushed her own hair back. "I wear things there."

The troll nodded and bent down again. Thankfully, this meant his fetid breath was no longer blowing at her.

She put one hand on his large, slick ear and then paused. "Where are the twins, Leaf?"

"Dead Tree," Leaf said.

"They're in a dead tree?" she repeated skeptically. "People don't usually live in trees."

Leaf made a loud, grating noise. He slapped the ground with one massive hand, and spit flew from his mouth.

Matt and Fen both surged toward her, and she backed away from the troll in fear. "I wasn't trying to insult—"

"God girl funny. Place called Dead Tree," Leaf rumbled.

That horrible noise had been *laughter*. She shook her head. A troll laughing was not funny. She slowly walked back toward him. As she did so, she saw that Fen stayed right beside her.

"Deadwood," Matt said. "They're in Deadwood."

"Leaf say that." The troll turned his gaze on Laurie. "Give Hammer now."

"Right." She looped the cord around a big wart on the troll's ear and tied it into a knot. The tiny silver unicorn looked funny on the creature, but it was hanging where the troll couldn't see that it wasn't really the Hammer, and that was the goal. They had their information, Matt had his Hammer, and the troll had an earring.

The troll straightened. It smiled, exposing teeth in serious need of scrubbing and flossing, possibly even sandblasting. Oral hygiene clearly wasn't a priority with trolls. After seeing that, she made a mental note to buy a toothbrush for her cousin, who undoubtedly had not packed one.

Cautiously, she walked over to Matt. Fen was tight to her side. Her wolfy cousin kept looking back at the troll, who was staring at them, but not saying anything.

"Laurie," Matt said quietly. He was looking past her, and she looked over her shoulder at the almost-lightening woods. Morning was coming, thankfully, and they had what they needed. She didn't see anything but trees, and all that was left was to walk away.

"What?"

Fen growled. His fur stood up.

"Family come." The troll grinned. "Show family god Hammer."

"Crud," Laurie muttered. Four more trolls were coming toward them. Two of the trolls were even bigger than Leaf.

"Run," Matt urged as soon as Leaf turned to see his family.

She heard Leaf grumble, "God Hammer on ear."

And she tried to run faster. Matt was in front of her, and Fen was behind her. They were running as fast as they could, but the trolls would still be able to catch them in minutes. Trolls weren't fast thinkers, but they certainly could *move* quickly.

She heard the weird sound of trolls laughing, and then the ground shook as the trolls came toward them.

They were almost at the edge of the woods. *Maybe they can't leave the woods.* She hoped that was the case. *Please let them be unable to follow us.*

Frantically, she looked for a place to hide, as if there were a place secure enough to be trollproof. She didn't see anything. Matt suddenly grabbed her arm and half pulled her forward.

Before she could ask him why, she heard a deep growl. *Fen.* She turned to look back just as she saw her fool cousin standing with his paws firmly planted, growling at the five trolls.

Matt shoved her behind him and yelled, "Run!"

The troll in the front had almost reached Fen when Matt used the Hammer and sent the troll sailing backward. He threw another and another thunder of energy at the trolls, and all the while Fen darted out of their reach, trying to keep them too distracted to chase Laurie.

"*Run!*" Matt yelled at her again.

She wanted to, but she couldn't leave them. She looked around desperately for something to use as a weapon. The nearest things were a trash bin and some rocks. She ran toward the bin and tried to tug it free.

Then she heard a sharp *yip*.

"Fen!" She whirled to see Fen being lifted into the air. "No!" she screamed. "Matt! *Help!*"

A massive clawed troll hand was wrapped around Fen's throat. He hung limp in the troll's grip.

"Do something!" she yelled at Matt. Tears slipped out of her eyes, and she started to race toward the trolls.

"Wait." Matt grabbed her arm as she ran past him. "Look."

As the sun rose, the trolls all turned to stone. They looked like a cross between massive sculptures and rock piles. If she hadn't seen them moving, she might've thought they were oddly shaped rocks—well, that and the fact that a wolf hung limply from what was basically a stone noose.

She ran over to Fen. He wasn't moving, and his muzzle hung open like he was gasping for air. His eyes were closed, and she thought for a second that he was dead.

"He's still breathing," Matt said. He was right beside her now.

"Not for long. He'll choke." Then she spun to face Matt. "Blast it."

"Blast it," he repeated.

"Break the stone with your energy thing, or Fen's going to die." She hated the thought of breaking the troll's hand, even though it had chased them and probably would've killed them, but she hated the thought of Fen dying even more.

Matt frowned, but he obviously couldn't see any other solution, either. The circle of stone that was the troll's hand had to be cracked to remove Fen. Their only other choice was to wait till nightfall, when it would wake back up—and then probably finish choking Fen anyhow.

The energy blast cracked the stone around Fen's throat, and he dropped to the ground with an awful *thump*. He didn't move.

Laurie pulled the motionless wolf into her lap. "Fen! Fen, wake up!"

As she did so, she petted his face. *What do you do when your cousin who is a wolf gets choked by a troll who is part of a mountain?* These weren't the sorts of things ever covered in health class.

"I'll carry him out of here and . . ." Matt's words faded as Fen shifted from wolf to boy.

Blearily, Fen blinked up at Laurie. "Did we win or die?"

She patted the top of his head like he was still a wolf. "Won."

"Oh, good," Fen murmured. Then he rolled over and went to sleep.

After Matt carried Fen into the woods to sleep, Laurie and Matt took turns napping. They were pretty sure that Fen was okay. He'd woken up a few times, asked a question, and then gone back to sleep. She wished that they had their tent and sleeping bags with them, but they'd stowed them near the Mount Rushmore parking lot because they were pretty sure that walking into the monument area with camping equipment would attract attention they didn't want. So now they had only the cold ground to sleep on, and their backpacks to use for any kind of pillows.

In one of his brief awake periods, Fen told her that going back and forth between wolf and human took a lot of food, and he was just exhausted—and also healing from injuries. She was leaning against a tree then, and Fen scooted over and laid his head in her lap. It was warmer with him cuddled against her, but it meant she couldn't move.

When Matt woke, he offered her his sweatshirt, so she slipped it on and, with Matt's help, moved so she wasn't Fen's pillow. Then she stretched out on the ground next to her cousin for a short nap.

By afternoon, during one of Matt's shifts, Fen woke, and

they'd woken her up, too. Her cousin seemed fine—tired, but okay.

They filled him in, and then they went to buy something to eat and figure out how to get to Deadwood. They were finishing their breakfast-lunch when Fen inclined his head toward a group of kids about their age, who were starting to board two buses with big DEADWOOD TOURS signs painted on the sides. A woman with a clipboard stood outside the bus, checking names off a list as kids boarded.

"We could go with them," he suggested. Now that he'd had food, he was a lot more alert.

"They *are* headed to Deadwood," Laurie mused.

Matt didn't say anything for a moment. He looked at the crowd, and then he stood. "Better than walking or trying to hitch a ride."

Fen grinned. "Excellent."

All of her father's side of the family had the uncanny ability to persuade people to do things. It made sense now that she knew that Loki was a relative, but it still made her uncomfortable, even though it was clear they'd have to use those skills to get on the bus without being noticed. Fen was obviously a lot like their ancestor, though: he had that trouble-ahead bounce to his step that always worried Laurie, but after seeing him almost killed by trolls, she didn't have the heart to say anything. Maybe a little bit of Brekke skills were justified after cases of near-death by trolls.

Fen looked over at her and noticed her expression. Quietly, he said, "You can do this." Then he glanced at Matt and said, "When we distract her, just get on the bus like you belong. Clear back. Head down."

Matt nodded.

Then Fen said very softly to Laurie, "You're a Brekke. It's in our blood."

"Right," she breathed. "I can do this."

As they approached the bus, Fen started poking at her and said loudly, "I get the window seat."

"You had it earlier." Laurie shoved him. "Jerk."

"You know it." Fen flashed his teeth at her, looking so wolfy that she wondered how she'd never noticed.

"Enough." The woman with the clipboard scowled at them. "Where are your badges?"

"He lost them," Laurie whined. "I told him, but—"

"You told me after I lost them. What kind of help is that?" Fen looked at the woman. "I don't want to sit with her on the way back."

Matt boarded the bus.

"Well, maybe I'll sit on the other bus." Laurie shoved his shoulder, and then she turned to walk away.

"Get on the bus." The woman sighed wearily.

Fen folded his arms. "Fine. *You* get on this, and I'll—"

"*Both of you*, on the bus." The woman looked at the line of kids waiting. "Now."

They went to the back, where Matt was seated. He nodded at them, but they said nothing else. Laurie might not be experienced at this like Fen was, but she *was* a Brekke. She knew instinctively that they'd used a distraction to get on the bus, but now they needed to avoid attention to *stay* on the bus.

They took the seat directly in front of Matt's.

A few kids looked at them, but this wasn't a school group. *Thankfully.* Blending into a school group would be harder. There, the kids mostly all knew each other. This was a group, but probably for something like a community center or church or youth group.

A girl sat down beside Matt. "Who are you?"

"Matt," he answered.

Beside Laurie, Fen smothered a sigh. They exchanged a worried look. Matt just wasn't used to trickery. Even though she tried not to use it, she still knew Tricks 101: don't use your real name. Laurie opened her mouth to intervene before he said something crazy like *We're runaways from Blackwell.*

But before she could, she heard Matt say, "Didn't we meet earlier?"

Fen looked at her and raised both eyebrows in surprise. Matt was taking the act-like-you-belong thing to a new level. In the seat behind them, they could hear Matt and the girl chattering away about the monument. It wasn't a strategy she would've used, but it seemed to be working. The kids in the seat across from Matt were talking, too.

"Laurie might know," Matt said, suddenly drawing her into the conversation.

"Know what?"

"How far to Deadwood?" the girl beside Matt said. She was smiling, but Laurie didn't think it was particularly friendly.

"Ummm, I don't know. Maybe an hour?" Laurie had a rough guess from trips she'd taken before, but that wasn't the sort of thing she usually paid much attention to.

"Which school do you go to?" the girl asked. "I don't think I've met any of you before."

"We were on the other bus," Fen said. He leaned his head back on the seat and closed his eyes before adding, "Do you mind not talking? I have a headache."

"Sorry, I forgot." Laurie was silently thankful for Fen's surliness, but she looked at the girl and mouthed, "Sorry."

The girl said, "Whatever."

Matt nodded.

Once they'd looked away, Fen leaned in and whispered, "Knew you could do it."

Laurie tried not to feel too excited by their success so far. They had a huge list of impossible things in front of them... but they'd already overcome trolls, wolves, and chaperones. They really weren't off to a bad start.

FOURTEEN

MATT

"ALL-POINTS BULLETIN"

On the bus trip, Matt relaxed for the first time since his grandfather had named him champion. He'd done well so far. Really well. They'd found the trolls, and they'd gotten the information they needed. His idea hadn't exactly gone as planned, but Laurie had figured out a solution, and they'd all worked together to escape. That's what it was about—working together. He wasn't a perfect leader, but maybe he wasn't totally faking it, either. Maybe he really could become the leader they needed.

When the bus stopped, they were in Lead, making an educational pit stop to visit the Black Hills Mining Museum.

Matt thought of just staying on the bus, but everyone was getting off.

"The chaperone said it's only three miles to Deadwood," Fen whispered as they filed out. "We're walking."

As they stepped off the bus, a tour guide was trilling, "And don't forget, if you decide to try the gold panning, you are guaranteed to find gold!" The older kids jostled past her, some mimicking her and rolling their eyes. The younger kids just trudged along, casting pained looks at the museum and the prospect of an hour of sheer boredom.

The museum didn't look like much. It was mostly a single-story building with a flat roof. Near the front, though, a weirdly shaped silo jutted out. A model of a mining shaft, Matt guessed. He was following along, gaze fixed on that silo, thinking maybe this could be interesting, when Fen stopped him.

"Did I say this is where we get off?" Fen whispered.

"Right, but—"

"But what? We're in the middle of saving the world, and you want to take a museum tour? You really are a geek, aren't you, Thorsen?"

Matt could see Laurie tense, and he struggled to keep his voice calm. "No, but we're only three miles from Deadwood. I don't see the point in bailing now."

"Right. We're *only* three miles, so I don't see the point in *not* bailing. Getting back on the bus again is risky."

"Fen has a point," Laurie murmured.

When Matt opened his mouth to argue, she directed his attention to his seat partner from the bus. The girl stood over at the side, talking to the adult leader as she pointed at them.

"Okay, we'll bail," Matt said.

"Glad we have your permission," Fen said. "Follow me."

Now it was Matt's turn to stop him. They were in the middle of a parking lot, with a single stream of kids flowing to the museum doors. If they broke from that stream, they'd be spotted. He pointed that out, then said, "We'll go inside and circle back. Just stick with me."

He continued on toward the museum. Laurie stayed beside him. When he realized Fen wasn't with them, he looked back. Fen stood there, staring at Laurie, looking shocked and maybe a little hurt. She waved him forward. He turned a scowl on Matt and fell in line with the other kids, making no effort to catch up.

Fen finally did catch up, right inside the doors, which was as far as he'd go. Laurie convinced him to chill out long enough for them to get into the museum's re-creation of an actual mine—a long, semidark "underground" passage. Once they were in there, Matt pretended to be fascinated by the next exhibit, and he and Laurie talked about it while the other kids and the grown-ups all passed. Then they backed out.

There were a guy and a girl on duty near the front, but they were too busy talking to each other to notice anyone else. Matt ushered Fen and Laurie past and out the doors.

Once they were outside, they didn't need to walk more than a block before they saw signs for the highway. That would be the easiest route to Deadwood, Matt explained. The Black Hills towered all around them, and that thick, mountainous forest was a really bad place to wander. Besides, it was less than an hour's walk. If they picked up the pace, they'd be in Deadwood before the bus even left the museum.

Lead wasn't exactly crowded, but it was busy enough, so they didn't have a problem blending in as they moved along. Matt kept one eye on the road, though, just in case.

"Side road!" Fen said suddenly. "Now!"

Matt glanced around, frowning.

Fen gave him a look like he was standing in the path of that tornado. Then he muttered under his breath and started steering Laurie quickly to the next side road. Laurie looked back at Matt and whispered, "Cop!"

Matt peered down the road. A police car was creeping along. Matt had seen it turn the corner, but to him, it was about as alarming as seeing a delivery truck. Unlike other kids, he didn't see a police car and immediately think, *Am I doing something wrong?*

No, that wasn't true. He did. But that question was

quickly followed by *Is it my Dad?* If the answer to both was *yes*, he was in trouble. Otherwise, if Blackwell officers saw him doing something he shouldn't, they'd just roll up and say hi, and Matt got the message.

So he'd seen the car, and since he was just walking and this wasn't his father, he hadn't reacted. Except they weren't in Blackwell. This wasn't some officer he'd known since he was a baby.

He broke into a jog and followed Fen and Laurie down the side road.

"You think the lady on the bus called it in?" he asked.

Fen shrugged and kept bustling them along. They turned another corner, getting into a residential area lined with row houses and pickups, both in need of fresh paint. Two kids on rusted bicycles watched them. Then the kids looked up sharply, pushed off, and rode fast, legs pumping, bikes zooming around the corner.

Matt glanced over his shoulder to see the police cruiser gliding along the side street they'd just left, slowing as it approached the corner.

"If it turns, we run," Fen said.

"Where?" Matt gestured at the road. The next side road was a quarter mile away, and he couldn't see a break in the row houses. "Just be cool. I've got this."

He kept his gaze forward as he strolled along the sidewalk. He heard the rumble of the engine as the car turned the corner and rolled toward them. Moving slowly, which meant the officer was checking them out.

"Be cool," he whispered. "Just be cool."

They were on the left side of the road. The police car crossed over, ignoring an oncoming truck as it slowed by the sidewalk. Matt pretended not to notice. He heard the window slide down. Then he looked over. He smiled at the officer, a heavyset guy in his twenties.

"Afternoon, sir," he said.

"Afternoon." The officer stopped the car and put it in park. "Where you kids heading?"

"Just stretching our legs. Our folks took my little brother to the mining museum. It didn't seem like our kind of thing, so we begged off." Matt peered down the street. "Someone said there was an ice-cream place down here, but I think we made a wrong turn."

"You did. Easy mistake, though. It's off the strip. Why don't you kids hop in, and I'll give you a lift."

"Thanks, but we've been in our minivan forever," he said. "We need the exercise. We'll just head back downtown and find it."

The officer swung open the door. "No, I really think you should let me give you a lift"—he unfolded himself from the car—"Matt."

Matt turned to run, but the officer grabbed his wrist. He

saw Fen take off, Laurie following. The officer whipped Matt around to face him.

"Do you have any idea how much grief you've caused, son?" he said. "As a sheriff's boy, you should know better."

"I—"

"Exactly how far did you think you'd get? Your dad put out a statewide APB on you. Any kid goes missing, we pay attention. Sheriff's boy? We *really* pay attention." He gave Matt a yank toward the car and opened the back door. "Get in there. If you behave yourself, I'll let you come up front. For now, you're going to be treated like any other runaway."

Matt looked over to see Laurie standing about twenty feet away. She was frozen there, as if torn between running and coming back. He waved for her to go. The officer saw him and glanced over at Laurie. Fen was behind her, jogging back to get her.

"Is that Laurie Brekke?" the officer said. "We have a report on her, too. Your dad said it wasn't connected to you. Should have known better." He called to Laurie, "Don't you try running, missy."

He put his hand on Matt's shoulder to prod him into the car. As he did, his fingers loosened on Matt's wrist, and Matt tensed, waiting until he felt that grip relax, the one on his shoulder still loose enough to—

Matt flung himself to the side, wrenching from the

officer's grip. Then he ran. Instinctively, he ran toward Laurie and Fen. When he realized what he was doing, he veered across the road. He had to head in the other direction and let the Brekkes get away. Which would have been a perfectly fine plan, if Laurie hadn't run after him. Fen shouted for her to come back, but she'd already almost caught up to Matt.

Matt looked back at the officer. The guy was in his cruiser, on the radio, as his car lurched out of park.

Matt raced up the curb and onto the lawns. Laurie followed. Fen was following, too, cursing Matt with every step. Fen was right: Matt had messed up. Really messed up. And he couldn't believe he'd been so stupid. He'd run away from home, and he hadn't known his dad would put out an APB? His only excuse was that, as crazy as it sounded, it wasn't until this moment that he really realized he *had* run away from home.

His family wanted to sacrifice him to a giant serpent. His only chance of survival was to hit the road and find help to fight the serpent. It wasn't exactly your typical *my-parents-are-mean-and-totally-unfair-so-I'm-running-away* situation. But to the rest of the world, that's exactly what he'd done.

The police car roared up alongside them as they raced across the lawn. The officer put the window down.

"Get over here now, Matthew Thorsen!" the officer snapped. "You're a sheriff's son. You're supposed to set an example. Do you have any idea how much you've embarrassed your father?"

Behind Matt, Fen snorted and muttered, "Well, if you put it that way..." his voice thick with sarcasm. Except that Matt did stumble a little. The officer's words made his heart slam against his ribs, a voice in his head screaming that he was right. Matt couldn't be irresponsible. He couldn't embarrass his family.

It was only a quick stumble, though, before Matt realized that the old rules didn't apply. Being responsible now meant saving the world, even if it meant disobeying a police officer. Even if it meant embarrassing his family. It also meant...

"There!" he shouted, waving at a gap between two row houses. "Go! I've got this."

Fen gave him a shove toward the gap. "No, Thorsen, *I've* got this. You've done enough."

Matt tried to argue, but Fen only shoved him, harder, and all three of them raced through the gap between the row houses. Then Fen ran into the lead. He took them through the yard and over the fence. Through another yard, this one on a street of detached homes. They raced across the yard, over the front fence, and down the driveway.

The police car was nowhere in sight...yet.

Fen looked around. Matt was about to make a suggestion when Fen waved toward a pickup across the road.

"In there," he said. "Take Laurie. Lie down and stay down."

They ran across and hopped over the tailgate while Fen stood guard. Matt saw the police car turn the corner. He ducked as he called a warning to Fen.

"Lie down. Stay down. Stay quiet," Fen hissed. "Can you do that, Thorsen?"

Matt was about to answer, but Laurie silenced him with a look. He listened as Fen's sneakers slapped the ground. He seemed to be jogging toward the oncoming cruiser. The car stopped, engine rumbling.

"Hey," Fen said.

Matt heard the officer grunt a return greeting. "Where are your friends, boy?"

Fen lowered his voice. "That's what I'm here to tell you. But we gotta make a deal."

Silence.

Fen continued. "I'm from Blackwell, too. Laurie's my cousin. She ran off with Thorsen after the fair. Got some crazy idea they'd go on an adventure together. Dumb, huh?"

Matt listened as Fen snorted a laugh and the officer responded with a chuckle, as if relaxing now.

"Anyway, I caught up with them this morning. Only my cousin won't listen to me. So I want you to catch her and take her home. Can you do that?"

"Sure can. Your folks will be proud of you, son, looking after your cousin like that."

"It's the right thing to do," Fen said.

"All right, then. Just hop on in."

"See, that's the problem," Fen said. "My cousin and me, we're kinda friends, and if I turn her in, she's not going to be happy with me. Could you pick them up first? Then I'll walk to the next street over, and you can pretend to corner me there?"

The officer agreed. Matt realized that Fen wasn't even surprised that there wasn't an APB on him. Matt strained to listen as Fen told him that Matt and Laurie had raced along the row of lawns, intending to circle back downtown and hide out in the shops. Fen was explaining that he wasn't sure exactly which shop, but "Thorsen's not hard to find, with that red hair." The officer thanked him and promised to meet up with him as soon as he could.

After Fen's trick, they got away easily. They did stay off the roads, though, walking just inside the forest, keeping an eye on the ribbon of blacktop so they didn't get lost.

"I'm really sorry," Matt said as he held back a branch for Fen and Laurie. "I screwed up. I didn't—"

"—see it coming," Fen interrupted. "*None* of us saw it coming, but we should've. You're the sheriff's kid. Of course the cops are looking for you. For both of you." Fen paused, and with more patience than Matt had expected, he added,

"We've had other things on our minds, though. Tornadoes, Raiders, Valkyries, and trolls. We'll just add cops to the list, right?"

"Right." Laurie nodded, and then she bumped her head against Fen's shoulder and laughed. "We just hadn't stopped to think of regular problems. Like the fact we're all runaways."

"We can't forget it again," Matt said. "We need to be extra-careful now. No more hitching rides or anything."

"Exactly," Fen murmured. He shot a look at Matt and then at Laurie and smiled.

And no one commented on the fact that only two of them had APBs out on them.

FIFTEEN

❖

LAURIE

"DEADWOOD"

L aurie was surprised that they'd had a reasonably calm walk, but they'd realized that once again they had no more than a vague plan: "go to Deadwood, find the twins." It wasn't all bad to get a few hours' peace. Neither boy admitted that they were becoming friends, but they obviously were. Between the cops and the creatures out of myths, their world was turned completely upside down, but they were working together as a team. After a few hours, though, Matt seemed worried, and Fen was fussing over food.

"Let's go up here first." Laurie motioned to Mount Moriah, the cemetery on the hill above Deadwood. She wasn't sure why, but it made perfect sense to her.

"Sure," Matt agreed. His eyes lit up in the same way they had at the museum.

"Whatever," Fen said, but he trudged up the hill in front of her.

Both boys obviously were scanning the area for threats as they had during the several-mile walk, but Laurie couldn't fault them for that. She could fault them for thinking she hadn't noticed, but she didn't feel like bringing it up just then.

Just inside Mount Moriah, Laurie saw them: two kids, a boy and a girl who were unmistakably siblings, doing grave-stone rubbings. There were other people inside the cemetery, and there had been plenty of people in town, but her feet had led her here. She wasn't sure how she knew they were the ones she needed to reach, but as soon as her gaze fell on them, she knew they were the descendants. She looked closer and confirmed that these two weren't just siblings: they were twins. *Like Frey and Freya. They are the ones we need.* The question was how to tell two strangers that they ought to join up with three kids they'd never met and plot to kill a big reptile to save the world. It sounded crazy any way she tried to phrase it.

"That's them," she whispered. "The twins."

The one holding the paper on the stone watched them approach; the one kneeling on the ground rubbing the chalk over the paper looked back at them briefly and then resumed rubbing. They didn't smile, say hello, or seem at all sociable. At school, she would've been a bit nervous approaching them.

But this wasn't school.

And after trolls...well, a couple of kids who were trying to be unfriendly didn't seem nearly as scary. She'd seen scary, and the bored, you're-not-worth-my-time looks she was getting weren't scary. She smiled, and they continued to ignore her. The one standing up said something to the one on the ground, who laughed.

"Are you sure?" Fen asked.

Laurie nodded, but she didn't take her attention off the twins. She had the sudden fear that they'd run. *They can't. We need them.* The problem was that she didn't know how to convince them to join the team.

She wasn't sure why, but she had sort of expected them to be like Matt or like Fen, but they weren't. From here, they seemed tall, and she thought they might be almost as tall as Matt. They both had shoulder-length, straight, pale blond hair. She wasn't entirely sure which of the twins was the girl and which was the boy because they were dressed almost identically in black pants with straps and zippers, big black boots, and jewelry flashing in their ears and on their fingers.

"Do we have a plan?" Fen asked.

Matt said nothing, but he shifted his path to walk toward the twins.

The twins, however, seemed completely unconcerned with the attention that they were getting. Maybe they were used to being watched, because they weren't uncomfortable about it. Then again, they hadn't faced wolves, Valkyries, or trolls. Laurie reminded herself that she probably ought not to mention any of those details just yet. The twins continued their studious not-paying-attention while Laurie and the boys continued walking through the hilly cemetery toward them.

She wanted to hurry. The cemetery bothered her more than she'd expected; as they passed graves of people long dead, she shivered. Maybe it was just the cold, or it was that she just now realized that they could die. Fen almost did die—and according to the mythology, Matt would die. The thought of either of them dying made her feel sick. She hadn't known Matt that well before the tornado, and what she thought she knew about him wasn't entirely accurate. After facing a few monsters at his side, they were becoming friends. *They can't die. They won't.* She was going to do everything possible to keep that from happening.

And that started with convincing the twins to cooperate.

She walked faster.

Matt sped up to keep pace with her. His voice was a low whisper as he asked, "What are you doing?"

"Talking to them," she said resolutely.

"You're just going to go up and tell them they need to

help us fight a big snake and stop the end of the world?" Matt asked incredulously. He wasn't whispering this time, but he was still too quiet for the twins to hear. "This isn't Blackwell. They might not even know who Thor and Loki are."

"So we ask what they do know," Laurie said.

Matt looked at Fen for help, but Fen just shrugged. Her cousin might not like her plan, but she knew he'd side with her. Fen always took her side. Okay, *almost* always. He would side with Matt if he thought it would keep her safe. She knew that. She also knew he'd pound anyone who was rude to her. He'd made that pretty obvious as far back as kindergarten. And maybe it made her a little braver knowing that, she admitted.

In another few moments, they reached the gravestone where the twins were and stopped. This close, Laurie could see that they both had short black fingernails and both wore black eyeliner. The twins still acted like Laurie and the boys weren't there. They didn't even glance at any of the three of them.

"Hi," Laurie said.

Neither twin replied.

"My cousin is talking to you," Fen said.

"And my brother and I aren't interested in talking to her . . . or you," said the standing twin, who, now that she'd spoken, Laurie could tell was the sister.

Fen growled.

The twin on the ground stood and moved so he was shoulder-to-shoulder with his sister. He said nothing, just glanced at her, a little uncertain.

"Look," the girl continued. "We don't know you, don't want to know you, and really don't care about whatever you want. Ray and I are busy." She turned her back on them and flicked her hand at her side as if to shoo them away. "Now go away."

Fen growled again.

"Fen," Matt started.

"I got strangled by a *troll* to find Goth Ken and Barbie here, so I'm not going to 'go away' so they can play with chalk or go do each other's makeup." Fen's eyes actually flashed yellow, and Laurie wondered briefly if he'd hidden a lot more of himself from her than she'd realized or if he was just exhausted.

"Excuse me?" the girl said in a tone that made it sound more like a challenge than a question.

"Reyna..." her brother said under his breath.

She ignored him and turned back around to face Fen. "Don't think our eyeliner means we can't kick your scrawny butt. Ask anyone in town. And trolls? Seriously. Go back to your video games."

"Whoa! Both of you, stop. We're not here to fight." Matt stepped between Ray and Fen. "We just want to talk to you.

We're tired, and some of us"—he glanced at Fen—"have had a rough trip. We don't care about the, ummm, makeup."

"Really? He's wearing nail polish and *guyliner,*" Fen grumbled.

"Stop it, Fen." Laurie put her hand flat on Fen's chest, and then she looked at Reyna and Ray. "Please? Just let us explain."

They all stood in an awkward standoff for several moments until Reyna said, "Fine. Say whatever you need to say and then leave." She linked her arm through her twin's at the elbow.

A strange tickle crept over Laurie, as if she had pins and needles all over. Whatever god powers these two had, they were stronger when they were connected. Apparently, Matt could feel monsters, and she could sense descendants? *And what? Trouble? Threats?* She wasn't sure, but there was something going on here and it increased when the twins touched.

"Right," Laurie started. "Do you want to sit down or walk or—"

"No. We don't," Reyna said. Apparently, she spoke for both of them. Ray stood silently at her side, more like an extension of her than an actual person.

"Fine." Laurie took a deep breath, but she didn't know how to start. She looked at Matt. "Ummm?"

He stepped in and said, "The end of the world is coming. We need your help to stop it."

Reyna took a step backward, pulling Ray with her.

Matt hurried on. "There's more, of course. That's the short version. I can tell you the rest if you just give us a few—"

"Come on, Ray." Reyna crouched down and started gathering up their stuff with one hand. Her other hand was still holding Ray's elbow. Ray stood staring at Matt.

"There's something different about you, something you can do that most people can't," Laurie blurted out. "It's because you're like us."

"We're nothing like you." Reyna released her hold on her brother and folded her arms over her chest. "We're—"

"Descendants of the Norse gods. You have some sort of power. I know you do," Matt said evenly.

"Or you will soon," Laurie added.

The twins exchanged a look, and then Ray murmured, "We don't know what you're talking about."

In the next minute, the twins had scooped up their art supplies and they all but ran away from the three of them. They were walking so quickly that if they went a single step faster, they would be jogging.

"That went well," Fen deadpanned.

After the walk to Deadwood from Lead and then up the hill to the cemetery—and after their failure with the twins—the walk into downtown Deadwood felt like punishment. It had been an awfully long couple of days, and Laurie was tired. She wanted a bath, her own bed, and to curl up on her own living room sofa with a book—or maybe to watch a movie with Fen and Matt. What she didn't want was to try to figure out how to convince the twins, who were obviously hiding something, to join them in a fight to save the world. In all honestly, she didn't want to sign up to save the world, either, but it didn't seem right to know that there was something that important at stake and not help out. Sure, she wasn't one of the people destined to be in the fight, but her cousin was and her friend was, and she was helping them get there. She *had* tricked the troll, and she *knew* she was right about the twins—at least that's what she told herself.

"What if I was wrong about them?" she asked.

Matt stopped and looked directly into her eyes. "Do you think you were?"

"No. Maybe. I don't know." She jumped as she heard a man yell something about "calling the law."

Suddenly, as they stood there on the sidewalk along the streets of Deadwood, two men were yelling at each other and aiming guns. For a brief moment, Laurie wanted to get involved, to protect... one of them. In that split second, she wasn't sure which one to help, but she was trying to figure it out. One of them was dressed in a suit and tall hat, and the other wore a brown fringed leather jacket, dirty trousers,

and a battered cowboy hat. A blink later, she realized that this was a sort of theater. These were actors, reenacting some of Deadwood's Wild West history.

"Wild Bill wasn't killed in the street," Matt muttered.

"What?" Fen asked.

"I don't think that guy's supposed to be Wild Bill. He might be the most famous person here, but he wasn't the only gunslinger," Laurie said.

She and Matt had both stepped forward to watch the show.

"Seriously? We're going to stand here? I'm bored." Fen stepped between her and Matt.

Laurie stepped closer to her cousin. He had always been a little bit of a jerk when she paid attention to anyone other than him. Her mom had told her that she only encouraged him to do it more by giving in, but someone had to encourage Fen, and in her family, the only two people who had in years were her and her dad. "Come on, Fen. I think it would've been cool to live here then. You don't?" she teased. "I thought you were a Brekke."

He was quiet for a minute while they watched the two men face off in their pretend fight. "Maybe a little cool, but these are just people pretending."

It was hard to tell which one they should be cheering for. She watched as the man in the suit drew his gun and the man in the cowboy hat drew his and twirled it around so fast it looked like a magic trick. She hadn't been paying attention to what they were saying, so she still had no idea which one was the one they were to cheer for. It would be easier—in plays and real life—if things were as simple as good guys and bad guys, heroes and villains, but right and wrong weren't always clear. She glanced up at Fen. What was clear was that her cousin was going to be a hero. She'd been right about him.

"Bet there were Brekkes here then, and"—Fen glanced at Matt—"Thorsens arresting them for every little thing."

Matt shrugged.

"Be nice," Laurie chastised Fen. "Not all Thorsens are the same, just like not all Brekkes are. Matt was running from the cops with us, and you jumped in to fight with him."

Both boys shrugged, and both looked uncomfortable.

Matt's interest in the pretend gunslingers seemed to vanish. "We should eat, and then figure out how to convince the twins to join us," he said.

"And find somewhere to sleep tonight," Fen added. "We don't have sleeping bags, and unless you want to break into a hotel room, we don't have rooms anywhere."

They started walking down Main Street, looking for a place to eat. To be safe, they stopped in a tourist shop and bought a hat, which Matt wore pulled down low. After their run-in with the police in Lead, a little extra precaution was in order. With their police situation and their age, getting anywhere comfortable to sleep wasn't likely. Trying to steal some sleeping bags wasn't a great idea, either. They'd left theirs hidden back at Mount Rushmore, first in order not to attract attention at the monument, and then they couldn't bring them on the bus. Laurie sighed. The thought of sleeping on the cold ground again was far from appealing, but she knew hotels didn't rent rooms to kids, and she wasn't sure they should spend their little bit of money on a hotel room even if they could get someone to rent it for them.

Her family members usually had pretty good luck with cons; she felt strangely proud now that she knew about her ancestry: her family's con and luck skills were because of Loki. In a way, her mom was right: she was just like her dad. But maybe that wasn't a bad thing, despite the way it sounded when her mom said it. Admittedly, her mom said it after there had been a call from the principal's office, but sometimes Laurie thought that her mother forgot the good things about her father. Being lucky—or clever—wasn't all bad.

"Maybe the twins would let us stay at their house," Laurie suggested, thinking about the possibility of convincing them through a mix of luck and tricks.

Fen laughed. "They don't even want to talk to us, and you think they're going to invite us to their house?"

"Maybe," she hedged. If it was just Fen, she'd tell him why she thought so, but she suspected that even though they were all friends of a sort, Matt still wasn't going to be too much in favor of trickery.

"I hate to agree with Fen, but he's right on this one. They ran off pretty fast." Matt paused. "When we brought up gifts, they spooked."

"Are we sure that they're on *our* side?" Fen asked. He rubbed his hands on his face like he was trying to wake up, and his words all sort of started to tumble out. "I mean, how much of the myth stuff is supposed to be what happens? If I could switch, they could, too. Could they be on the snake's side? And also, aren't people going to notice a big monster snake and do something about it? I get that in whenever it was, big snakes were probably hard to kill so call in the gods, but today, there are tanks, bombs, and all sorts of stuff."

Laurie didn't say anything beyond, "Fen has a point... or points, or whatever. He's right. We don't know what we're doing or where to go." She paused and then said, "And I'm tired and hungry."

Fen's burst of frustration seemed to vanish. "We'll eat. We'll figure it out."

He gently bumped his shoulder into hers.

Matt was silent as they walked. He stayed that way while they ate at a little diner. Then, as they left the diner, he looked at Laurie and casually asked, "Which way are the twins?"

Without thinking, she pointed to the left.

Fen and Matt both grinned at her, and once she realized what she'd done, she smiled, too. "I *can* find them," she said. "It is them, and I can find them."

"We can do this," Matt said. "The three of us, and then we'll convince the others. We're a good team."

Laurie half expected Fen to flinch away at Matt's words, but he just looked at her and said, "Lead on."

They walked away from the tourist-filled, casino-filled heart of Deadwood to the streets they'd skirted on the way from Mount Moriah to downtown. She didn't speak and neither did the boys as she followed the instinct that told her where the twins were—until she realized that they were headed back to the cemetery. That was weird.

Matt must've figured out the same thing, because he was frowning.

"Wait, maybe I'm wrong." She glanced at the boys. "I was so sure this feeling was leading us to them."

"Maybe the people we needed are still in the cemetery, and we just missed them," Matt suggested helpfully.

The frustration and fear that she was leading them on another long, pointless walk made her let out a small scream of frustration.

Fen squeezed her hand. "It's cool."

"Not really." She closed her eyes and tried to concentrate.

The same sensation was there, urging her, telling her which way to go. She turned away from the cemetery, but the directions remained unchanged.

She shook her head. "I don't know. Maybe they went back there, or maybe it is someone else we're supposed to be looking for."

With the boys behind her, she continued walking, but the trail ended a few moments later—not at Mount Moriah, but on Madison Street. She felt the end so strongly that it was as if she could see a trail dead-ending on the ground. The house in front of her was a sprawling mess. It looked like the owners had bought several houses on the street, demolished them all, and constructed one of those garish oversized houses that screamed "more money than we need." Laurie gestured toward the house and said, "I think they're inside there."

"Well, then." Fen snorted. "Looks like Goth Barbie and Ken are loaded, too."

Matt shook his head. "We walk in there and they get nervous again, we'll end up needing to deal with police. I'm guessing if they're looking for me in Lead, they'll be looking here, too."

Fen gave Matt an appraising look. "Not a bad point, Thorsen. So now what?"

With surprise, Laurie realized that Fen was still looking to her to lead them. "I don't know."

After a moment, Fen suggested, "We need to move away before someone reports us for loitering."

The house was near the cemetery, and the twins were obviously fond of it, so the three of them decided that the best thing to do was tuck in there and wait. Either the twins would come back, or when they went somewhere else in Deadwood, Laurie could find them. It didn't help with the convince-them-to-join-the-fight part, but convincing them meant finding them first.

SIXTEEN

MATT

"UNMARKED GRAVES"

When they got back to the cemetery, Matt couldn't resist the chance to take a look around, so he said they should walk through and make sure the twins weren't already there. Fen grumbled that the twins had been right up front last time and Laurie's hound-dogging had led to their house, but Matt insisted. Finally, Fen bought it and followed him inside.

They passed through the black gate. Matt walked into the cemetery proper, moving at a decent speed, but after the fourth time Matt stopped to read a sign, Fen growled.

"What?" Fen said. "Are you prepping for a history paper, Thorsen? Those twins aren't hiding in that sign."

"There are almost four thousand marked graves in here," Matt said, reading. "And that's only a third of them. Lots more are unmarked."

"They're not hiding in one of those, either," Fen drawled.

"I'm just saying it's interesting."

"Interesting?" Fen scowled. "It's a cemetery."

"In *Deadwood*." Matt swept a hand across the hills, dotted with graves. "Think how many of these guys died in gunfights at high noon. Isn't that cool?"

Laurie laughed softly. "I don't think it'd be too cool if you were the one dying."

"You know what I mean," Matt said. "It's a cemetery from the Wild West. *That's* cool."

He looked down the hill toward the town of Deadwood at the base. Trees blocked enough of it that if Matt squinted he could picture it the way it should be, with saloons instead of coffee shops and gambling dens instead of casinos. He was relaxing now, for the first time since leaving Lead. He'd messed up there. Really messed up, and he'd been sure Fen and Laurie would figure out he wasn't the leader they needed. But they'd just carried on. So now he was relaxing, feeling more like himself. Even kind of feeling like he was around friends.

"Deadwood was the last frontier," he said. "I remember reading letters on it for a project, and someone said they didn't fear going to hell because they'd been to Deadwood."

"Why was it the last frontier?" Laurie asked as they resumed walking. Fen rolled his eyes, but she gave him a look and said, "I'm interested, okay? As long as we're here, might as well get the unofficial tour."

Matt smiled. "I can do that. Never been here—my parents don't approve of Deadwood, past or present—but I know all the stories. They called Deadwood the last frontier because the town itself wasn't even legal. The land was supposed to belong to the Native Americans, but General Custer found gold here and that started a gold rush, which started the town of Deadwood. Because it was illegal, though, there wasn't a whole lotta law and order, not until Seth Bullock— a Canadian guy who became the first sheriff—came along."

Matt continued with the tour as Fen trailed along behind, shaking his head.

As they walked, Matt managed to find all the famous graves— Wild Bill, Calamity Jane, Seth Bullock, Preacher Smith, and Potato Creek Johnny—but they didn't find the twins. And they took so long getting to the back of the cemetery that they then had to search on the way out, in case the twins had come in during the meantime. Fen complained about that…and about the fact that Matt continued to stop for things he'd missed the first time, including Potter's Field. He explained to Laurie that was where most of the unmarked graves were.

"I'm going to put *you* in an unmarked grave if you say one more sentence with the word *dead* in it," Fen muttered.

"Does that include *Deadwood*?" Matt said, grinning.

"Yes."

Matt laughed, but Fen had a point. They really should get back to the front of the cemetery and watch for the twins.

They found a place to hide behind a monument and waited. An hour passed. Then another. Dark began to fall. Matt was out stretching his legs when he heard something cracking and snapping. He looked up to see a flag whipping in the wind.

"See something?" Laurie whispered as she crept out from behind the monument.

Matt shook his head. "Just the flag." He squinted up at it in the twilight. "It's weird. They don't lower it at sunset like most places. I read that they leave it up twenty-four hours a day and—"

"Are you at it again?" Fen said. "I swear I'll find you a nice empty grave if you keep it up."

"I'm not too worried," Matt said. "Cemetery's full." He thought of stopping there, but really, it was fun to push Fen's buttons sometimes. Especially when there wasn't much else to do for entertainment. "You know, though, there actually might be some empty graves. Back in frontier days, they'd bury prospectors here, and then sometimes their families would find out and want the bodies sent home. Except, of course, by that point, the person had been dead awhile, so digging them up and mailing them would be pretty gross. They'd just send back the bones, which meant they had to boil—"

"Hey!" Fen jabbed a finger at Laurie. "You think she really needs to hear this?"

"Actually..." Laurie began.

"No." Fen swung his scowl on Matt. "Shut it, Thorsen. Or I'll shut it for you."

"Before or after you put me in the empty grave?"

Fen growled. Matt grinned back.

Laurie stepped between them. "He's baiting you, Fen." She turned to Matt. "Stop that." Then to Fen. "You stop it, too."

"But he started—"

Her look silenced Fen, and she stalked back behind the monument. Matt and Fen followed. As Matt stepped behind the monument, though, he thought he heard something. He looked around. When he didn't see anything and turned away to ignore it, he felt a ... brain twitch. That was the only way he could describe it. Like the weird sense of someone watching you, except it wasn't the hairs rising on his neck, it was a *ping* in his brain that said *Pay attention.*

Then he really felt the ping as his amulet jumped and began to heat up. He opened his mouth to say something, but wasn't sure what exactly to say and leaned out from the monument instead, peering into the growing darkness. That's when he saw two figures making their way toward the cemetery.

Norns? Valkyries? Trolls? His amulet had reacted to all three. As the figures drew closer, though, he saw that it was the twins—Ray and Reyna. So he could detect descendants, too? That hadn't happened before. Maybe it was a new power.

He tapped Laurie on the shoulder and pointed. She saw the twins and murmured that they should wait until they got closer. Fen shuffled impatiently, but he didn't argue.

Matt wasn't sure what to make of the twins. They weren't the kind of kids you saw in Blackwell or Lead or even Deadwood. Not that there was anything wrong with being different. He just...he didn't know what to make of them. That meant he didn't know how to talk to them or how to convince them to join the fight.

But that's your job, isn't it? That's the test the Valkyries gave you. Find the others and get them to join up.

The fighting part was so much easier.

He sized up the twins. The answer seemed to be to ignore the weird clothes and the makeup and just talk to them. But Laurie had already tried that.

The heat of his amulet flared, as if to remind him that he could *make* the twins join up. Scare them into it. The very thought made him queasy. That wasn't how a leader acted. It wasn't how Thor had acted, either. Sometimes people thought he had, but in the old stories, he always used his strength for good. To help others, not hurt them.

Matt watched the twins, now close enough for him to see their faces, set in that same the-world-bores-me look they'd had earlier. And he realized he had no idea what they could do now that they hadn't done earlier, and Fen and Laurie were expecting him to do more, to find the right words, except he didn't know them and now they'd gone through all this for nothing and—

He took a deep breath. He'd talk to them. He'd be reasonable. Use logic.

Logic? They were telling these kids that they had to help them save the world. Fight a giant serpent before wolves ate the sun and moon and plunged Earth into eternal winter. Logic didn't even—

His amulet began to vibrate now. He tugged the new cord and flicked it outside his shirt so he could concentrate. Only even as he was moving it, he felt the vibration, and it wasn't coming from his warm amulet. He dropped quickly and pressed his fingers to the ground. *It* was vibrating. Which meant it wasn't the twins making his necklace react.

Matt leaped up. "Tro—!"

He didn't even finish the word before two headstones sprang to life. They vaulted over the wall before Matt could get out from behind the monument. The twins turned and gaped.

The trolls scooped them up and swung them over their shoulders. The boy—Ray—froze. Reyna pounded at her captor's back and shouted. Matt raced from the monument, Fen and Laurie behind him, but the trolls moved lightning-fast, swinging back over the wall. As the trolls ran, another headstone jumped up and followed, and the three tore through the cemetery. All the while, Reyna was howling and struggling.

Matt raced after them, but by the time he reached the spot where they'd jumped the wall, they'd vanished into the dark cemetery. He ran in the direction they'd gone. There was no sign of them, though, and he slowed, squinting as he kept jogging forward. Finally, he saw something move over by the monument to Wild Bill Hickok.

He stopped Fen and Laurie and pointed. The troll who'd been playing backup for the kidnappers had stopped at the fence surrounding Wild Bill's grave. He was trying to shove his hand through the chain-link fence to grab at something.

"The coins," Matt whispered, remembering Laurie throwing one to the troll at Mount Rushmore.

As he moved from headstone to headstone, he could see he was right. Earlier, they'd noticed that people had reached through the fence to leave "offerings" on Wild Bill's grave. There were a couple bottles of whiskey, a flower, a set of aces, and coins. It was the last that had caught the troll's attention.

As Matt watched the troll struggling to get the money,

he had to stifle the urge to laugh. It was kinda funny, like watching a six-hundred-pound tiger stop chasing a gazelle to bat at a butterfly. The other trolls were long gone.

"I'll circle around," Fen whispered. "When I give the signal, we'll both run out and jump him. Make him tell us where they took the twins."

A day ago, Matt would have thought this was a perfectly brilliant plan. But he'd fought the last troll. He knew that, as silly as this one looked, grunting and grumbling and straining for pocket change, it was still a living pile of rock...with a sledgehammer punch. Forcing Leaf to reveal the twins' whereabouts hadn't worked so well. So he motioned for Fen to hold off and just watch.

The troll spent about five minutes trying to get its oversized arm through the wire before it realized that the fence barely came up to its chest. Then it took a few more minutes to figure out how to climb over.

"Not too bright, are they?" Laurie said with a soft laugh.

That was an understatement. And something Matt needed to remember if they had to take this guy on. They didn't, though. It got the money, climbed back over the fence, and loped off. Matt motioned for them to follow.

With the other two trolls long gone, this one didn't seem to be in as much of a rush, and they were able to keep up. The troll continued over the hills, occasionally disappearing behind clumps of trees or melding with gray headstones then emerging a moment later, still on the move. Finally, nearly at the far side of the cemetery, Matt heard the twins.

"Do you really think we're stupid?" Reyna was saying. "You're working with those kids. They tell us stories about gods and trolls, and you guys show up wearing troll costumes. *Lame* troll costumes. I can see the zipper in the back, you know."

"I don't see a zipper," Ray's whispered voice drifted over on the breeze.

"Well, there must be," his sister said. "They've put on costumes to kidnap us for ransom. That's what you want, isn't it? Ransom?"

"Treasure," one of the trolls rumbled. "Aerik want treasure."

"See?" Reyna said.

Matt darted along the headstones until he could see the trolls. The third one had joined its companions, and all three crouched around the twins, who sat, bound back-to-back. Ray looked terrified; Reyna looked furious.

Now that they were closer, Matt recognized one of the two trolls who'd taken the kids. He'd know the crags of that ugly face anywhere. Leaf.

It was Leaf who spoke next, turning to the one who'd been delayed and saying, "Where Sun go?"

The troll—whose skin was veined with dark red, like rusty iron—opened his hand, revealing the coins.

"More?" Leaf asked.

Sun shook his head.

Leaf grunted and turned to the twins. "You have treasure."

"Money?" Ray said. "Sure, our parents have money. Our dad runs one of the casinos."

"Don't—" Reyna began.

He shot her a look that silenced her, then he turned back to the trolls. "Our dad will pay. I can give you his cell phone number. Or..." He looked them up and down. "I can call on mine."

The trolls stared blankly at him. Then Aerik said, "Treasure. Aerik want treasure. Leaf say girl daughter Freya. Boy son Frey. God kids want. Frey and Freya have treasure."

Laurie leaned over and whispered, "They know the twins are valuable because we wanted to find them so badly."

Matt nodded. "And to them, valuable means treasure."

They listened for a few more minutes, as the two sides tried—without much success—to understand each other.

"They'll be at this for a while." Laurie turned to Matt and asked, "Should we wait until they turn to stone?"

Matt looked up at the sky. The stars had just appeared about an hour ago. It was a long way from dawn. He glanced over at the trolls. One they could handle. Two might be okay if they could free Ray to help. Three? Not happening.

Matt nodded. "We have to."

A half hour later, the twins finally started to get what the trolls meant. Kind of.

"No paper money?" Reyna said. "How do you get a ransom without paper money? Bonds or something?"

"Gold," Ray whispered to his sister. "They said shiny treasure, so I think they mean gold."

"Then why don't they say gold?"

Ray looked at the trolls, and Matt could see by the way he studied them that he'd figured out they weren't guys in costumes. But when he glanced at his sister, he seemed to decide this wasn't the time to argue with her about it.

Ray wriggled in his bonds and pulled off a ring. Then he held it out as best he could, pinched between his fingers. "Is this what you want? More of this? Treasure?"

Aerik made a move to snatch the ring, and Ray quickly tossed it onto the grass. All three trolls dove for it. Leaf came up victorious, chortling in that scraping-rocks way that made Matt's teeth clench.

"That's what you want then?" Ray said. "That's treasure?"

"Yes," Aerik said, bouncing. "Treasure. More treasure. Aerik want treasure."

"Give them your ring," Ray whispered to his sister.

"What? I am not—"

"Reyna!"

230

Reyna grumbled, but managed to yank it off and tossed it. Again, it was like a football tackle as all three went for it. Leaf got this one, too, but Aerik snatched it away, and they argued in wordless rumbles before Leaf gave in.

"There," Reyna said. "Now, if you can untie us..."

"More treasure," Sun said, rolling forward to crouch in front of her. "Want more."

"We don't have more with us," Ray said.

Reyna wriggled her fingers. "See? No more rings. That's it."

Now Leaf sidled forward, rocking from side to side, knuckles dragging. "More treasure."

"We don't have—"

"More treasure!" Aerik roared as he shot forward and grabbed Ray by the throat.

Aerik swung Ray up, Reyna dangling behind him by her bound hands. He lifted Ray overhead and started to squeeze. Ray gasped and kicked. Reyna shouted and tried to twist around.

"Treasure!" Aerik shouted. "Give treasure or Aerik break son Frey. Break his bones. Grind his bones. Do now!"

Matt yanked off his amulet and lunged from his hiding place. "Did someone say treasure?"

Aerik turned, the other two turning with him, and Matt found himself facing off with three trolls. He swallowed and found his voice.

"Remember me?" Matt said.

"Son Thor." Leaf held up an injured hand. "Cracked Leaf fingers."

"Right. And the son of Thor has a very special treasure, doesn't he?" Matt unclenched his fist and let the amulet fall. "You remember this, too?"

"Hammer," Sun said. "God Hammer."

"And the god Hammer is a very special treasure, isn't it? Better than a whole mountain of rings and coins. It has power. Thor's power. Giant-killing power."

He swung the amulet. All three pairs of beady eyes tracked it, back and forth.

"You want this?" Matt asked.

Three ugly heads nodded.

"Then put those kids down."

Aerik dropped them, Ray landing on Reyna, who let out an *oomph*.

"Good. Now, I know all three of you want it, so we have to make this a race. I'll throw it. First one who gets it wins the power of Thor. Is that fair?"

They nodded again. Leaf inched forward. Aerik shot out a long arm to stop him, and they grumbled at each other for a moment before Leaf moved back in line.

"Everyone ready?" Matt said. "On the count of three. One." He pulled his hand back. "Two." He flexed his arm.

"Three!" He pretended to whip the necklace, instead tossing it up, hidden, in his fist.

None of the trolls moved. Matt lowered his fist to his side and waved with his other hand. "It's out there. Go get it."

"Is in hand," Sun said.

"What?" Matt held out the hand he'd waved. "No, it's empty. See?"

"Other hand."

Aerik took a long stride forward. "Son Thor think Aerik stupid. Aerik not stupid. Hammer in hand."

Matt opened his other hand and faked surprise at seeing the necklace there. "Huh. It must have gotten caught on my finger. Sorry about that. Let's try again."

He waved Aerik back in line between the other two. Behind them, Ray and Reyna were working furiously to get free. Reyna had one hand out and was pulling at the knot. Matt tried to stall, but the trolls started grumbling and rocking back and forth, as if ready to attack.

"Okay, okay," he said. "Here we go. I'll throw it this time. Everyone ready?"

The trolls nodded. As Matt had been stalling, hoping the twins would get free, he'd tugged the amulet off the cord. Now he gripped the cord, letting it dangle, but held the amulet firmly between his thumb and palm. He counted down and then whipped the cord as hard as he could.

Again the trolls just stood there.

"Didn't you see it?" he said, waving with one hand as he slid the amulet into his pocket. "I threw it this time."

"I saw it!" Ray piped up. "I can still see it, on the base of that grave over there."

"Is black strap," Aerik said. "Thor son threw black strap. Not want black strap."

Why isn't it working? Laurie tricked them easily. Panic swirled in his gut.

Laurie moved forward. "But the black strap is what holds the Hammer on his neck. It's over there. Just like Frey's son said. See it?"

"Is trap," Aerik said. "Hammer in pocket."

"What?" Matt said, patting his pockets, hoping his hands weren't shaking. "How would it get in there? I threw it. It's—"

Aerik charged.

Matt shoved Laurie out of the way and hit Aerik with a Hammer blast. A perfect hit, almost instantaneous, and he couldn't help grinning as the troll sailed to the ground. Unfortunately, there were two others with him, and they were charging now. Matt dove to the other side, away from Laurie, hitting the ground and rolling.

"Hey!" Fen shouted. "Ugly number two! Over here!"

As Matt got to his feet, he started motioning for Laurie to get to safety, then stopped himself: they needed to get the twins untied. She was a step ahead of him and already racing toward them as her cousin baited the trolls.

Matt hit Sun with the Hammer as Fen dodged Leaf's charge.

Fen ran up beside Matt as Aerik lumbered to his feet. "Word of advice, Thorsen? Stick to fighting. You have no future as a magician."

"Yeah, yeah."

Aerik rushed them. Matt sent him flying with the Hammer, but by then, Sun was on his feet and Leaf had wheeled, and they were both running at Matt and Fen. They dove opposite ways, and the trolls went after them.

As Sun lunged, Matt launched the Hammer. Or he tried to. Nothing happened. He rolled as Sun's fist came down, hitting the ground with a boom. He tried the Hammer again, focusing harder, getting madder. Sparks fizzled and drifted to the grass, barely even making it smolder.

Matt saw that massive fist coming at him again and tried to scramble up, but he was too late. It caught him in the shoulder, and he crashed into the nearest grave, his head striking it hard enough that he blacked out for a split second. When he came to, he was hanging three feet off the ground, staring into Sun's face as the troll held him by the collar.

Matt clenched his fist and called on the Hammer. His hand barely glowed.

"You're out of juice!" Fen yelled. "Think of something else."

Matt started to yell back that he could use a little help, but Fen was facing off with Leaf. The twins were free and now with Laurie. The three of them were dancing around Aerik, trying to keep him distracted.

Sun shook Matt. "Give Hammer. Give Hammer now."

"Wish I could," Matt muttered. "But I seem to be running on empty."

"Sun break Thor son. Break him—"

Matt swung at Sun and hit him square in the jaw. A knockout blow...that barely made Sun flinch and sent white-hot pain stabbing through Matt's arm, like he'd punched a brick wall.

That's what he is. A brick wall. Like Fen said. They're monsters made of stone. You can't fight—

"Give Hammer!" Sun roared. "Give now!"

He shook Matt so hard his teeth rattled and his stomach lurched and all he could see was the blur of Sun's beady eyes and open mouth and—

Yes!

Matt clenched his teeth and waited for Sun to stop shaking him. Then he pulled back his fist and punched the troll in the eye. Sun let out a grating howl. Matt hit him in the other eye.

Sun dropped him, and Matt hit the ground as Sun staggered back, yowling a nails-down-chalkboard yowl.

"Sun no see! No see! Sun blind!"

"Thorsen!" Fen yelled.

Matt struggled up and wheeled to see Laurie in the grip of Aerik. The twins batted at the monster, who ignored them. Fen was twenty feet away, facing off with Leaf, who stood between him and his cousin.

"Thorsen!" Fen shouted again.

"Got it!"

Matt ran and launched himself at Aerik. As he did, he remembered why he hadn't done this the first time—because it was like leaping onto a smooth rock face. There was nothing to grab. No, wait, maybe...

As he jumped, he managed to hook one arm around the troll's neck and hold on. He reached around to grind his palm into the troll's eye.

Aerik roared and dropped Laurie. He whacked at Matt, his claws catching Matt's T-shirt. Matt lost his grip and fell off before he was hooked.

The troll spun as Matt jumped. He landed with Laurie, Ray, and Reyna. When Matt realized that, he tensed to run, to draw attention away from them, but Sun had recovered from his temporary blinding and blocked Matt's path. He turned again, looking for a way out. Fen ran at them, Leaf right behind them, and then noticed that he was running straight for Sun and stopped.

The five of them stood together, three trolls circling around them, gnashing their teeth and rumbling with rage and frustration.

They were trapped.

SEVENTEEN

LAURIE

"A DOOR OPENS"

Laurie's heart was racing, and her lungs felt like someone was trying to suck the air out of them. They were surrounded by trolls, and they hadn't fared well the last time they'd tangled with trolls. There *were* more of them, but Ray and Reyna were huddled together, Matt was low on energy, and Fen's other form wasn't too much use against creatures made of stone.

As the trolls' circle grew tighter and closer to them, the pressure in Laurie's chest intensified until she thought she was going to fall or throw up. She saw Fen and Matt both reach out to steady her, and she lifted both of her hands to signal them to keep back. As she did so, the air in front of her started to ripple. She widened her hands, staring at the oddly colored space in front of her. It was as if the space between her hands was taking on the colors of an opal.

"Laurie?" Fen stepped closer, but didn't touch her. "What are you doing?"

"I don't know." She felt light-headed as the space grew, and she wondered abstractly how long had passed because she felt disconnected from her skin as she stared at the flashes of color in front of her and tried not to puke.

Beyond the light, she knew trolls waited. They had stopped and were staring at the portal that had appeared between her hands. Behind her were the twins. And in front of her, on the other side of the doorway she'd somehow created, was a room filled with plants. "Go on," she said.

Ray said, "Where?"

"Who cares, as long as it's somewhere without trolls," Reyna muttered. She grabbed Ray's hand and dove into the doorway, tugging him with her.

It hurt. Laurie's body felt like she was being squeezed, and she thought for a moment that the trolls had grabbed her. They were all staring at her, the trolls and the boys.

"Go *now*," she demanded.

Matt exchanged a look with Fen, but he said nothing as he went through the doorway. Then Laurie shoved Fen through the door and jumped in after him, leaving Deadwood and the stupefied trolls behind.

They weren't inside the doorway long, but it felt like space was folding in on her. The pressure of letting others through the doorway was completely different from the sensation of going through it herself. It was as if she were being folded inside out, and the temptation to close her eyes was almost overwhelming. Fen's hand held tightly to hers, and she tried to concentrate on that.

In either a moment or maybe a piece of forever, they stumbled forward into a giant open room filled with tropical plants and brightly colored birds. Overhead was a dome window, and through it, she could see trees outside. Around her in the room were orchids, and something scaled with a long, thin tail vanished under a plant she couldn't identify. They were in a greenhouse or something; they were alive; and she was not, in fact, inside out.

There were also no trolls here. That alone was enough to make her want to sit down and relax for a minute. However, Matt and Fen stood on either side of her, looking around for dangers. Fen still had hold of her hand, and the twins were behind them. As Laurie looked around at their little group, she realized that everyone looked like they expected trolls or some other monster to jump out at any second, and considering where they had been mere minutes ago, that wasn't an altogether unrealistic fear. They also, she admitted to herself, were darting looks at her like she was something peculiar.

"I'm going to puke," she whispered to Fen.

As Laurie slumped to the ground, Fen said, "Put your head between your knees."

"It's all real," Reyna said quietly. "There weren't any zippers, were there?"

Without seeing him, Laurie knew Fen rolled his eyes or scowled at them.

"Slow much?" he said.

"Be nice," Laurie whispered, not because she was trying not to be heard but because speaking any louder seemed impossible right now.

"Don't puke on my feet," Fen said just as quietly.

"I'm okay," she lied to him—and herself. There was nothing okay about how she felt. She had the horrible feeling that her insides had been turned wrong side out by whatever she'd just done. They were safe from trolls, but she wasn't sure what had happened. Maybe the Norns or Valkyries or whatever else was out there had given her a weird gift. Right now, though, she wasn't so sure it was a *gift* and not a curse.

"That was unexpected," a boy said. "I've never seen a portal open before."

Laurie looked up to see a boy who looked about their age watching them. She hadn't noticed him at first when they'd arrived, but the whole making-a-gateway thing was dizzying. The others were staring at the boy, too, so maybe even going through the portal was unsettling for everyone.

"Where did you come f—"

"Around the corner as you portaled in." The boy pointed at the walkway, which had, in fact, curved just out of their line of sight.

The boy himself was taller than her and Fen, but not quite as tall as Matt and the twins. He was almost as big as Matt, bigger than either Fen or Ray. Sand-colored hair, somewhere between light brown and blond, flopped in his face. Freckles dotted his cheeks, and brown eyes stared at them with open curiosity. He had on a T-shirt with what looked like an advertisement for a skateboard.

When he took a step closer to them, Fen growled.

"I got it." Matt stepped in front of Fen and Laurie. "There's nothing here to see, so—"

"He's the person we're looking for," Laurie interrupted. The pins-and-needles feeling was back, and she suspected now that it meant that she'd found a descendant of the North. She smiled at the boy.

"You're like a homing pigeon, aren't you?" Reyna said from behind her.

Laurie looked over her shoulder, but said nothing. The sudden movement made her dizzier, and Fen was starting to look like a dog straining on a leash, ready to attack everyone. He leaned away from the twins and toward the new boy.

As she stood, she reached out for his hand as much for her stability as to keep him restrained.

"Come on." Reyna pulled her twin farther away from them.

Fen and Matt stayed beside Laurie, but they kept an eye on the twins. Laurie noticed—with a not-insignificant amount of pride—that the twins didn't move so far away that they couldn't see the rest of the group. She and the boys had saved them from trolls, and while the twins might not entirely like the situation, they had enough common sense to know that keeping the girl with gate-opening skills and the two warriors in sight was a good idea. *That's what they are*, she thought with a smile. *Warriors.* They might be kids, but they were going to do something amazing.

"Are you sure about this?" Fen prompted her.

She nodded. "I am."

It felt good that they were all working together, and now that they had found this boy, they were even closer to having the whole monster-fighting team assembled. Everything was working out.

"I'm Laurie. That's Fen, Matt, Reyna, and Ray." She pointed at them as she said their names.

"Baldwin." The boy smiled again. Unlike the twins, he seemed thrilled to see them, more so as he started talking. "This is so cool. I've never met anyone with weird powers like me before. I knew there had to be others. It's like knowing inside that there's something different about you, and then realizing you can't be the only one. I mean, my parents took me to doctors, but I just knew that it wasn't sickness. I just don't ever feel pain or get injured. What are your powers? Are we like superheroes? I don't read a lot, but I like comics."

Everyone stared at him. Even the twins stopped whatever quiet conversation they had been having to look at him. Baldwin was excited, accepting the oddity of their situation with a happiness that was different from any of their reactions.

"Weird powers?" Fen echoed.

Baldwin nodded. "Well, most people can't open portals...or *can* you? Can all of you do that? I bet I could get some epic air on my board if I could go through a portal."

Laurie laughed. "This is *so* much easier than the twins." She winced and looked over her shoulder. "Sorry."

Reyna pursed her lips like she was trying not to say anything.

Laurie turned back to Baldwin. "I open portals. They do...other stuff."

"Cool." Baldwin kept smiling. "Like what?"

Laurie was half afraid that Fen was going to snarl at Baldwin. Cheery people got on his nerves, but before she could reply to stop Fen from being mean, her cousin said, "We'll get to that later, but first—"

A noise nearby made Baldwin say, "Hide."

The descendants, by habit or common sense, all stayed silent until Baldwin popped up from behind a giant fern.

"Sorry. I thought it might be a guard. I can usually smile at them and they'll be cool, but I'm not sure how it would be if there are other people here. I'd hate to get them or you in trouble."

"A guard? We need to get out of here." Matt looked around. "Wherever *here* is."

"Reptile Gardens, Rapid City, South Dakota." Baldwin swept his arms out. "I love it here. I keep hoping they'll let me see the venomous snakes up close, but every time I get near someone freaks out." He paused, and for the first time, his cheeriness faded. Then his grin was back. "I thought maybe at night, though, since it's just a couple of guards here..."

"The snakes aren't on display?" Laurie frowned. She wasn't exactly a snake fan, especially right now, when she kept thinking about the Midgard Serpent, but it seemed odd for a place calling itself a "reptile garden" to not have venomous ones on exhibit.

"Oh, no, the snakes are on exhibit, but I want to *touch* them, so I stayed after hours tonight." Baldwin looked at them as if his explanation made sense—which it didn't.

"Great," Fen muttered. "He might be nicer than the makeup sisters here"—Fen pointed over his shoulder—"but he's mental."

Baldwin laughed. "No. Not at all. I just wanted to experiment with the snakes, but now you're here. The snakes will wait."

"It's like the myth," Matt said.

They all looked at him, and Matt continued, "He's *Balder*. The god couldn't be hurt by anything except mistletoe... and he was really nice. Always happy."

"Huh?" Ray and his grumpy twin sister rejoined them.

"You mean he's impervious to injury?" Reyna pointed at Baldwin. "From everything?"

"Except mistletoe," Matt repeated.

"I'm a god? Cool...Huh. I've never seen real mistletoe." Baldwin looked dangerously interested. "So, if I poked myself with it, it would hurt?"

They stared at him. Fen's mouth opened to say something, but then he closed it and shook his head. After a moment, he walked away. The twins followed him.

"No, really," Baldwin said as he caught up to Fen. "Do you snowboard? Skate? I have a ramp." His words never seemed to end, but instead of Fen growling, he had slowed down so Baldwin could keep pace with him.

Matt looked at Laurie questioningly, and she shrugged. She could find the descendants of the North well enough, but that didn't mean they were going to make a lot of sense to her. The twins were still keeping some sort of secret; she was sure of it. Baldwin apparently wanted to poke himself with a stick to experience pain. All she really wanted was to hide away somewhere, get a shower, and maybe put on some clean clothes—or at least wash hers.

After they left Reptile Gardens, they walked to Baldwin's house. Along the way, Matt filled him in on the coming of Ragnarök and what it meant that Baldwin was a descendant of the god Balder. Maybe it was because of his inability to feel pain, like Fen's wolf thing and Matt's Hammer power, but he had already known there was something special about himself, so he accepted their explanation with the good-natured ease that Laurie suspected was his response to most everything. If anything, he was too eager. He wanted to fight, loved the idea that his invulnerability was because of an upcoming battle, and—perversely, in Laurie's opinion—was crazy excited at getting to see a giant snake.

"It's even better than the little ones at the Reptile Gardens," Baldwin was saying as he opened his house door. "And unless the snake is made out of mistletoe—which would be weird, right?—it'll be just like everything else. No pain. No injury. This is just too epic."

As they followed him inside, Laurie was secretly glad it wasn't like the oversized place where the twins lived. She was pretty sure that neither she nor Fen would be comfortable somewhere like that. This was just a regular-sized place surrounded by other normal houses.

Fen flopped down on the sofa. The twins sank gracefully to the floor in movements that mirrored each other. Matt paced the room, looking out windows and locating exits.

"You could all stay here if you want tonight. My parents

are away for the weekend. I'm supposed to sleep at the neighbors' house, but they don't ever make me. People are always weird like that, letting me have what I want. Is that a descendant thing too? Do you all get treated like that?" Baldwin went into the kitchen as he was speaking, his words all hyperfast. "You're probably hungry, too."

"No, but yes, hungry," Fen said, but Baldwin was already gone. Fen rubbed his face and then called out to Matt, "Thorsen? What's the myth on him?"

"Aside from the can't-be-hurt-by-anything-but-mistletoe part, everyone likes him because he's just so nice. I bet that's why he gets what he wants. People just want to make him happy." Matt looked away from the window at them. "In the myth, all the gods liked him. They made a sport of throwing weapons at him, but it wasn't to *hurt* him, though."

Baldwin poked his head around the doorway. "Maybe we could do that."

"No," Fen and Matt said at once.

"Okay. Maybe later." Baldwin shrugged. "I don't know much about myths, so who are you?"

Matt pointed at Fen, "Fen's a descendant of Loki, trickster and troublemaker. Laurie is, too."

Laurie smiled at Baldwin.

Then Matt gestured at the twins. "They're Frey and Freya. She was goddess of love and beauty; he was weather and fertility. And I'm, uh, a descendant of Thor. I'll... umm... fight the Midgard Serpent."

"Thor smash," Reyna interjected.

"That's the Hulk, not Thor," Matt started to explain.

"Whatever," Reyan muttered.

Ray laughed, but then Fen said, "At least Matt's powers are useful—unlike the power of eyeliner and baby-making."

For a moment, Matt's expression was of total shock at Fen's stepping in to defend him, but he wiped it away before Fen could notice—not that he would've. Fen was already headed toward Baldwin, asking, "What do you have to eat?"

Laurie wasn't sure she'd ever seen Fen quite so friendly with a stranger, but Baldwin was really likable. The whole extreme sports thing would appeal to Fen, too. He wasn't exactly bookish. She glanced at Matt, who was beckoning her. They went into the foyer.

Matt stared directly at her and said, "In the myths, Loki kills him."

When she didn't reply, Matt continued, "Loki gave Balder's blind brother a spear of mistletoe, and that spear killed him. That's the main version. There are others. They also say that the gods tried to get Balder back from Hel—the lady in charge of the afterlife—because everyone was so upset. Hel said that if everyone mourned Balder, he could go back to life, but Loki wouldn't cry at all, so Hel wouldn't let Balder go. Loki was responsible for Balder's death and his staying dead. But that's the real Loki. It doesn't mean anything for *us*." He looked toward the kitchen, where they could hear Fen and Baldwin laughing. When he continued, he sounded almost angry, as if she had argued with him. "The Seer and my family say the myths are true. After everything we've seen, I believe some of it is, but we're ourselves, not god clones. The Norns say we aren't destined to lose, so that means the rest doesn't have to happen like it does in the myths, either."

Laurie weighed the details out in her mind. She wasn't entirely sure what to think of a lot of things, but she was certain that they could win. What would be the point in doing all the stuff they were if she thought they were going to be trapped by what the myth said happened? That was just a story; this was *real*. She called, "Do you have any brothers, Baldwin?"

"No." Baldwin came into the foyer, swiping at his floppy hair as he did so. "Do you want to borrow some clothes? I can throw yours in the washing machine."

They both smiled at him. He really was the nicest person she'd ever met. She liked him, but it was sort of the way she liked Matt—with the sense that he could be a brother, that he was important to her the way Fen was. She didn't feel that way about Reyna or Ray, though, and that made her nervous...more so because Reyna was the only other girl. She'd mostly had boys for friends, because of Fen, but still, she *wanted* to have girls as friends, too.

As she followed Baldwin, he chattered about the pictures on the wall as they went upstairs, the first time he'd jumped out of the second-floor window, and something about trying to order a sword on eBay, which had gotten him grounded.

Upstairs, he grabbed a T-shirt and jeans to lend her—and a belt to keep them from falling off. At the door to the bathroom, he pointed at the towels. "I'm going to see how many pizzas Mom left in the freezer. Probably better than going anywhere, right?"

"Yes, please." She yawned. "It's been a long few days."

"Right." He walked away humming.

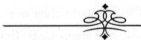

It was a blurry couple of hours of everyone getting food and claiming spots to sleep. Matt had tried to talk about the next part of the plan, but Fen had threatened to bite him if he didn't give them a few hours of peace. The twins appeared to be in a daze over everything, and Baldwin peppered Fen and Matt with questions. As the boys relayed mostly accurate stories of Mount Rushmore, tornadoes, trolls, Valkyries, and all the rest, Laurie dozed—until the doorbell rang.

At first, Laurie was confused. She was in a strange house, sleeping on an unfamiliar sofa, wearing someone else's clothes.

The ringing was followed by a knocking, and then Baldwin was standing beside her. Seeing him made her remember where she was.

"Trolls don't ring the bell, right?" he said.

"I don't think so." She got to her feet and went with him to the door. They both took turns looking through the peephole in the door.

A girl stood on the porch. She had short dark hair that was dyed pink at the tips and was wearing the sort of clothes that screamed "not from here": a funky cropped jacket with a fur collar, a skirt that looked like it was sewn together from all sorts of different materials, and a pair of tall pink boots.

"Is she with you?" Baldwin asked.

Laurie shook her head.

"Huh." Baldwin opened the door. "Hello."

The girl beamed at them and said, "Hi, I'm Astrid. I hear you're looking for my boyfriend."

EIGHTEEN

MATT

"WAKING NIGHTMARE"

After talking to Baldwin for a while, Matt had drifted off. Now he was dreaming that he was back at home, before Vetrarblot, his mother making rakfisk in the kitchen.

"I'm quitting boxing," he said to his mother as he took milk from the fridge. "Wrestling, too."

His mother looked over, knife raised, frowning. Josh and Jake stopped eating. All three stared at him.

"I'm thinking I'll join the football team," he said. "Be a team player." He put the milk back. "I'm not very good at fighting anyway."

"Of course you are," his mother said. "You're the best in middle school."

"You'll be the best in high school, too," Josh said, shooting him a thumbs-up. "You're a natural, Mini-Matt."

Matt slammed the fridge door. "No. No, I'm not. I'm a lousy fighter. You need to find someone else."

"Find someone else for what, dear?" his mom asked.

"Matt?" his dad called from the hall.

"In here!" his mom called back.

Dad walked in holding a box with holes punched in the top. "Got you something today. I know we've always said you can't have a pet, but I think you're finally ready."

"Finally responsible," his mom said.

"*Finally* responsible," his brothers echoed.

Dad handed him the box. Matt opened it to see a small snake curled up in the bottom. It lifted its tiny head, red eyes flashing as it hissed at him.

Matt dropped the box onto the counter. It toppled, snake spilling out as he backed away. The snake uncurled, and when it did, it was half as long as the counter, its head as big as the box it had come in.

"Matt!" his mom said. "You'll hurt the poor thing."

"It—it's a serpent."

Dad scooped up the snake, draping it over his arm. "It's a very special serpent, Matt. It's *your* serpent. You need to take care of it."

The doorbell rang. Everyone ignored it and just watched Matt, shaking their heads in disappointment as he recoiled from the box. The serpent stretched until its head touched the floor, then it swung over and wrapped around his father's legs.

"Dad!" Matt shouted.

He tried to leap forward, but he couldn't move. The serpent wound its way up his father's body, wrapping around and around like a python, green scales glittering, red eyes gleaming.

The doorbell rang again.

"Aren't you going to take your serpent, Matt?" his mom said. "You won't make your father look after it, will you? That isn't very responsible."

The serpent's coils now enveloped his father's entire body, its head poised over his father's. Its jaws opened, fangs flashing. It looked at Matt, who couldn't move, couldn't even shout now, but was frozen there, watching the serpent's giant jaws hover over his father's head.

"You really should take care of it," his father said . . . right before the serpent devoured him.

Matt's eyes snapped open, and he found himself staring up at a white ceiling with a weight on his chest, pushing him down, pressing the air from his lungs. He struggled to breathe, but he couldn't open his mouth. He couldn't move. It was like he was still in the dream, paralyzed. He couldn't

even blink. His eyes stung, and his chest was on fire, and he couldn't breathe.

Somewhere he heard Laurie's voice and Baldwin's and he tried to yell for them, but he couldn't get words out. He was trapped there, on the floor in Baldwin's living room, suffocating.

"You need to take care of it," a voice said behind him. His mother's voice.

She leaned over him, and her face was gray and pale.

"Are you going to take care of your serpent, Matty?" she asked. She leaned down farther, until he could smell her breath, stinking like rotted fish. "You really need to take care of it."

She kept bending, her mouth opening, eyes glowing red dots now, skin green scales, teeth sharpening to fangs, forked tongue flicking out.

Matt bolted upright like a slingshot. He bent over, coughing and sputtering as he caught his breath. Then, slowly, he turned. The serpent was gone. He blinked and rubbed his eyes and looked around.

He was in Baldwin's living room, on the floor. Fen was fast asleep, curled up in the recliner. The couch where Laurie had been was empty now, her blanket draped over the side, and he could hear her talking to Baldwin at the front of the house. Just like in his dream.

So it wasn't a dream?

No, it must have been. Some weird kind of waking nightmare.

He blinked again and rolled his shoulders, then squinted at the blue numerals on the DVD player. Past midnight. Why was Laurie up and talking to Baldwin?

He gave a soft laugh as he thought it. Dumb question. He'd seen Reyna sneaking looks at Baldwin earlier. He supposed if a girl *that* pretty was checking Baldwin out, the guy must be good-looking.

Matt yawned and rubbed down the last goose bumps on his arms as the wisps of the nightmare finally floated away. He was stretching out again when he heard another voice— a girl's. *Reyna?* It didn't sound like her. As he sat up he dimly remembered the doorbell in his dream—the one no one else had seemed to hear.

Matt got up and padded barefoot toward the front hall. The girl's voice came clearer now, saying something about Odin. Baldwin asked her to come inside, and the voices retreated to the dining room. Matt followed. When he drew close, he could see the girl through the doorway.

She had...pink hair. He blinked and rubbed his eyes. Okay, it wasn't completely pink, but the ends definitely were. She wore pink boots, too, ones that went right up to her knees. Weird, but cool-weird.

She looked up. When she saw him, she smiled, a smile so bright and wide that it made her whole face light up. Laurie was saying something, but the girl started toward Matt, as if she didn't hear Laurie. If it was possible for her smile to widen, it did. Matt felt his cheeks heat.

"You must be Matt," she said. She looked him over, and he was sure his face went as red as his hair. "Wow. You really are Thor's son, aren't you?"

"N-no. Just a descendant. A distant descendant."

She smiled. "You know what I mean."

"Matt?" Laurie said. "This is Astrid. She's Odin's *girlfriend.*"

Laurie emphasized the last word, and Matt yanked his gaze away, cheeks flaming now. Had he been checking Astrid out? He hoped it hadn't looked like that. He wasn't. Or, at least, he didn't think he'd been.

"Odin's girlfriend," he said quickly. "Cool." He walked in and leaned against the wall, as casually as he could. "So what's going on?"

"Odin sent her," Laurie said. "He's busy doing stuff to get ready for Ragnarök, so he sent Astrid here to help us."

"Cool."

"Is it?" Astrid sighed in relief. "Good. Odin said you'd be okay with it, but I wasn't sure. It's your call, right? You're the guy in charge." She was looking right at Matt.

Matt managed a laugh. "I wouldn't say that."

She shot him a small, secret smile, as if they knew better.

Matt cleared his throat. "So, how exactly can you—?"

Something drifted past the window, wispy, like a puff of smoke. He instinctively reached for his amulet. When his fingers touched bare skin, his eyes widened.

"Matt?" Laurie said.

"My Hammer. It's—" He stopped and patted his pocket. Then he paused again, thinking back. "Right. I left it on the end table so I wouldn't lose it."

"Because we need to get a new cord again," Laurie said. "I'm starting to think we should buy them in bulk."

"Yeah, yeah." His gaze rose to the window again. It was empty.

"Did you see something?" Laurie said.

"Just fog, I think." He gave a short laugh. "Getting jumpy. Too many trolls."

"No kidding, huh?" Laurie pulled out a chair. "Okay, so—"

"Did you say fog?" Astrid cut in. She looked at Laurie. "Sorry. I didn't mean to interrupt. But..." Her gaze shot to Matt. "Fog?"

"Or something," he muttered. "Maybe nothing." He pulled out a chair.

"No, it could be something." Astrid walked to the window and tugged the curtains back more, her hands clenching the fabric, voice going tight. "What exactly did it look like?"

"I dunno. Fog. Smoke." He walked over and peered out into the night. "It's gone now."

Astrid turned. "Was everyone sleeping okay?"

"I just heard the doorbell," Laurie said. "I wasn't sound asleep, but that's it."

"Everything was fine with me," Baldwin said.

They all turned to Matt.

"Um, sure," he said. "All good. Just sleeping."

Astrid's eyes bore into his. "Really? This is important, Matt. Was anything going on when you woke up? Were you dreaming anything?"

He flinched. "Sure, I guess. Kind of a bad dream, but I don't see—"

"A nightmare?" she asked. "And then when you woke up? Did you feel anything?"

He looked from one face to another.

"Matt," Laurie murmured. "She said it's important. Don't play tough guy."

"Yeah, I was having a nightmare," Matt admitted. "I thought I woke up, but I didn't really. Not completely, anyway. I couldn't move, and I was seeing things, and I couldn't breathe."

"Because it felt like something pressing down on your chest?"

"Yeah," he said. "How'd you—?"

"Mara." Astrid yanked the curtain closed. She spun. "I thought I'd gotten rid of them."

"Gotten rid of what?" Laurie said. "What's a mara?"

She looked at Matt for the answer, but his brain just

spun, whipping through all the old stories and finding nothing.

Astrid strode into the hall and looked around, tense, as if braced for attack. "Odin warned me, but I thought I'd lost them. I am so sorry. If I knew they'd followed me, I would never have come here."

"What's a mara?" Matt asked, as she strode to the window and peered out.

"Mara. Mares," Astrid muttered.

"Horses?" Baldwin said.

Matt shook his head as he pulled the answer from some half-forgotten saga buried deep in his brain. "Spirits of confusion. That's where the word *nightmare* comes from. *Mares*, or *mara*."

"Okay," Laurie said. "But are they outside?" She cast a slow look around. "Or in here?"

"I-I don't know," Matt said. "I don't know anything about them, really. It's minor stuff in the stories. Just a mention or two in the sagas. Astrid?"

He glanced toward the front hall, but she was gone. He jogged into the hall and found her at the front door, hand on the knob.

"I need to go," Astrid said when he walked up to her. "I brought them here. If I leave, they'll follow me."

"What are they after?" Matt asked.

She frowned up at him.

"What are the mara after?" He repeated.

"The same thing all the monsters are after. You guys. The descendants of the North."

"Right. Me, Laurie, Fen, Baldwin, the twins... they followed you here to get to us. Your leaving isn't going to help," Matt pointed out.

"Right. Of course. I'm so sorry. This is—" She took a deep breath. "I'll handle it. Get everyone in the basement."

"What? No. We've fought trolls and Raiders. We can do this. If you want to get in the basement—"

Her chin shot up. "I don't hide. Especially not when I'm responsible."

"Okay," Laurie said, walking into the hall, Baldwin trailing behind. "So how do we fight these things? What exactly are they?"

"Spirits, right?" Matt said. "Like ghosts. That's what I saw outside."

Astrid nodded.

"But they're inside, too," he said. "Or they can get inside us somehow. In our brains. Mess us up. You said you thought you'd gotten rid of them. What did you do?"

"It won't work for you," Astrid said. "That's why you guys should go down—"

"We're staying," Matt interrupted. "Just explain."

"Quickly, please," Laurie said, glancing out the side window.

"I'm descended from Queen Gunnhild of Norway, who was believed to be a witch. She was—and I have her powers. Dispelling the mara takes magic. Special magic. I'll handle that part. You guys just...do what you can."

"Laurie, can you wake Fen?" Matt said. "I'm liable to get my hand bitten off if I try."

"Like Tyr," Astrid said, struggling for a smile.

Something crashed in the living room. They all ran in, Matt pushing into the lead.

It was Fen. He'd fallen off the chair and lay on the floor, still sleeping.

Matt laughed under his breath. "Have fun trying to wake him up, Laurie. He's dead to—"

Matt saw Fen's eyes then, wide and staring, and he ran over, dropping beside him. Fen lay there, frozen, eyes filled with terror, mouth open, too, chest heaving as if gasping for breath.

"Sleep paralysis," Astrid said. "Like you had."

Matt shook Fen's shoulder.

"Don't!" Astrid said, leaping forward. "You'll only make it worse. You have to let him snap out of it naturally."

Matt turned to say something to Laurie. But she wasn't there. He turned and saw her across the room, staring into nothing, and he thought she was frozen, too. Then her lips parted, and she whispered, "Jordie?"

Jordie? Who was—? Her little brother.

"She's hallucinating." Matt leaped up. "Laurie? It's not—"

"Jordie!" she shouted and ran from the room, as if chasing her invisible brother.

Matt looked back at Fen, still frozen and wide-eyed on the ground.

"We've got this," Astrid said. "Baldwin and I will be here when Fen snaps out of it. You go get her."

Matt ran after Laurie. He could hear her, her voice choked with sobs, saying, "I'm sorry, Jordie. I had to leave. I had to."

Matt followed her voice to the kitchen. She was standing in the middle of it, looking toward the counter, tears streaming down her face as she begged her brother for forgiveness.

"I didn't know," she said. "I thought I was protecting you. I didn't know."

"Laurie?" When she didn't turn, he said, louder, "Laurie? It's not him. It's not Jordie. Whatever he's saying happened, it didn't. It's a mara, remember?"

"No," she said, shaking her head. "No!"

Matt thought she was talking to him, until she said, "I would never do that. I was trying to stop Ragnarök. Protect you."

"Laurie!"

Matt strode over and stood between her and the counter. He was right in front of her, but she couldn't seem to see him. Trapped in a waking nightmare, like the one he'd had.

"No!" she screamed. "Jordie, no!"

She rushed forward and plowed right into Matt. When he tried to hold her back, she clawed and kicked, and finally, he moved out of her way and she dropped to the floor, sobbing and reaching out, as if there were someone there, lying on the floor.

"Laurie." Matt took her shoulder and shook her. "Laurie!" When she didn't respond, he grabbed her under the arms, heaved her to her feet, and said, as sharply as he could, "You're dreaming. Jordie's fine. He's miles away. You know that. You *know* that."

She started to struggle, but weakly, as if she could hear him. He said it again, even sharper, then he gave her a shake and pulled her away from her brother's imaginary body.

"Wh-what?" she said, looking up at him. "Where—?" She looked up at him and shoved him away. "Thorsen!"

"You were hallucinating. I think you thought Jordie died and it was your fault."

"Jordie . . . ?" She swallowed and swayed, as if it was coming back, but when Matt reached for her again, she pushed him away and straightened, then took a deep breath.

"Everything's fine," Matt said.

"Is it?" said a voice behind him.

Matt turned slowly. There stood his father, his hair and clothes soaking wet, his face almost . . . melted.

"Do *I* look fine?" Dad said, stepping forward. "You let

268

your snake swallow me, Matt. You let it *eat* me, and you did nothing to stop it."

"I couldn't. I—"

Matt stopped himself and squeezed his eyes shut. Hallucinating. He was just hallucinating. He knew that, but it felt real. That was the magic, like with Laurie. She knew Jordie couldn't be there, but it *felt* real.

"Matt?"

He heard Laurie's voice, but dimly, as if she were across the house. *She's right there. Focus on her. Pull yourself back.*

He kept his eyes shut as he turned back toward Laurie's voice.

"Keep talking," he said.

"Talking about what?" It was Jake now. "What's there to talk about, Matt? You messed up. I knew you would. You always do."

"Laurie? Talk. Please."

He could hear her saying something, but her voice was drowned out by another—Josh.

"Why'd you let this happen, Matt?" Josh asked. "I thought you could do it. Even when Jake said you couldn't. Even when Dad thought you couldn't. I believed in you."

"Laurie? Louder."

He felt her fingers wrap around his arm. "Snap out of it, Thorsen. Get a grip. You know it's not real. Fight it!"

His eyes snapped open, and he saw her standing there, glowering up at him.

"I'm back," he said.

"*Stay* back."

"Yes, ma'am." He looked around, blinking away the last of the vision. "Okay, we need to get to—"

A scream from upstairs.

"The twins." Matt pushed Laurie toward the door. "You check on Fen. I'll go help them."

As they ran for the door, something hissed to Matt's left, and he looked to see a serpent's head coming through the window, red eyes glowing.

"It's not there," he muttered under his breath. "Nothing's there."

Laurie shrieked, hands flying up to cover her head as she ducked from some unseen monster.

"It's not—" Matt began.

"I know," she said, already uncovering her head. She cast an angry look around the room. "Not real. You hear me? You're not real."

"You got it." Matt put his hands on her shoulders and steered her, in front of him, toward the doorway.

When a puff of smoke appeared in the doorway, swirling, he instinctively stopped and pulled Laurie back. The smoke took the shape of a woman—so thin she looked like a skeleton with skin stretched over her bones. Long white hair swirled around her. Her eyes were empty pits. When she opened her mouth, it was filled with rotting stumps of teeth.

"You're not there," Matt said, pushing Laurie forward. "You're a figment of my imagination."

The apparition hissed and reached out a long, bony finger.

Laurie dug in her heels. "Uh, Matt? Are you seeing a really ugly woman pointing at us?"

"Yeah…"

"Then she's actually there, because I see her, too."

"A mara," he said. "That must be what they look like." He stepped in front of Laurie and squared his shoulders. "But it's still just a spirit. It can't hurt you. Remember that. Close your eyes and hold my shirt, and we'll walk right through—"

Something shot from the hag's finger and hit Matt like a jolt of electricity, knocking him to the floor and stunning him.

Laurie pulled him up. "Your theory is wrong."

"No kidding."

The mara pointed again, this time at Laurie. Matt pushed Laurie to the side and dove after her. The bolt hit the wall, leaving a sizzling hole in the plaster.

"Other door!" Matt shouted.

He pushed Laurie and ran behind her. When he heard a sizzle, he shouted a warning and dodged. The bolt whizzed past into the wall again. They raced out the other door and found themselves at the foot of the stairs.

From above, they could hear Reyna shouting and Ray gibbering.

"Guess I'm going up with you," Laurie said.

They raced up the stairs, the mara in pursuit, seeming in no hurry, as if just herding them along, cackling and throwing her bolts. When a figure appeared on the steps, Matt almost fell backward. It was his mother—her face gray and dead, like it'd been in his dream.

"I believed in you," his mother said. "I told them you could save us."

His father appeared at the top of the stairs. "You let her down, Matt. You let us all down."

"Not real," Matt whispered. "Not real."

Laurie shrieked, seeing some apparition of her own, and she turned as if to run back down the stairs, but Matt pushed her up, his voice getting louder as he chanted, "Not real. Not real!"

The more he fought the nightmares, the harder the mara tried. His parents came first, then his brother, then his grandfather, then friends at school. All dead. Devoured by serpents and rotting in graves. All dead. All blaming him.

But Laurie was getting it just as bad. He could tell by her yells and cries, but all he could do was keep pushing her forward and deal with banishing his own nightmares. When they finally reached the top, the apparitions fell in behind with the mara chasing them.

Laurie ran to a closed door and yanked it open. Inside,

Matt saw Baldwin's parents' room, and he almost stopped her, ready to say they shouldn't go in there. But now wasn't really the time to worry about being rude. So when she pulled him in and slammed the door, he let her.

On the other side, he could hear his family, shouting at him. A bolt from the mara went right through the wood and burned his shoulder. As he stumbled back, Laurie spun and raced into the room. She ran to the balcony door and yanked it open.

"Wait!" Matt yelled.

"We have to get outside. They won't follow us there."

She raced through. Matt ran after her. The balcony was long and narrow, with a wooden railing that overlooked the backyard. Laurie climbed onto the railing.

"No!" Matt shouted, lurching forward.

"We need to get over the fence," she said. Her eyes were blank again, and he knew she was dreaming.

He ran for her. "That's not a—!"

She dropped over the side. Matt let out a cry and raced for the railing. He looked down to see Laurie lying on the ground. He scrambled over the railing, stood on the edge of the balcony, crouched, grabbing the edge, then dropped.

He hit the ground hard enough to let out a gasp, pain shooting through his legs. Then he scrambled over to Laurie. She was sitting now, cradling her arm. It was bent at a weird angle. Broken.

"Are you okay?" he said. "Other than your arm, are you—?"

"There you are," said a voice from the house.

They both looked up as Fen barreled out the patio door, his face twisted with rage. "Did you really think I'd let you take my cousin away?"

NINETEEN

FEN

"TROUBLE IN PINK BOOTS"

Fen saw the two of them and realized they were trying to ditch him. His cousin, his almost-sister, was leaving him because he wasn't as strong as Matt. He'd known it could happen, but he'd believed in her. She was the only one who'd ever stuck by him.

"So what, you creep out while I'm sleeping? Leave me here while you go save the world?" Fen advanced on them, growling deep in his throat like he wasn't on two legs anymore.

"It's a dream, Fen." Matt had his arm around Laurie, and she was leaning on him.

"You and Thorsen?" Fen reached for her, but she flinched away. "You're going to be heroes and leave me behind?"

"No." Laurie pushed away from Matt. "This is a *dream*, and we're all having nightmares about the things we fear."

"They're called mara. They're attacking us with nightmares." Matt stepped closer to them and pointed up to the second floor. "Laurie jumped from there thinking it was a fence."

Fen looked at Laurie, and she nodded and then looked pointedly at the arm she was holding tight to her chest. "I broke it. *That's* why I pulled away."

He started to answer, but then Kris walked out of the shadows and stood behind Laurie. "You believe this trash? You always were dumber than the rest of the family, boy. You know they offered to pay me to take you in? And I still said no." Kris laughed and then tossed a half-empty beer at Fen. "I lost the betting pool, though, and now I'm stuck with you."

Fen ducked to avoid the can.

"Fen." Laurie stepped up to him. "Whatever you're seeing, it's not real. Focus on me. Please. I need you to help me."

He shook his head, and Kris vanished. "How do we fight illusions?"

"Focus on what's real." Matt looked back toward the house. "The bony women inside aren't illusions, though, and my Hammer is in there. If we're going to fight them..."

"Let's go get it, then." Fen marched up to the door and went back inside. His dad was on the floor in the kitchen,

276

being kicked in the sides and stomach by Skull and Hattie. They grinned at him.

"You're next," Hattie said. "Wait till I tell your little friends about how we got the shield and how you're going to help us get Matt, too. Bet we won't have to hurt you then. They'll do it for us."

Beside him, he heard Laurie repeating, "Not real. Not real. Not real."

Fen squared his shoulders and looked away from the Raiders in the kitchen. They needed to find the mara and get rid of them. Baldwin ran toward them. "There are monsters in my house." He held out a hand to Matt; cupped in his open palm was the Hammer amulet. "Here. You left this in the living room."

"Thank you!" Matt folded the tiny Hammer in his hand so tightly that Fen thought it might cut the skin. Baldwin really was a good guy: he'd brought them what they needed without even being told.

"Where are the twins?" Laurie asked.

"They're shooting something at the mara. I can't *see* it, but every time they hold hands, the air ripples, and the illusions near them vanish." Baldwin shook his head. "The bone people don't, though. They're not going away."

"And Astrid?" Matt asked. "Is she okay?"

"Who?" Fen asked.

"New girl. With us when you woke," Baldwin said, and

then he looked at Matt and shook his head. "She's some-where in the house, said something about magic."

Fen, Laurie, and Matt made their way up the stairs and to the guest room, where the twins were to be sleeping. They stood arm-in-arm, staring out the door. Between the twins and them were five bony, ugly old women. The women couldn't get in the room, but they weren't retreating, either.

Reyna and Ray looked tired, but they kept flinging their free hands as if they were throwing things. The mara flinched, but they weren't destroyed. Laurie had been right that the twins had a secret. They were witches of some sort.

A girl—presumably Astrid—opened another door and peered out at them. "Matt!" She grabbed Matt's arm. "I couldn't get in to the twins."

With a sudden smile, Baldwin started to walk up to the mara. The mara didn't look their way, even as Baldwin tried tugging them back from the doorway.

Then Fen heard the growls. He looked over his shoulder and saw at least three wolves coming up the steps. "Wolves! Get into the other room!" He started trying to herd them into the bedroom across from the twins' room.

"Not real," Laurie murmured. "Fen. Not real. Jordie's not here. Mom's not here. The wolves aren't here." She was too pale, and he knew she was going to pass out. The break in her arm meant they needed to go to a hospital, but he couldn't leave Baldwin out there alone.

"Come on." Fen shoved Matt aside, pushing him closer to Astrid and helping Laurie over to sit on the bed. "Need a plan, Thorsen. The twins and Baldwin are buying time, but we need a plan."

"Let me see," Astrid offered.

Fen snarled at her. He wasn't going to let a stranger near Laurie when she was hurt.

"Plan, Thorsen," he half snarled, half spoke.

Through the open door, Fen could see Baldwin clinging to the back of one of the mara like a cheerful monkey; the mara ignored him. The twins were making no progress, and Fen wasn't keen on leaving Laurie's side.

"Trying, Brekke," Matt said. He was staring past Fen at something only he saw.

One of the mara turned and advanced toward the door.

"Not real," Matt muttered.

Astrid came to Matt's side and slammed the door, like a thin piece of wood would keep out a monster.

"They're on their own out there, Thorsen. Either you go or I go. One of us has to stay in here to protect Laurie." Fen gestured at her, and for the first time since they'd faced the Raiders in Blackwell, Laurie didn't argue. That alone meant she was in real pain.

Matt must've noticed, too. He grabbed Astrid's wrist. "Whatever you did before, you need to try it again."

"I don't know if it will work, but"—she put her hand on

top of Matt's hand, who quickly yanked away from her—"I can try."

"Now!" Fen demanded.

"Fen's right." Matt was at the door, ready to yank it open. "If you can't do it, he and I need to go out there."

"I'll try," Astrid said.

Matt yanked the door open. Astrid shot Fen a grin before she followed Matt into the hallway and started saying something unintelligible. The mara shrieked, horrible shrill noises that made Fen cringe, and then they vanished.

Astrid collapsed, swaying into Matt, who caught her and helped her sit on the floor. He stayed crouched beside her.

The twins left their room, stepped around Matt and Astrid, and came to the bedroom where he and Laurie were.

"Who is she?" Reyna asked.

"Astrid. Witch or something," Baldwin sang out as he came bouncing past them into the room. "Did you see? She just zapped them away. I told you we were like superheroes. Bring on the next villain!"

Despite everything, Fen couldn't help smiling at Baldwin's attitude. "He's as bad as us, Laurie," he said.

When she didn't even smile, a cold spike of panic rushed through him. "Laurie?"

She gave him the least convincing smile he'd ever seen. "Sorry. Maybe there's aspirin or something here. Baldwin?"

"Sure, but we should call a doctor," Baldwin said. "That's

what people do when they get hurt, isn't it? I never have, but there are kids at school and..." His words dwindled. "I'll get aspirin and the phone."

"No phone," Laurie objected. "Aspirin. Then we can wrap my arm or something. If we go to a hospital, they'll call the cops, and we just can't."

"We'll fix it." Ray stepped closer to the bed.

Fen put himself in front of Laurie and bared his teeth. The only thing keeping him on two legs was the realization that he couldn't speak if he became a wolf.

"It's okay, Fen," Laurie said. When he didn't reply, she snapped, "*Fen!*"

He glanced over his shoulder at her. He whimpered before he could stop himself.

"We've got this one, puppy." Reyna walked over to stand beside her brother. "No hospital needed. Honest."

"Let them pass," Laurie said gently.

And Fen wanted to say something rude, but the truth was that if they could take that too-pale look away from Laurie's face, he would owe them. He did, however, look at Matt—who had now left Astrid to stand with Fen beside the bed.

Matt looked as worried as Fen felt. That, at least, made Fen feel a little better. If there was trouble, he wouldn't be alone in dealing with it.

"Don't touch her while we do this," Ray cautioned.

And then the twins stood on either side of the bed where Laurie lay. They clasped hands, right-to-left, so they were a circle of two over her. Then they lowered one set of clasped hands to her oddly angled arm and began whispering words in a rising-falling-rising way that made Fen's skin prickle.

Baldwin came to stand with him, and Astrid walked over and leaned on Matt. He awkwardly put an arm around her waist to steady her, and Fen had a prickle of unease. Matt, despite Fen's years of disliking him, had turned out to be a really good guy. Like Laurie and Baldwin, though, he was too trusting. That left Fen with several people to protect. He wasn't sure what he thought of the twins, but he knew he didn't like Astrid.

"Thank you," Laurie whispered, drawing his attention. Her arm was looking straight again.

The twins stood in one movement, as if their very muscles somehow communicated and had to move as perfect mirrors.

"You saved us from the trolls; we fixed you. We're even now," Reyna said.

"You'll need to sleep, but it's healed," added Ray.

"I knew you had a secret," Laurie murmured drowsily.

As Fen stepped closer to her, both twins backed away. Ray held up his hands disarmingly, but Reyna snorted. Fen wasn't entirely sure how much magic any of the three witches had, but he didn't care just then. They all needed to step away from Laurie.

"Thanks." He remembered to say that part first, and then he added the important words, "Now leave." A small growl slipped out, and he was pretty sure his eyes weren't all the way normal, either. Laurie being hurt had scared him enough that he wasn't feeling very in control. He'd learned that when he felt like this, he shouldn't be around people. They *had* helped her, though, so he tried to sound a little nicer. "She needs to sleep."

Matt said, "If you need us..."

Fen only nodded because he wasn't quite sure he could talk. Too many strangers were in the room near Laurie, and Fen's instinct to protect his cousin was making everything else unimportant. He trusted Matt and Baldwin, but the other three were threats until they'd proven otherwise. One battle didn't make them allies.

Threats should be removed.

Baldwin stayed at the door, standing like a sentinel awaiting orders. Matt led the twins and Astrid away. As they left, Matt said to the twins, "Thanks for healing Laurie. What else can you do? Does the magic work for offense, too, like Astrid's?"

There was a part of Fen that wanted to know, but mostly he was glad that they were gone. He and Matt weren't friends, but they'd gone to school together long enough that Matt knew Fen was overprotective. The only thing new there was that Matt knew now that they could be tangling with a grumpy wolf if Fen got too angry. Matt had done exactly what Laurie would've: taken the people away so Fen didn't have to try to be nice.

He felt like something heavy fell off his shoulders as he walked to the doorway, where Baldwin waited. "Thank you," he said again, and then he closed the door and lay down on the floor. The only way to get near Laurie was to get past him, and even as tired as he was, he'd wake if anyone came in.

TWENTY

✦

LAURIE

"WITCHING AND WHINING"

W hen Laurie and Fen came downstairs at almost lunchtime the next day, she felt more rested than she had in days. Her arm felt a little tender, but it seemed to be healed. The twins had definitely had a secret: they were witches. From what Fen had said had happened with the mara, so was Astrid.

That should mean that Laurie was happier. Having three witches along seemed like it should be an asset in stopping Ragnarök, except it didn't feel like that. Laurie hated admitting it, but she was nervous. They'd gone from a group of three to seven in a single day, and they hadn't had any time to stop and recover from the craziness before they were attacked again. It felt like they were getting battered at every turn, and if Astrid hadn't arrived, they would have had no idea how to defeat the mara. Laurie was grateful to the new girl, but she also realized that they couldn't keep counting on surprises to save them.

As they walked into the living room, Fen ordered, "Sit."

"I'm fine, Fen. Honest! It's just a little sore, but not broken." She held out her arm. "I can—"

Fen growled and pointed at the sofa.

"You're being silly," she objected, but she still sat. She was tired, and she was sore, and they both knew it. He'd spent almost an hour trying to convince her to go home. Even if her mom couldn't keep her safe, he was sure that Kris and a few other wolves would protect her from the Raiders. Fen's biggest objection to her coming along was that it was dangerous, and here she was, already injured— not that he hadn't been as well. Strangulation by troll had to have been pretty painful. The problem with arguing with Fen, though, was that he didn't see injury to *himself* as a big issue.

So Laurie sat on the sofa while Fen wandered off to get her something to eat. It would make Fen feel better to look after her, and it didn't hurt her to let him. She could hear him talking to Baldwin, and she smiled. That was good for him, too. Whether it was because of the other boy's god powers of likability or something else, Fen obviously really liked Baldwin. Matt and Astrid were talking as they walked in the room, and the twins were absentee. Laurie felt oddly alone.

Then Matt headed to the kitchen, and Astrid walked toward her.

Laurie tried for a cheerful voice as she said, "Hi."

"Hello." Astrid sat down beside Laurie.

"Thanks for the save last night," Laurie said.

Astrid laughed. "They followed me here, so it's not actually a *save*, right?"

At that, Laurie relaxed. "Well, you defeated them, so that's the important part."

The smile Astrid gave her was as friendly as one of Baldwin's. It made Laurie feel less alone. Astrid was like her, too: not really one of the important descendants, but still a part of it all. Maybe that's why Reyna and Ray weren't as friendly as Astrid—maybe they didn't think she should be here. Fen and Matt certainly thought Laurie ought to go home. It was only Odin who had seemed to believe that she should be there. *Kinda like Astrid. We're both here because of him.*

"I met Odin. He seemed...nice," Laurie told Astrid. "You must miss him."

Astrid laughed. "Nice? Odin? He's a freak, but it's not all his fault. I mean, we are who we are because of some story that was written forever ago."

"I hope not!" Laurie shook her head. "He was a little different, but like Fen and Matt and...everyone"—she gestured toward the kitchen and upstairs—"he's got a huge responsibility. We're lucky that we don't have to do what they're going to. I mean, we'll help, but it's not the same."

Fen had come back while she was talking. He handed Laurie a plate and then glared down at Astrid like she was a bug he didn't know whether to squash or eat.

Astrid seemed oblivious. She smiled at him and said, "Hi." But she didn't move to a chair so Fen could have her seat.

Laurie didn't say anything. They could figure it out; she was going to eat. As she chewed her sandwich, she wondered briefly if his protectiveness was a result of his wolfyness. Now that she knew that he was *wulfenkind*, so many of his behaviors seemed logical to her. He had declared himself her protector when they were little, but he'd gotten worse when her dad left. Fen—and her father—both knew that there were seriously scary things out there because they were aware of the shape-shifting thing. Knowing there were big bad wolves out there *and* being wolves had to make them more worried about the family members like her who weren't wolves.

But none of that meant that he should be so snarly to a girl who had done nothing but save them last night. He still hadn't moved, and now Astrid was staring up at him.

"Can you scoot over?" Laurie asked. "He's still acting like I'm hurt."

"Sure," Astrid said. She slid to the other end of the sofa, and Fen flopped down between them.

He sat there silently, and conversation suddenly seemed impossible as a result.

After a few moments of tense silence, Astrid said, "So you and Laurie are Loki's great-great-whatever kids?"

Fen looked at her, but all he said was, "Yeah."

Laurie smiled gratefully at Astrid. This was a topic they could discuss, one that would lure Fen out of his silence. "We are. That's why Fen does the wolf thing. I'm not a shape-shifter, though. Fen's going to fight with Matt against the serpent." She smiled at Fen. "I'm not going to fight, but I'm not too bad at tricking trolls."

"Or you could go home," Fen suggested.

Instead of arguing with him in front of Astrid, Laurie took another bite of her sandwich. She was sick of everyone trying to get rid of her. Just because she didn't need to be present to fight the serpent didn't mean she couldn't help.

Matt walked toward them. He looked so much more confident than Laurie ever felt. Maybe that's what it was like to be a champion. She had moments of feeling sure, but those were when she was doing something worthwhile, not when Fen was acting like a crazy guard wolf.

"At Ragnarök, Loki led the monsters." Astrid glanced at Matt. "But like Matt says, we don't have to follow the stories, so you shouldn't worry about that."

"Okay..." Laurie said. That seemed like an odd thing to say. Of course Fen wasn't going to lead the enemies! Astrid was probably trying to be reassuring, but she had sounded a little suspicious.

Instead of sitting, Matt stood behind the chair with his hands on the back of it. "We're all awake now, so let's plan. We can't sit around waiting for monsters to keep attacking us." He raised his voice and called, "Ray? Reyna? Baldwin? Conference time."

Baldwin came in and flopped down on the floor beside Fen. The twins strolled lazily down the stairs and into the living room. They stayed back a bit, but they were technically present.

Matt stood beside the empty chair and looked at all of them. "We have our team, so now we need our stuff."

"What *stuff*?" Reyna asked.

"Feathers, Hammer, shield," Matt recited. He turned to Astrid. "Can you reach Odin?"

"I wish," she said with a sigh. "He's wandering around as usual. That's why he sent me here. He'll show up eventually, but until then you're stuck with me. But I do know where we should start. Mjölnir. Our champion needs his Hammer."

Matt blushed and shook his head. "We're a *team*, Astrid."

"Oh, I know. But the serpent is the big baddie in this fight, and you need to defeat it alone." She gave a little laugh. "You're the lead singer in this band, Matt. We're the backup. Hopefully, really good backup, but still backup."

Matt looked uncomfortable and opened his mouth to answer, but before he could say anything, Fen spoke up, "Pinkie here has a point. Might as well get Thorsen's Hammer next." He slouched back into the sofa then and folded his arms. "I'm ready when you are."

"Excuse me?" Reyna said. "If this is your idea of planning, it's a wonder you survived a minute."

"What?" Fen drawled. "You and Ken have a better plan?"

"Who's Ken?" Baldwin whispered.

"Hold on," Matt said. "Reyna, are you objecting to going after the Hammer? Or are you objecting to focusing on me? Because I never said I was special or—"

"Chill, Thorsen." Fen shook his head. "I was serious. You need the real Hammer. Your little whatsit is only good so long."

"But do we know where Mjölnir is?" Laurie asked. "We do know where the shield is, so I say we get that first." She looked at Astrid. "Unless you know where the Hammer is, since you suggested getting it..."

"I was hoping you guys did." Astrid looked at Matt. "Did the Valkyries give you any clues? The Norns maybe?"

He shook his head.

"Can you contact them? Ask?"

"I can ask if and when they show up. Until then, we're stuck...." Matt straightened. "No, we aren't stuck. Laurie's right. We know where the shield is."

"Great, but we need the Hammer more," Astrid said.

Fen growled loudly enough that Reyna and Ray exchanged a look, and Laurie hoped that she wasn't going to have to step between them. His temper was never good, but today it was worse than usual because he was worried about her.

"Being Odin's girlfriend doesn't make you a part of this," Fen said.

Astrid jumped up, glared at him, and ran out of the room.

Casually, Fen looked at Matt. "So how do we find the Hammer?"

No one said a word. Matt glared at Fen, and then he walked out. Laurie wasn't sure what to do. The twins fled back upstairs, and Baldwin looked from the doorway to Fen to her. He didn't say anything or follow Matt and Astrid.

"Fen..." Laurie started, but she wasn't sure what to say.

Fen stood. "Tell me when there's a plan," he called as he left the room.

He was being a jerk, but Astrid was going to need to be less sensitive if she was going to be around them. If she was going to run away every time Fen said something rude, she might as well never sit down. Laurie liked her, and she liked

the idea of having another girl around in addition to Reyna—who hadn't warmed up to Laurie...or anyone else, either. However, Laurie was going to have to talk to her. No one had run away when Astrid pointed out that Laurie and Fen were descendants of the god who fought on the other side—or when trolls, Norns, Valkyries, or mara appeared.

TWENTY-ONE

MATT

"RAIDING THE RAIDERS"

Matt needed to make Astrid feel better. It was like being on the boxing or wrestling team. You might fight the other guys at practice, but at a tournament, you had to support each other. Help each other. Cheer each other on. Whenever there was a problem—like one guy razzing another—Coach Forde would send Matt in to cool them down. He supposed that meant he was good at it. Now it was up to him to make things right. Bring the team back together.

But what if Astrid took it the wrong way? What if she thought he liked her? He did like her, as a person. But the way she kept looking at him and talking about him...his cheeks heated just thinking about it. She probably didn't mean it like that. She had a boyfriend. She was just being super-nice to him because he was being nice to her. Like at school sometimes, when he was nice to new kids and all of a sudden they were sitting beside him at lunch and walking home from school with him.

But what if, by chasing her, she thought he meant something else. He'd have to tell her it wasn't like that. Or, worse, she'd tell *him* it wasn't like that for *her*—*You're a great guy, Matt, but I have a boyfriend*. He'd probably burn up with embarrassment.

So he followed her for a bit. Then he imagined her looking back and seeing him *following* her and how much worse that would be.

"Hey, Astrid," he called, as calmly as he could. "Wait up."

She turned and when she saw him, her whole face lit up in this smile that made him stumble over his feet.

"I'm sorry about that," he said, pointing to the house. "Fen didn't mean to snap at you. Everyone's just really tired and freaked out. You're right about Mjölnir."

She walked toward him. "Thank you. You're the brains *and* the brawn of this operation, aren't you?"

"No, we all are. It's a team effort. Fen has a point. We don't know where Mjölnir is. But we do know where to find the shield."

Her shoulders slumped, and she let out a deep sigh.

"Sure, I can't wait to get Mjölnir," he said. "But the Valkyries say the shield is just as important."

"But if you know where it is, you can get it anytime." Her fingers touched his arm. "You need Mjölnir."

He brushed back his hair, "accidentally" dropping her fingers from his arm.

"There must be someone you can ask," she continued. "The Norns. The Valkyries. I bet you could call them. Ask them for help finding Mjölnir."

Matt shook his head. "I need to find it myself. It's part of the test."

"Test?" She gave a scornful laugh. "If they're testing you, they don't know you very well. Anyone can see that you're ready. And who are they to test the mighty Thor? You're the important one. You always have been. Even these days, everyone knows the name of Thor. Can they name a Norn? A Valkyrie? Most don't even know what they are."

Except he wasn't Thor. He was only the god's representative, which meant he had to prove himself worthy of the honor. He wasn't ready to meet the serpent. It was nice that Astrid thought so, but she was wrong.

She moved closer again, lowering her voice as if they might be overheard. "I suppose you've heard that Odin was king of the gods."

"He was."

"True...but he wasn't the most popular one. He wasn't

the most-worshipped one. Look it up. Odin was the god of the nobility. Thor was the god of the common man. He was the most popular. The most worshipped. The most beloved. It's not Odin who got to be a comic-book hero, is it? There's a reason for that. It's all about Thor. It's always been Thor." She met his gaze again. "And that's you. You are Thor and you need Mjölnir, and if your friends are saying you don't, it's because they're jealous. You're Thor. They're... someone else."

"If you're upset about what Fen said, that you're not really a part—"

"I don't care about that. I care about getting that Hammer for you, Matt."

That seemed a weird thing to be concerned about, and Matt suspected she really was hurt over what Fen had said, but he decided not to push it.

"No one's saying I don't need the Hammer. I know you're trying to help, but we should get the shield first." Now it was his turn to meet her eyes. "I understand if you don't want to help with that, but it would be great if you could."

Did he imagine it, or did *she* blush now?

"Of course I'll help, Matt."

The others had gathered in the kitchen. Matt walked in, Astrid trailing after him.

"Fen? You know where the Raider camp is, right?" Matt asked.

"Uh, I did. If your dad and his posse haven't rousted them," Fen said.

Matt turned to Laurie. "If Fen knows where it is, can you open a door?"

"I can *try*, but I'm not entirely sure how I did it the first time." She paused and smiled. "You're going after the shield. We'll have one of the weapons then."

"*If* we get it."

"You want Laurie to open a door into the Raider camp?" Fen said. His voice wasn't a full-out growl, but it was pretty close. "Seriously?"

"Not into the actual camp," Matt said. "We'll touch down a little ways from it and walk."

"All of us?" Fen paused, and then he shook his head. "I'll handle this, Thorsen. Laurie opens the door, and I'll go through and get your shield."

Even Laurie looked over sharply, as if shocked. Matt was a bit surprised, but it was nice to see Fen finally becoming a team player.

"I appreciate the offer," Matt said. "But I've fought them with you. You'll need backup. Lots of it. We're all going in."

"All?" Reyna repeated.

"Yes." Matt fixed her with a look. "All of us."

300

Fen locked gazes with Matt. "Not Laurie. She was *just* hurt. She's not going in there, and she doesn't have fighting skills like everyone else." He glanced at his cousin and snapped, "Don't argue."

Laurie folded her arms over her chest and glared at him, but Matt was just glad she was mad at Fen, not him.

After a few failed attempts, Laurie opened one of her portals. She was shaking by the time she did it, and Fen looked ready to bite someone. Matt didn't want to step between them, and he wasn't sure who he'd side with anyway. Laurie was right that they needed her help, but Fen was right that she looked like she was going to be sick.

They stepped through a door that brought them out in a forest. After a quick look around, Fen declared the Raiders camp was about a quarter mile away. Blackwell was nearby, too. Matt thought about that—how close he was to home. He could be there in a half hour. But he couldn't. Not now. Maybe not ever again.

At this moment, all that was important was that they were far enough from both Blackwell and the Raider camp that no one would stumble on them as they plotted. As evening fell, the forest shadows lengthening, Matt explained his idea.

"I don't get it," Baldwin said. "You said you needed us for a fight."

Matt shook his head. "I said we needed everyone for backup. That's *in case* of a fight. This is more than a couple of dumb trolls. These guys outnumber us, and they're *all* good fighters. Plus, some can change into wolves. Big wolves."

"So . . . there's no fight?" Baldwin said.

"Thorsen's right," Fen said, probably because he was still angling to keep Laurie out of danger. "We don't want a battle if we don't need one. Better to sneak in and grab it while the rest of us watch for trouble."

"Actually, I was going to ask you to come along," Matt said. "You know the camp."

"Just what I've told you already. I have no idea where they're keeping the shield."

Fen looked at Matt with a strange expression, half challenge and half pleading, and Matt realized that Fen must have been *really* shaken up by Laurie getting hurt. It made sense, considering how close they were.

"I think it's better for everyone if I stay here," Fen continued. "I'll change to a wolf so I can listen for trouble, and I'll run in if I hear anything."

"I guess that's okay." Matt looked at the others, ignoring Laurie, who was staring suspiciously at Fen as he studied his feet. "So who wants to come with me?"

Baldwin and Matt peered out from behind a bush, having left the others back in the forest grove. Matt started sneaking around it when Baldwin motioned for him to wait.

"Before we go, I just want to say thanks for picking me."

Matt shrugged. "No problem."

He didn't want to add that no one else had exactly jumped at the chance. Laurie had offered, but Fen gave Matt a look to say he'd better not pick her…or else. Ray volunteered, which earned Matt the same kind of look from Reyna. Astrid offered, but Matt didn't know enough about her skills—her powers or her ability to defend herself. He probably would have picked Baldwin anyway. He couldn't get hurt, and he'd promised not to try to cause a fight.

"I just wanted to say thanks," Balwin said. "I'm usually not the guy anyone picks."

Matt peered at him. "Why not? Everyone likes you."

"Oh, I'm never left until the end or anything. But I'm never the *first*. If it's math teams or spelling bees, I do okay, but lots of kids do better. Same with sports. Art. Music. Whatever. I'm never first." Baldwin gave a small laugh, a little sad.

"I know what that's like."

"But we were definitely someone's first pick now, huh?"

Baldwin grinned over at him. "Those Norns or Valkyries or whoever. Someone picked us first."

Matt smiled. "Yeah, I guess so."

"They did. Anyway, we should get going. I just wanted to say thanks and that I won't make you regret it. Not you. Not the gods. Whatever I need to do, I'll do it, and I'll do it well."

Fen had warned Matt to sneak in downwind so none of the *wulfenkind* smelled them. There wasn't much of a wind that evening, so Matt had to keep stopping and checking. When they were close enough to see the camp, he motioned that they'd stop behind another bush.

While Baldwin waited patiently, Matt pushed aside branches and peered out. He always thought of Raiders as Boy Scouts gone bad. Now, seeing their camp, he realized that wasn't far off. He'd spent a year in Scouts himself, and part of the reason he'd taken up boxing and wrestling was to have an excuse to quit. His leader used to be in the army and ran his troop like they were cadets. Especially when they went camping. Everything had to be just right. A pile of logs beside the fire pit at all times, with the logs just the right size, piled just the right way. No garbage anywhere, which made sense, but the rule applied to anything you weren't using at the time. Put down a mug and leave on a hike and you'd get fifty push-ups. Even though they stayed at the same campsite all week, they had to roll their sleeping bags and pack their gear every morning. In case, you know, the enemy swooped in and they had to evacuate. Crazy.

Now Matt was wondering if his Scout leader had been a Raider, too. The camp looked the same, with only the tents left up. Even those tents were arranged in a perfect circle around the fire pit.

"Looks like nobody's here," Baldwin whispered. "They must all be off on a raid." He paused. "Was Fen serious about that? They really raid towns? Like the Vikings?"

"More like vultures. They break into empty homes and steal anything that's not nailed down. I'm sure they've left a guard here, though. We need to find him before we go in."

Baldwin didn't ask how Matt planned to go in. He just seemed to accept that Matt knew what he was doing. He was wrong. Matt looked at the camp and felt a weird sinking sensation in his stomach. There were at least a dozen tents that all faced the campfire in the middle, so how would he sneak into one without being spotted? And which was the right tent? Fen said it would probably be in Skull's or Hattie's—they were the leaders. But Fen also said that their tents looked just like all the rest. Supremely unhelpful.

"Oh!" Baldwin whispered, pointing. "Something moved over there. Did you see it?"

Matt hadn't, but as he squinted, he spotted a glowing red dot, hovering in the air. Then he saw a dark figure holding out the dot to another, who took it and lifted it to his lips. Two guys sharing a cigarette.

The two guards were on the far side of the camp, downhill a little, by a stream. When Matt hunkered down, he couldn't see that red dot anymore. Meaning they couldn't see him. He smiled.

He whispered for Baldwin to stick behind him and stay quiet. He didn't really need the warning—that's what Baldwin had been doing the whole time. The perfect team member. Maybe the others could take lessons.

As they drew closer to the ring of tents, Matt's amulet began to tingle. It didn't exactly warm up, and it didn't exactly vibrate, either. He wasn't sure how to describe it, except as a tingle. Like it was reminding him it was there.

Was it reacting to the shield? But it was the shield from the longship, and he'd been around it lots of times and his amulet had done nothing. But it had done nothing around the Raiders before. So . . .

Follow the weird feeling. That's what his gut said. So that's what he did. They circled around the outside of the tent ring. The amulet tingled more with each step, until it started tingling less. Matt backed up and found the tent that seemed to produce the most tingle . . . which sounded completely ridiculous, and he sure wasn't saying it to Baldwin. Again, he didn't need to. Baldwin didn't ask. He just trusted that Matt knew what he was doing.

Matt knew he couldn't just sneak into the tent and expect Baldwin to *know* he should stand guard. Fen would; Laurie would. Baldwin had to be told, but once he was—in a brief, whispered exchange—he got it, and Matt had no doubt he *would* watch his back.

Matt crept around the tent with Baldwin. Then he undid the ties on the flap, lifted one, and slipped in while Baldwin stayed outside. The only thing inside the tent was a pile of blankets. As Matt walked over, he swore his amulet was practically jumping with excitement. Sure enough, under that stack of blankets, he found the shield. He smiled, clutched his still-twitching amulet. Another power, then. Something that must have "turned on" after Hildar had told him what he needed. It would be nice if she'd explained. But, he had to admit, it did feel good, figuring this stuff out for himself.

He pulled out the shield. It was definitely the one from the longship. It was lighter than he expected, the wood smoother, too, as if polished by years of handling. He imagined it in the hands of a real Viking warrior, setting off to battle—

A nice fantasy, but this really wasn't the time for it. He hefted the shield and, without even thinking, swung it over his shoulder, arm through the strap, letting it rest on his back. It felt good there. Comfortable. Protective, too, like he had someone at his back. Now all he needed was Mjölnir, and he'd be set. He grinned to himself and headed from the tent.

Baldwin was right there, waiting, on guard like a pointer,

scanning the horizon for trouble. When Matt whispered, "Got it," Baldwin stumbled, nearly tripping over his feet.

He saw Matt and looked almost disappointed for a second, like he'd been hoping for a real threat to fight off. Then he saw the shield and his eyes rounded.

"Is that...?" Baldwin said. "Wow. That is so cool." He grinned. "Looks good on you."

"Thanks. No sign of trouble?"

"Nah. Cancer boys are still down by the steam, sharing a smoke." Baldwin paused. "I didn't think kids smoked anymore."

"Only the evil ones," Matt murmured.

Baldwin started to laugh, then swallowed it and settled for a grin. "That's so we can recognize them, right?"

Matt smiled. "Right. Now let's head out. Mission..."

A figure stepped from behind a tent across the circle. Then another and another. Matt wheeled. More were behind him. A Raider stood in every gap between two tents. In every escape route. He turned fast, evaluating the least threat, ready to barrel through—

A familiar figure strolled between two tents. Skull—the biggest of the Raiders, the one Matt fought outside the fair. Matt looked over his shoulder to see a girl about Skull's age. She was even taller than Reyna, with wide shoulders and blond braids. That must be Hattie—Fen had mentioned her. A half dozen of the biggest Raiders followed them.

TWENTY-TWO

MATT

"BATTLEGROUND"

ou wouldn't be stealing from me, would you?" Skull
said. "Not Matt Thorsen, son of Blackwell's finest."

"You're the one who stole it!" Baldwin said,
jumping in front of Matt. "You swiped it from that
longship."

Skull laughed, Hattie echoing him. "Is that what Fen
said?" He leaned around Baldwin to look at Matt. "Ask Fen
again, Thorsen. Ask who really stole the shield. Better yet,
ask why he sent *you* to get it."

"It doesn't matter," Baldwin said.

Skull's laugh rippled through all the Raiders. "Really?
Huh. Fen delivered the shield...and now he's delivered the

champion." He looked at Baldwin. "You can go. Tell Fen he's all paid up."

Matt replayed Skull's words. He'd misunderstood. He must have. He could believe Fen stole the shield—this whole thing had started when he'd caught Fen trying to swipe it—but delivering the champion? Matt couldn't believe that. It must be a trick.

It's not. That's why he agreed with Astrid about getting your stuff. That's why he didn't want to come into camp with you. He wasn't helping get the shield; he was turning you over to the Raiders.

Baldwin stepped forward. "If you want him, you have to go through me first."

Matt heard a noise behind him. He turned, but too late. A half dozen of the Raiders were running at him. He took out the first with a left hook as Baldwin raced in, fists flying.

"Ignore blondie!" Skull called. "You can't hurt him, so don't bother trying."

Matt hit another Raider and sent him flying, but as he did, at least four others tackled him from behind. They swarmed over him, forcing him to the ground as he kicked and punched. Baldwin tried to pry the Raiders off Matt, but they'd just backhand him or elbow him away, which only made him madder, fighting like a whirlwind, yelling, "What about me? Hey, you, zit-face, come on! I thought you guys were Viking warriors! Fight me!"

When one finally swung around, as if ready to take Baldwin up on that, Skull shouted, "I said ignore blondie. He's Balder. Can't be hurt unless you have some mistletoe handy. Just keep swatting him off like the annoying little fly he is."

That made Baldwin furious, and he fought so hard that Skull finally ordered a few of the Raiders to grab him and pin him down. Matt was already pinned. Lying on his back, spread-eagle, a Raider holding down every limb, a fifth one sitting on his chest. He'd struggled at first, but realized they had him and stopped, conserving his energy and waiting for his chance.

"Get him up," Skull ordered.

The Raiders obeyed. They dragged Matt to his feet, two holding each arm. Matt felt his amulet, red-hot against his chest, and knew it was charged up, ready to go. But for what? He could take out one guy. That wouldn't stop the other dozen standing around. He needed a better plan. A smarter plan.

"Now, where's my shield?" Skull said.

A Raider had taken it from Matt's back before they'd pinned him. The kid held it up.

"Put it in my tent."

The Raider did as he was told. When he'd disappeared into the tent, Skull strolled toward Matt.

"There's someone you need to meet," he said. "But first I think you need a lesson about stealing."

Skull's gaze dropped to Matt's stomach, and Matt knew what was coming. A blow to the solar plexus against a defenseless target. Except Matt wasn't defenseless. He readied his Hammer as he watched Skull, ready to launch it as soon as he pulled back for—

Someone hit Matt from behind. A hard, fast hit to the kidney that sent pain jolting through him. He twisted to see the girl—Hattie—grinning. Then another blow, this one from the front, the hit he'd been waiting for. Straight to the solar plexus. The air flew from Matt's lungs, and he doubled over, wheezing and hacking.

"Hey, Skull!" Baldwin shouted, struggling against the Raiders holding him. "What kind of name is that, anyway. Do you think it makes you seem tough? It better work with these guys, because you need all the help you can get, loser."

Skull slowly turned on Baldwin.

"Yeah, I'm talking to you!" Baldwin shouted. "The loser who won't even take a swing at Thor's kid unless four guys are holding him down. You call yourself a Viking Raider? The Vikings wouldn't have let you clean their toilets. You won't even fight Matt without help from your girlfriend there. I can see where she comes in handy, though. One look from that ugly face and guys probably run before you *need* to hit them, right?"

Hattie advanced on Baldwin.

"I said to ignore him," Skull said. "You can't hurt him."

Hattie punched Baldwin in the stomach, making him cough. "Maybe not, but it makes me feel better."

"Truth hurts, doesn't it?" Baldwin said as he caught his breath and bounced back, grinning. "Do you turn into a wolf, too? I bet you don't. You don't need to. You're already a dog."

Hattie hit him. Matt winced and wanted to tell Baldwin to stop, but reminded himself that Baldwin couldn't feel it, couldn't be hurt. If Baldwin could draw off Hattie and Skull with insults...

"Enough!" Skull roared. "You want to hit someone? Get back here and hit Thorsen. I bet blondie will feel *that*."

Skull advanced on Matt again. When he pulled back his fist, Matt launched his Hammer. It knocked Skull to the ground, flat on his back. He scrambled up, face twisted in rage.

"You little brat," he said, charging Matt. "I'll teach you not to—"

Fog swirled between them, so thick Matt couldn't see Skull, could only hear him cursing as he fought his way through it. Matt stared at the fog. Had he done that? He did get a few wisps with his Hammer, but this was like smoke from a raging bonfire, spreading over the camp so fast—

Don't just stare at it. Use it!

Matt realized the holds on his arms had slackened, and when he looked over, he saw that the Raiders holding them

were gaping into the fog themselves. He yanked one arm free easily, then swung and plowed his fist into the jaw of one guy holding the other. The guy flew back and knocked over the Raider next to him, the two falling like bowling pins.

Matt dove into the fog, the gray wrapping around him, everything else disappearing. He heard a grunt to his left and turned to see a Raider girl charging him, knife raised. Something hit her from behind, and she fell face-first, Fen on her back. Fen plucked the switchblade from her hand, folded it into his pocket, and leaped up.

"Come on, Thorsen," Fen said.

Matt didn't move.

"I'm rescuing you," Fen said. "Again. Don't make me regret it. Come on."

Matt backed away.

"What the—?" Fen began.

A Raider leaped through the fog. Just a kid. Matt took him down. Then Fen grabbed his sleeve.

"We need to go," Fen urged. "The twins can't hold the fog forever."

Matt paused. "That's them?"

"No, it's natural. Just does that out here." Fen sighed in that annoying way of his before adding, "Yeah, it's them."

Matt hesitated. His brain said he shouldn't trust Fen, but he did. He just *did*.

He took a deep breath. "Okay. Is Laurie safe?"

Fen's face darkened, and Matt felt a stab of annoyance. Fen seemed to hate it when Matt worried about her. Did he think Matt had a thing for Laurie? He'd set him straight on that later. Maybe Fen's world was different, but in Matt's, you could have a girl as a friend without thinking of her as a girlfriend.

"'Course she's okay," Fen snapped. "I take care of her."

And so do I, Matt wanted to say. But he knew better.

"Okay, we need to get Baldwin and—"

"Got him," said a voice. Laurie appeared with Baldwin beside her.

Fen scowled. "I thought I told you to stay—"

"Yeah." Laurie rolled her eyes. "And someday you'll learn that I don't always—"

Two Raiders lunged from the fog. Matt took out one. Baldwin and Fen nearly knocked heads going for the other. A right hook from Fen sent the Raider back into the fog with Matt's.

A growl sounded somewhere in the fog, another joining it.

"I need to get the shield," Matt said.

"What?" Fen said. "All this and you don't have it?"

"They took it back," Baldwin said.

"I'll grab it," Matt said. "Laurie, open a door. Take the others through. I'll follow."

Laurie said nothing, and Matt peered through the thin curtain of fog between them. "Laurie?"

"That's what I've been trying to do," she said. "Open a door. I can't."

"Okay." Matt took a deep breath. "Um, I'll get the shield. You guys just... go back to where you were hiding before."

"Can I go with you?" Baldwin asked Matt.

"Fen?" Laurie said. "I want you to go with Matt."

"No. I'm making sure you get back—"

"Go with Matt. *Please.* If they're changing to wolves, you need to do that and stay with Matt." She stared directly at her cousin. "I'm going to catch my breath and open a door for us. Baldwin will be with me."

Fen seemed to realize there wasn't time for arguing. He nodded and gruffly told Baldwin to watch out for Laurie. Baldwin promised he would, and they slipped off into the fog. Fen went away, too, leaving Matt to fend off a Raider before returning in wolf form and quickly dispatching another.

They made their way to Skull's tent. Matt had no idea where to even find it in the fog, but Fen must have been able to smell it. Matt wondered if the Raider would have put the shield somewhere else, but as he followed Fen, he could feel his amulet's tingle, telling him they weren't quite that bright. The shield was still in Skull's tent.

Matt emerged from the gray to see the tent... and two hulking Raiders standing guard.

The bigger one grinned. "Skull said you wouldn't leave without getting what you came for." He raised his voice. "Hey, Sk—"

Before he finished the word, Matt hit him with the same blow Skull had used on him—straight to the solar plexus. Never anything he'd use in a fair fight, but this wasn't fair. And it shut the guy up fast. Before the second one could raise the alarm, Fen burst from the fog and took him down. Then he snapped at Matt, and Matt didn't need a canine translator to tell him what Fen had said. *Get your butt in that tent and grab the shield.*

Matt found the shield right where it had been the last time—under the blankets. He didn't heft it over his shoulder; he held it the way it should be held, protecting his body as he stepped out. He was just letting the flap fall behind him when a small Raider came charging from the fog. As if instinctively, Matt raised the shield...and the kid plowed into it headfirst and staggered back, dazed.

Matt motioned for Fen to follow him into the fog, but Fen motioned back, jerking his muzzle from the shield to the kid. Telling Matt to bash the guy again. Matt looked at the kid— maybe eleven—holding his head and blinking hard, and when he thought of hitting him again, he felt a little sick. He might have come a long way in a few days—he had no problem hitting a little kid or a girl if he had to—but that was too much.

He shook his head. When Fen started to lunge at the

dazed kid, Matt grabbed him by the scruff of the neck. Fen snarled and snapped, then snorted, yanked free from Matt's grip, and ran into the fog. Matt followed.

They'd barely gone three steps before the kid shouted, "They're here! By Skull's tent! They have the shield!"

Fen growled back at Matt, as if to say *That's what I was afraid of*, but didn't slow down. It was okay anyway. They were deep in the fog, and as long as they kept running *away* from the camp . . .

Matt caught a glimpse of a dark shape to his right. He turned to hit his attacker, only to realize the guy was about twenty feet away, running in the other direction. There were more shapes around him, some in human form, some in wolf. The fog was lifting.

Of course it was. It wasn't smart to split up any more than they had already, so Ray and Reyna would have gone back through the doorway with Laurie. There wasn't anyone casting the spell.

At least the Raiders were running in the opposite—

"There!" a girl shouted.

Matt and Fen sped up. As they did, Matt mentally calculated how many he'd seen. Four Raiders and two wolves, he thought. None were bigger than him. Maybe they could fight before others joined—

He glanced back to see at least nine shapes, two more appearing from the left. Okay, *not* stopping to fight, then.

"Fen!" It was Laurie's voice from somewhere ahead. "Matt! I've got it. The door is open!"

"Go through!" Matt shouted back. "We're coming!"

"I'll get the others through and hold it open!" Laurie called.

"No! We've got Raiders!" Matt glanced back at the growing mob behind him. Two wolves were leading the pack, closing the gap. "And wolves! Get through!"

Silence. Was she going to listen? Or would she think he was exaggerating? Wanting her out of harm's way because she was a girl? A week ago, he'd have done that, but he'd come to realize Laurie was pretty good at taking care of herself. She might not be big, and she might not be able to turn into a wolf or launch Thor's Hammer, but she was smart.

The problem was that he'd given her the *You're a girl—we must protect you* line so many times that when there was real danger, like now, she might not believe him. It was like the little boy who cried wolf—he glanced back to see the two big canines almost at his heels now—or wolves.

Go through the door, Laurie. Please just go through the door.

Ahead he could see the clearing. And in the middle of it, a shimmering circle of color—the door. There was someone standing outside of it. A figure barely distinguishable through the last veil of fog.

"Laurie!" Matt shouted. "Jump through—"

"It's me!" Baldwin called. "I stayed to help fight in case

this thing closes—" He looked behind them, and his eyes rounded. "Whoa!"

Matt couldn't help chuckling as he ran. "Go through. We're right behind you."

Baldwin waited until they were there. Then, with Fen, they dove through together. They hit the other side, tumbling together, Matt catching a claw scrape across his arm, Fen letting out a grunt as Baldwin's foot connected with his stomach. They lay there for a second, catching their breath, until Matt heard Laurie say, "Um, guys..." He looked up to see the door gone. And in its place? Two very confused wolves were sitting in Baldwin's backyard.

"How do you like *that* trick?" Laurie said to the wolves. "Maybe I can't change into a big, hairy monster, but you have to admit, that is cool. And useful."

The wolves started, as if just realizing they weren't alone. They looked from face to face. One bolted, racing across the yard and vaulting the back fence. The other growled, fur rising, head down. But after another sweep of the seven faces in front of him, he turned tail, too.

"Grab him!" Matt shouted as he launched himself onto the wolf's back.

Baldwin let out a whoop and grabbed the wolf by the tail. The wolf spun and dislodged Matt, but he grabbed a handful of fur with one hand. Then Matt twisted and clocked the wolf on the top of the muzzle. It was a trick his dad taught him for dealing with strays or coyotes. The wolf let out a yelp of pain. With both hands holding on now, Matt dropped over the wolf's side and yanked the beast down. It didn't stay down, but after some wrestling—with help from Baldwin—Matt got the wolf pinned. Then Baldwin sat on it, grinning like a big-game hunter. Astrid laughed. Even Ray and Reyna smiled at the sight.

Fen walked from behind the shed. He was in human form and shaking his head.

"Yes, I know," Matt said. "I keep attacking things that can kill me. It is kinda fun, though."

Baldwin grinned. "See, I'm not crazy."

"Yeah, you are," Fen said. "Thorsen's just the same kind of crazy. I guess we should be happy you two didn't try taking on the whole Raider camp yourselves."

"We were working on it," Baldwin said. "But you totally ruined our fun. Spoilsport."

Fen rolled his eyes. Then he pointed at the wolf. "What's with the captive?"

Matt looked at the captive Raider, and when he did, he felt like letting out a whoop of his own. He didn't, of course. That wasn't very leaderlike. But he still felt that whoop deep in his gut. The sweet thrill of success.

We did it. We got the shield. We got the descendants. We're close to getting Odin, and he'll help us with the rest. We did it, and I led the charge, and I didn't screw things up. I made mistakes, but I learned from them.

I can do this. I really can do this.

"Hey, Thorsen," Fen said. "I asked you a question. What's with the captive?"

Matt smiled. "I want to question him."

"Question him? What are you? A cop? Oh, wait..." He gave a disgusted snort and walked over to the wolf. "What do you expect him to tell you?"

"Everything he can. What the Raiders' plans are. Why they wanted the shield. Why they wanted me. Why they want Ragnarök to happen." Matt paused and stared at Fen. "Most of all, who they're taking orders from."

"Orders?" Fen said. "The Raiders don't take orders from anyone."

"I think they are. Skull said something about taking me to meet someone."

Fen shrugged. "Other Raiders, I guess. There are more of them. Packs."

Astrid stepped forward. "I think Fen's right. From what Odin told me, the Raiders are on their own here. They're representing Loki in the final battle. Loki was in charge of the monsters. No one *made* him do anything."

"On second thought," Fen said, "Thorsen might have a

324

point. Skull's a good Raider leader. But leader of all the monsters going into Ragnarök? No way."

Astrid turned on him. "You can't give it up, can you? I say something, and you disagree. I agree with you, and you change your mind. I could say the sky was blue, and you'd insist it was purple."

"No, it's not." Fen pointed up at the night. "It's black."

Astrid went to stalk away, and Matt started leaping off the wolf to go after her, but Laurie motioned for him to stop.

She grabbed Astrid's arm. "We need to work together. I agree that we should question the Raider. I have no idea if there's some big, bad puppet master pulling the strings, but even if there isn't, this guy can tell us something useful. I'm sure he can."

Baldwin nodded. "I agree. So how are we going to do this?"

TWENTY-THREE

FEN

"THINGS FALL APART"

The Raider, Paul, had turned back into a human shape, and Matt had dragged him over to Baldwin's shed. Fen and Matt stood staring down at the Raider. Behind the prisoner, Baldwin dug around in a big cardboard box, muttering as he did so.

Matt asked a bunch of questions—all of which Paul completely refused to answer—while Fen assumed the job of enforcer: he knocked Paul back to the ground every time he tried to get up and escape.

Although he'd been raised around fights and harsh discipline, Fen felt horrible all the same. At least Laurie wasn't at the shed to see him like this. He hadn't even hurt Paul, just kept him from escaping, but Fen knew that Matt was too much of good guy to beat answers out of anyone. Not that Fen was *bad*. He just wasn't as good as Matt. Plus, there was a pack order here; whether anyone admitted it or not, Fen knew that Matt was in charge. So Fen stood silently and waited for Matt to decide what they needed to do.

"Aha!" Baldwin blurted.

Fen glanced at him and shook his head. At least Baldwin wasn't freaked out by the whole capture-the-enemy thing. He'd tugged out a dingy shirt with straps on it and was untangling it from a string of Christmas lights.

"It's a straitjacket," Baldwin said in reply to Fen's glance.

All the while, Matt kept talking, asking about the Raiders' plans, their travels, where Mjölnir was, and why the Raiders wanted the shield. It was a waste of time; Raiders didn't betray their packs. Fen knew that, and he respected it. If the situation had been reversed, if it had been Matt or Fen taken captive, Fen was positive they wouldn't talk, either.

"He's not going to talk," Fen said quietly. "Skull and Hattie will kill him if he does."

"We won't let them," Matt insisted. He turned to Paul and added, "You tell us, and we'll protect you."

Paul snorted and made a rude gesture.

"Here." Baldwin held up the straitjacket thing in one hand. He looked utterly unabashed as he announced, "I went through a Houdini phase. This is an escape-proof jacket." In his other hand he had a roll of duct tape. "And this will keep him from yelling. My parents aren't back till tomorrow, but if the neighbors heard yelling out here, they might call my mom."

"I'm ... not sure ..." Matt began.

"Let him sit out here and think about it," Fen suggested. "We can go in, eat, and try to reason with him later."

"I could eat," Baldwin interjected.

After a moment, Matt said, "Okay."

With relief, Fen slapped a piece of tape over Paul's mouth, and then he and Matt wrestled him into the jacket.

"Go ahead in," Fen suggested to Matt. "Let me give him some wolf-to-wolf advice."

"Okay, but then I want to talk to you," Matt said very quietly.

With as little emotion as he could, Fen said, "Sure."

Then Matt nodded, and he and Baldwin left.

Fen stared at Paul, trying to force the younger *wulfenkind* into submission, and said, "Think about it, Paul. Whether you tell us or not, Skull will beat you to find out if you did tell. You could stay here. Don't be stupid."

Paul snorted through his gag and rolled his eyes.

"You're making a mistake," Fen said, and then he stepped out of the shed and pulled the door closed behind him.

There weren't a lot of times in Fen's life that he'd ever felt like he belonged. Sure, with Laurie, he had, but even there, he'd had to keep a lot of secrets. Being part of a team, being one of the descendants of the North, being destined to do something real and important felt awesome—and Fen had a sinking feeling that it was also about to end. The way Matt had looked at him when he said he'd wanted to talk made it pretty clear that one of the Raiders had told Matt about Fen.

As he walked toward Baldwin's house, Fen admitted to himself that he should've told Matt and Laurie about the Raiders and the deal with delivering Matt, but he couldn't. Now, he wasn't sure what to say *or* what Matt knew. He liked Matt well enough, all things considered, and even if he didn't, he respected him. That didn't mean he wanted to have their little talk in front of everyone. A trickle of fear crept over him at the thought of not only being kicked out, but of everyone hating him.

What if Matt thinks I'm a traitor? I didn't do it, at least not the worst part.

Fen wasn't sure what Laurie would do. She'd been the most important person in his life for as long as he could remember, his partner in trouble, but it wasn't just the two of them anymore. She trusted Matt now. Fen paced across the porch and back into the yard, thinking about the situation. Baldwin was cool. He'd be decent no matter what. The twins were unpredictable; they were growing on him, but they were still pretty apart from the group. Astrid gave him a bad feeling; he didn't care what she thought of him, but the others seemed to like her. If the Raiders said something that Matt believed, if the others listened to the Raiders, things could easily turn against him, and although he wasn't going to admit it aloud, he didn't want to be kicked out. He needed to talk to Laurie and Matt.

He had his hand out to grab the doorknob to go into the house when the door opened. Laurie stood there, scowling, and the trickle of fear exploded. "What?"

"I'm tired of this," she started. She closed the door behind her and walked over to Fen.

"Of what?"

"You acting like I'm unable to take care of myself at all!" she exclaimed. "You can't keep doing that."

Every worry about being asked to leave intensified. If he left, he was taking Laurie with him. There was no way he could leave her here without him. Uncle Stig, Kris, the whole family really, they'd all hate him if Laurie got hurt—or worse.

"Yeah? Well you could've been hurt," Fen growled.

Laurie poked him in the chest. "So could you, or Matt, or Baldwin—"

"Actually, I couldn't," Baldwin interrupted.

Fen looked around in confusion.

"Up here," Baldwin said. He was leaning out of an upstairs

window, staring down at them. "Matt could've been hurt, and both of you. The wolves really seemed to hate you, Fen. They said you were on their side and you gave them the shield."

Fen and Laurie turned to stare at Baldwin at the same time.

"If we have time, like later or something, could you open a door so I can see some mistletoe?" Baldwin asked.

Without looking at his cousin, Fen knew she had the exact same incredulous expression on her face.

"No," Fen said levelly.

Baldwin held up both hands in a placating gesture. "Just a thought!"

"A dumb one," Fen snapped, but then felt instantly guilty when Baldwin looked crushed. Of all the descendants, Baldwin was the only one who didn't actually irritate him. It was some strange result of who he was—*everyone* liked Balder in the myths—but knowing that there was probably weird god stuff in the mix didn't make it less real.

"I'm going to order pizzas," Baldwin blurted. "That's what I came to ask. Do you want anything special?"

"Whatever you want," Fen said, as nicely as he could. He felt embarrassed because Laurie was watching, but it wasn't Baldwin's fault he was weird any more than it was Laurie's fault she opened doors or Fen's fault he turned into a wolf. Fen glanced up at Baldwin. "I'm sorry."

Baldwin grinned. "It's fine." And then he wandered off, calling out questions about pepperoni and olives.

Once he was gone, Fen and Laurie were left alone on the porch. It was hard being around Laurie now that she knew his secrets, hard being around all these people, and hard trying to be himself without upsetting any of them. He braced himself for her to yell at him about the Raiders.

But instead of jumping on the things Baldwin had just said, Laurie continued on with the rant she'd started when she'd come outside: "You need to trust me, Fen. I don't want to die, and I don't want any of you to, either, but if we don't stop Ragnarök, we all will. So, if we are going to stop this, we all have to do the things we can do. I'm part of this, and you need to deal with it."

"I just want to keep you safe. Thorsen does, too," Fen muttered.

"Matt's coming around. Maybe you could try to do the same thing," she suggested.

Fen grunted. "Maybe you could stay where it's safe. I'm the descendant who *has* to fight, not you."

She stood up and glared down at him. "Fine! You fight, but don't you even try to act like I'm not helping, too. I opened that door that got us the shield that *you* gave the Raiders."

Fen glared right back. She had heard what Baldwin had said; he'd thought for a moment that she'd missed it. He shook his head. "Your skill is to open doors, to *escape*. How are you going to protect yourself from the monsters that keep coming?"

She blinked away the tears he could see forming in her eyes. "We're a team. We rescue each other and fight together. That's what teams do. That's how we'll stop Ragnarök. You're a wolf. Think of it like a pack."

Thinking about packs was the problem. For most of his life, the most important person in his life was Laurie; he'd always figured they'd be a pack of two once she transformed—or that he'd hide what he was to keep her safe if she didn't become a wolf. He might not have parents, but he did have a sorta sister in her. If he was going to be a good packmate, a good almost-brother, he'd have to keep her safe, so if she wasn't going to let him protect her, maybe it was best to go home, leave the world-saving to Thorsen. "Well, maybe I don't want to be part of this pack! Maybe we ought to both go home, where it's safe."

"You're such an idiot! There is no *safe* anymore. The world is ending." She went inside, slamming the door and leaving him outside. He was alone, and he told himself that it was what he wanted, that he didn't want to be part of any team—except that the moment she left, he had to admit to himself that it wasn't what he really wanted at all. He just didn't want Laurie to get hurt—or to find out what he'd done and hate him.

Fen rubbed his hand over his face. He was sore, bruised, tired, and, if he was totally honest, he was scared. It was one thing to deal with the Raiders, but it was another to think that if he failed—if *any* of them failed—the world would end. That was a lot worse than getting smacked around a little. At first, he'd thought Skull and Hattie were crazy, talking about the end of the world, but now that he was in the middle of a fight against them to stop the end of the world, it felt so... *big*. What if Matt asked him to leave? What if he didn't, but they failed? What if the serpent killed Matt? What if they went up against trolls or mara or who knew what else and Laurie got hurt? What if Baldwin died, like in the myths? What if he or Laurie somehow turned evil or whatever because they were Loki's descendants? *How do you even know if you're turning evil?* He closed his eyes and tried not to think about any of the questions he couldn't answer, especially the last one. He wasn't sure how long he sat there before the door opened. He expected it to be Laurie or Baldwin, but when he turned his head to look, he saw Matt.

"Did you think I wouldn't find out you stole the shield?" Matt asked. "You could have told me. Then you could have come into the camp with me."

"I *was* in the camp. I saved your butt, Thorsen. Again. I'm not sure what you mean, but—"

"Don't," Matt interrupted. "I get it now. You offered to get the shield back alone. Then you didn't want to come into camp. You didn't want me to know you were involved with the Raiders."

"Wolves pay dues," Fen said. "That was mine and

334

Laurie's. I didn't know the shield mattered, just that I needed to get it."

"And the part about delivering *me*?" Matt asked.

Fen froze. He'd known it was a bad idea to go after the shield, but he hadn't thought Skull would actually tell Matt. *What? Did he stop midfight for a heart-to-heart?* Fen growled low in his throat. "I didn't, though! I fought at your side against *Raiders*. I tramped all over with you and fought monsters at your side. I mighta agreed to deliver you, but I didn't do it."

They faced off. Fen's heart was racing like they were fighting, even though all they were doing was staring at each other.

Finally, Matt rolled his shoulders and nodded. "Okay. I believe you. But no more secrets. We've gotta be a team now, trust each other, watch each other's backs so no one gets hurt."

Fen wanted to say something smart, to pretend he hadn't been wrong, but he couldn't. He would feel horrible if someone got hurt because of him, and he did want to save the world. He lifted a shoulder in a small shrug, but he stayed silent.

"At Ragnarök, Loki was Thor's enemy," Matt said. "But in other stories, they were friends. They traveled together. They fought side by side. We need to be that version. Friends."

And Fen didn't know what to say, so he settled on, "Whatever."

Matt turned and left, and Fen half expected Ray, Reyna, and Astrid to all come out to lecture him about something else. It felt like everyone wanted to tell him what he had done wrong or, worse yet, what he would do wrong.

Twenty minutes later, when the pizza arrived and Baldwin came out to pay for it, Fen took one of the two boxes and followed Baldwin into the kitchen. Astrid was already in there.

"I got everything out," she said. She pointed at the counter where plates, napkins, glasses, salt, pepper, Parmesan cheese, and red-pepper flakes were all lined up neatly.

"Thank you," Baldwin said.

Astrid beamed at him. "You did everything. This part was easy."

"Suck-up," Fen muttered.

Instead of snapping back at him, Astrid turned her supercharged smile at him. "Oh, and thank you, too, Fen, for being *you*!"

He snapped his teeth at her, and she left the kitchen.

After Astrid had left, Fen said, "I don't trust her."

"You don't trust anyone," Baldwin said.

"Not true." Fen picked up a slice of pizza and took a bite. "I trust Laurie, Thorsen... and you."

Baldwin shrugged. "Sure, but everyone trusts me. It's

like the not-getting-hurt thing. I don't think I count. Matt's our leader. You might not like Astrid, but she was right about that. He's the one who's going to lead us into the big battle, right? You kind of *have* to trust him, or you wouldn't be here."

Fen knew Baldwin was right, but he still didn't like Astrid or the twins. *Maybe wolves don't like witches?* He chomped the pizza while he thought about it. He'd ask Matt about that later. Right now, he just wanted some downtime. Baldwin was cool about the talking thing, too. He wasn't pushy, like Laurie and Matt were.

"Food?" Reyna—or maybe Ray—said as the twins came in. They were more of a single entity than made sense to Fen.

Everyone else followed. Laurie, Matt, and Astrid were laughing at something, and Baldwin stood there grinning in that way of his that made Fen want to get along with the witch kids. Maybe he was just being difficult.

"Do you want to pick a movie with me?" Baldwin gestured toward the door with a slice of pizza.

Fen nodded and grabbed another slice.

They abandoned the kitchen to the others and headed to the living room to figure out what to watch. They had a better chance of avoiding some girly nonsense if they picked it while all three girls were in the kitchen. It was nice to have someone on his side, too. Laurie seemed so mad at him, and Matt wasn't exactly *mad*, but Fen thought that was only because he'd decided not to be. He'd looked pretty hurt over the whole Raiders thing.

I'd like to pound Skull.

"Fen?"

He looked at Baldwin, who was pulling movies out of a cabinet.

"You're growling again," Baldwin said. "It's a little weird." Then he held up both hands so Fen could see the options. *Star Wars* was in one hand; in the other was a movie with an explosion on the cover and another with a cowboy on it. "Space or Earth? Monsters or humans?"

"Any of them. Just nothing about dances or anything"— Fen made air quotes with his fingers—"heartwarming."

They got the movie set up just as everyone was coming into the living room. Astrid flopped down on the floor. Ray and Reyna were on the sofa with Laurie. That left two chairs. Matt, being Matt, offered one to Astrid—who laughed and told him, "You take it. I'm happier on the floor."

Fen opened his mouth to make a remark, but Baldwin spoke hurriedly, "Come on. They didn't bring out the red-pepper flakes or cheese."

After they both snatched pieces out of one of the boxes, Fen offered, "I can grab it."

"Okay," Baldwin agreed—but he still headed to the kitchen.

They found the jar of red-pepper flakes sitting on the counter right where it had been.

"I love this stuff," Fen said.

"Me, too! Mom doesn't, but I go through jars of it." Baldwin held out his slice of pizza, and Fen shook pepper flakes onto it.

As they walked back into the living room, Baldwin took a bite of pizza and immediately started coughing.

"Baldwin, are you okay?" Matt asked.

Baldwin clutched at his throat.

Laurie grabbed her water and held it out. "Here, wash it down."

But Baldwin lunged toward Fen, grasping his arm so hard that he all but knocked Fen to the ground.

"Maybe he swallowed wrong." Fen pounded Baldwin's back.

Fen took Laurie's glass of water and tried to help Baldwin drink.

That wasn't helping either, so Fen switched to trying to do that Heimlich maneuver they talked about in health class. Matt understood and pushed everyone else back. As Baldwin flailed his arms around, the glass of water fell and shattered on the floor. Baldwin was clawing at his throat with one hand and grabbing Fen with the other.

And then he ... stopped.

He stopped grabbing Fen, stopped moving, and stopped breathing. He just stopped.

Fen felt Baldwin's body droop and lowered him to the

floor. He tried to feel for a pulse and didn't find it. Frantically, he pounded on Baldwin's chest like he'd seen in TV shows. In movies, that worked. People pushed on the chest and *what*...? Fen thought for a moment. They blew air in the person's mouth. Fen put his hands into a fist and pushed hard in the middle of Baldwin's chest. Nothing happened.

While he was doing that, Matt reached out and felt for a pulse.

As Fen leaned over to blow air into Baldwin's mouth, Matt caught hold of Fen's shoulder. "He's dead."

"No, no, no! He can't die. He can't even feel pain. No," Fen said.

Matt met Fen's eyes, and then he shook his head. "Fen..."

"No," Fen snarled. "He's fine. You, witches, *do* something."

Reyna said, "Magic can't change death."

Astrid started sobbing. She collapsed on top of Matt, who put his arm around her to steady her.

"It's like the myth! Balder is dead!" Astrid pointed a finger at Fen. "What did you *do*?"

As Fen kneeled there beside Baldwin's motionless body, no one spoke up to say Astrid was wrong, that it wasn't Fen's fault. Matt held Astrid, who was sobbing. Reyna and Ray looked at Fen with wide-eyed shock. Laurie stood motionless. She didn't say anything, didn't do anything. She only stared at Baldwin.

"Help me," Fen said.

It was Ray who came over and helped lift Baldwin.

Silently, Fen and Ray carried Baldwin up to his bedroom.

"I've got him. Pull back the covers." Fen shifted so he held the whole weight of Baldwin's body.

Once Ray did so, Fen lowered Baldwin to the mattress. Without looking back at Ray, he said, "Get out."

"It's not your fault. You tried to save him," Ray said quietly.

"Get out *now*," Fen growled.

And then he sat on the floor beside Baldwin. "I don't understand." Tears started falling. "Stupid freaking myths. How could you *choke* to death?" Fen arranged Baldwin's body so it looked like he was sleeping, and then he pulled the sheet up over his face.

The myth had come true: Baldwin had died…which meant that it was somehow because of Loki's actions, because of *his* actions.

TWENTY-FOUR

MATT

"GRIEF-STRICKEN"

Matt wandered through the house, unable to stop moving, not going anywhere, not looking for anyone, just moving.

Baldwin was dead.

Dead. Really dead. Not sleeping upstairs in his bed. Not knocked unconscious. He was dead.

Just like in the myth.

This was Matt's fault. He'd known the myth, and still he'd brought Baldwin into it. He'd told himself that it wouldn't turn out like that. It couldn't. That's what they were here for—stopping the old stories from coming true.

In the myth, Loki was responsible for Balder's death. He

hadn't killed the god himself, but he'd set it up. Matt had been sure that wasn't what happened here. Fen liked Baldwin. Really, honestly liked him, in a way Fen didn't like anyone except his cousin.

Even if it had been someone Fen didn't like—Astrid maybe—Matt would never think Fen might have killed her. The thought wouldn't cross his mind.

No one had killed Baldwin. It had to be an accident. But how could it be an accident? The only thing that could hurt Baldwin was mistletoe. There was no way that the pizza just happened to have mistletoe on it.

So if it wasn't an accident . . .

Someone had put mistletoe on the pizza. Shaved the wood to look like a spice and served it to Baldwin.

Wait—Baldwin had gone in to the kitchen for red-pepper flakes. The shavings could have been in them. But who'd put out the pepper flakes? Fen and Baldwin were the ones who'd set up—

No, Astrid had begun setting the table. Then she left, and when she left, the pepper flakes were out.

Matt shook his head. That was crazy. He wouldn't believe it. Couldn't.

Whatever the situation, he needed to talk to Astrid. He couldn't go around making accusations like that. No matter what you thought of a person, you didn't accuse them of murder.

Matt stopped wandering aimlessly and set out with a purpose now. Find Astrid. He went through all the upstairs bedrooms first, even Baldwin's, though he only glanced in fast, trying not to look at the body on the bed.

The body. Not Baldwin. Not the guy who'd been talking to him, laughing with him, fighting beside him only a few hours ago.

Matt took a deep breath and started to close the door. Then he stopped. Something was missing. His shield. He'd put it there, propped up against his bag earlier. Now there was just his backpack.

Matt strode into the hall and almost bumped into Laurie. When he opened his mouth, he was ready to ask where Fen was, but instead what came out was, "Have you seen Astrid?" And once he'd said it, he didn't correct himself. He knew what he was asking, and he knew, in his gut, that it was the right question.

"Um, I don't know. I heard the back door close, and I thought Reyna said it was Astrid, but..."

Matt took off at a jog.

By the time Matt got outside, Astrid was hopping down from the fence. Across her shoulder was an oversized gym bag, the fabric stretched by some large object within.

Some large object? No, it was his shield. Matt knew that even before he started across the yard and felt his amulet tingle.

He waited until he was on the fence before calling, "Hey! Astrid!"

She was in the neighbor's yard, partly hidden behind a rose garden. Matt saw the bag strap fall from her shoulder as she lowered her burden to the ground. Then she stepped from behind the roses without it.

"Hey," she said. She gave him a sad twist of a smile, her gaze downcast, swiping her fingers under her eyes as if she'd been crying.

"Where are you going?" he asked, as casually as he could.

"I just..." Another swipe of her dry eyes. "I just needed a few minutes to myself."

"Oh. Okay. I thought...well, it looked like you were leaving. For good."

She paused. Then she walked back to him and looked up. A deep breath, then she spoke carefully, as if the words pained her. "I think I *am* leaving. I'm sorry, Matt, but this isn't working out. Fen...he scares me. I'm sure he killed Baldwin. I don't know how, but..." She shuddered. "He's a monster. I know you don't see that now, but you will. Just..." She laid her fingers on his arm. "Be careful. I don't want him to hurt you."

"He won't. I just…I can't figure out why he killed Baldwin." He tried to say it like he thought it was true.

"Because it's in the myth. He was destined to. You know that." She tightened her fingers around his arm. "You have a traitor in your midst, and I just pray to the gods that you'll figure it out before it's too late. But in case you don't, I'm going to find Odin and tell him and let him warn you. In the meantime, forget what I said about getting your Hammer. Fen will only steal it. Protect the shield, too. He'll go after that, if he hasn't already."

"I'm not worried about that. I know exactly where the shield is," Matt said.

"Are you sure? I really think you need to check and hide it."

"It's already hidden. Right over here." Matt broke from her grip and walked over to the rosebushes.

Astrid raced after him and grabbed his arm, but he shook her off. When he reached down to grab the bag, she jumped on his back, grabbing his shirt and wrenching it so hard that the collar tightened around his throat. He started to choke and spun, fist out. It hit her and when it did, his amulet seemed to ignite, blazing so hot he gasped.

She ran at him, her face twisted into something so ugly that it stopped him in his tracks. She jumped on him, and he fell back with her on top of him. The amulet blazed again, scorching his skin.

Why couldn't you have done that sooner? A little warning would have been nice.

Matt hit Astrid with a fast jab, followed by a second. As he pushed up, she started falling off him, then grabbed him again, both hands wrapped in his shirt. She hissed, and he caught a flash of her white teeth heading straight for his neck. He managed to push her away before she could bite him. One good heave and she went flying to the ground. When she tried to scramble up, Matt knocked her down again.

She seemed ready to bounce up. Then she stopped. Her shoulders folded in, and her hands flew to her face. She started to sob.

"It's not my fault," she said. "He made me do it. He said he'd kill my family if I didn't."

"*Who* made you do it?" Matt asked.

"H-him," she sobbed. "He made me do it, and if I don't come back, he'll kill my family." She lifted her face to his and her eyes seemed genuinely red now. "Please, Matt. Let me go, and I'll tell him you're heading to North Dakota. You'll be safe."

She reached out and wrapped her fingers around his arm, and when she did, the amulet's heat scorched again.

Matt shook his head. "You're going to answer a few questions. Then, if I think you've told me the truth, I'll let you go."

She looked up, and the red shot right through her eyes,

through the whites and through the irises and even the pupils.

"You just don't know when to give up, do you?" She lunged to her feet and gave him a shove.

He'd been crouched on his toes, and the push knocked him off balance. When he saw her going for the bag, he shouted, "No!"

His hand shot out, Hammer launching, but she veered at the last second before grabbing it, and was heading across the yard, for another neighboring yard.

Matt hesitated for a second. He looked at the bag. Then he raced to it, grabbed it, and went after Astrid. He pursued her over three fences, but she was a faster runner, and with each one, he fell farther behind, until he climbed the fourth, looked out, and saw no sign of her.

"You!" a voice boomed.

Matt followed it to a second-story window, where a man glowered down at him.

"Get out of my yard now, or I'll come down there and—"

Matt didn't hear the rest. He was already running for the gate.

Matt spent twenty minutes searching for Astrid. There was no sign of her. He'd have to go back to the house and see if Fen could track her. In the meantime, at least they had the shield. And they still had Paul. Whatever Astrid knew, Matt bet the Raiders did, too.

Matt walked to the shed. He opened the door, looked in, and saw a pile of cords and discarded duct tape. Paul was gone.

TWENTY-FIVE

LAURIE

"LET'S GO TO HEL"

When Matt had gone upstairs to Baldwin's room to talk to Fen, Laurie had followed him. They didn't talk, but she knew as well as Matt did that Fen had tried to save Baldwin. She wanted to tell all of that to Fen, but he was gone. She walked over to the window—which was still open—but she couldn't see her cousin outside anywhere. Matt had taken off after Fen had, but Laurie wasn't really sure if Matt could say or do anything to bring Fen back to them.

Laurie had been to funerals, so it wasn't the first time she'd been in the room with a dead person. It was different with Baldwin. He'd just been alive, laughing, and being his goofy self. Staying in the room with Baldwin now that he was gone wasn't like being at a viewing at the funeral home with her dad. This was her friend, one of the descendants, and he was dead.

The whole thing felt unreal, more than trolls or mara. Monsters were one thing, but a dead friend was another. Laurie felt like she was in a haze, too shocked to even cry, though tears kept falling from her eyes. She'd gone downstairs to wait. By then, Fen, Matt, and Astrid were all missing. She was alone in the house with the twins, who retreated to another room. On the heels of their victory in getting the shield, they'd lost in a way no one could have seen coming.

Who dies eating pizza? It was insane. It should be impossible. They weren't even at a battle.

Laurie half sat, half flopped down on the sofa, thinking about how quickly everything changed. It was wrong to be here in Baldwin's house now that Baldwin was gone. She imagined his parents coming home and finding him. The boy who was impervious to injury had died—which didn't make *any* sense.

The only thing that could kill or injure Baldwin was mistletoe. Pizza wasn't made with any sort of mistletoe. It simply didn't make sense.

A door opened, and she scrambled up to see who it was.

Fen walked into the kitchen.

"I'm sorry," Laurie murmured. She started to go to him, to grab him and hug him, but he looked so angry that she stopped.

Fen looked at her, and she knew he wanted to tell her it was okay, but it *wasn't*. If someone had blamed her for anything, Fen would've jumped to her defense—even if she'd done it. She didn't think he had done anything wrong, and she hadn't thought it when Astrid had implied he'd caused it. She'd been shocked, scared, and crying. By the time she'd thought to speak, Fen was already gone.

"I didn't think you did anything wrong," she swore. "I just…I didn't have time to tell you. I would've. It was just that Baldwin was just here, and then he was…" Her words trailed off, and she swatted at the tears that were on her face again.

"Dead," Fen finished.

He grabbed the jar of red-pepper flakes and unscrewed the top. Silently, he poured it into one hand and poked at the flakes with his finger.

"It's not all pepper," Fen said flatly.

Her gaze flickered between his upraised hand and his red, swollen eyes. He might not be crying right now, but she could tell that he had been.

"Mistletoe?" she asked.

"It has to be. Someone put mistletoe in there and left it on the counter for him to…Astrid." Fen looked at Laurie

with fury in his expression. "She said it was easy. She *thanked* me. She thanked *him*."

He slammed his hand down.

"She poisoned him, and she knew I couldn't stop it." Fen looked like he was going to snap, and his voice sounded increasingly like an animal's growls were twisted around his words. "She watched him die. She *killed* him."

Laurie could hear the anger seething in Fen's voice, but she couldn't bring herself to speak. Astrid had poisoned Baldwin. She'd put mistletoe in the pepper shaker, and Fen had put the poison on Baldwin's pizza without knowing he was killing him.

"I couldn't save him," Fen whispered.

Laurie grabbed Fen and pulled him to her. "It's not your fault."

Although Fen didn't pull away, he didn't hug her back, either. "It's just like the myth. I had a part in killing him."

Laurie squeezed her cousin, as much to let her buy time as to let him calm down. She wasn't entirely convinced that Fen could contain himself if he saw Astrid. *What if she comes back?* The reality of it was that one of their group had been murdered by another. She didn't know if she could handle Fen doing the same thing—or if *Fen* could.

They were still standing there when Matt walked into the room. He looked as devastated as Laurie felt. Fen pulled away from her and squared his shoulders, bracing himself for a fight.

"Astrid's gone," Matt said.

At the same time, Fen said, "Astrid poisoned Baldwin."

There was a long moment of silence as the boys looked at one another. Then Matt took a deep breath. "You were right," he said. "About not trusting her. I should have listened."

Fen shrugged. "I didn't have any proof."

Matt met Fen's gaze. "I still should have listened."

Fen nodded and shifted uncomfortably. Laurie cleared her throat and rescued him by asking Matt, "What happens in the myth? After Balder died, what did the gods do?"

Matt paused, and then, slowly, he smiled. "They went after him."

"Went where?"

"To Hel, the land of the dead." Matt looked from Laurie to Fen and back again. "Do you think you can open a doorway there?"

Laurie took a deep breath before she could answer. This wasn't some little thing they were considering. Go to *Hel*? Could they even do that? What kind of monsters were there? All sorts of fears swirled through her, but in the middle of the fear was hope. If they could do this, they could bring Baldwin back. She nodded. "I *do* find descendants of the North."

The horrible look of sadness slipped from the boys' faces, and Laurie felt herself smiling, too. They didn't need to discuss what would happen next. They *knew* what to do.

The twins walked into the kitchen. "We should probably take off before Baldwin's parents get home," Ray suggested.

"We are," Laurie said, and then she turned to Matt. "Did the gods succeed?"

"No," Matt said slowly. "The myth says Hel wouldn't give him up because Loki didn't mourn." He clapped Fen on the shoulder. "But you *are* mourning."

Fen grinned. "Well, then it looks like we need to go to Hel."

ACKNOWLEDGMENTS

We want to thank the following people for making this book possible:

- Sarah Rees Brennan, for suggesting one sleepy morning over an airport breakfast of donuts that we needed to write a "Kellissa book";

- Meghan Lewis, Breanna Lewis, and Dylan Marr, for coming up with titles for the books;

- our agents, Sarah Heller and Merrilee Heifetz, for believing in the project (and us);

- film agent Sally Wilcox, and foreign rights agent Cecilia de la Campa, for enthusiastic support;

- Megan Tingley, Kate Sullivan, Samantha Smith, and the rest of the team at Little, Brown and Atom, for taking a chance on us;

- Xaviere Daumarie, for creating gorgeous art; Deena Warner, for building a great website; and Azoulas Yurashunas, for constructing traditional Viking shields;

- and our kids (Marcus, Alex, Julia, Dylan, and Asia), Kelley's assistant (Alison Armstrong), and our friends (Jennifer Lynn Barnes, Ally Condie, and Margaret Stohl), for feedback on the book at various stages.